Forever Friend

JANICE PLUMTON CHASSIE

© Copyright 2021 Janice Chassie

Publisher: Headstone Publishing: ON Canada

All rights reserved. Neither this publication nor any part of this publication may be reproduced or transmitted in any form or by any means, electronic or mechanical, including photocopying, recording, or any information storage and retrieval system, without written permission from the author.

Unless otherwise indicated, all Scripture taken from the Holy Bible, New Living Translation (NLT), Copyright ©1996, 2004, 2007 by Tyndale House Foundation. Used by permission of Tyndale House Publishers, Inc., Carol Stream, Illinois 60188. All rights reserved.

Scripture marked AMP taken from the Amplified® Bible, Copyright © 2015 by The Lockman Foundation, La Habra, CA 90631. All rights reserved.

Scripture marked BSB taken from the Berean Study Bible, Copyright © 2016–2020 by Bible Hub and Berean Bible. Used by permission.

Scripture marked CEV taken from the Contemporary English Version, Copyright © 1991, 1992, 1995 by American Bible Society, Used by Permission.

Scripture marked ESV taken from The Holy Bible, English Standard Version® (ESV®), Copyright © 2001 by Crossway, a publishing ministry of Good News Publishers. Used by permission. All rights reserved.

Scripture marked GNT taken from the Good News Translation, Copyright © 1992 by American Bible Society.

Scripture marked ICB taken from The Holy Bible, International Children's Bible® Copyright© 1986, 1988, 1999, 2015 by Tommy Nelson™, a division of Thomas Nelson. Used by permission.

Scripture marked ISV taken from the International Standard Version, Copyright © 1995–2014 by ISV Foundation. All rights reserved internationally. Used by permission of Davidson Press, LLC.

Scripture marked KJV taken from the King James version, which is in the public domain.

Scripture marked MEV taken from The Holy Bible, Modern English Version. Copyright © 2014 by Military Bible Association. Published and distributed by Charisma House.

Scripture marked MSG taken from The Message, Copyright © 1993, 1994, 1995, 1996, 2000, 2001, 2002 by Eugene H. Peterson.

Scripture marked NASB taken from the New American Standard Bible, Copyright © 1960, 1962, 1963, 1968, 1971, 1972, 1973, 1975, 1977, 1995 by The Lockman Foundation.

Scripture marked NIV taken from The Holy Bible, New International Version®, NIV® Copyright ©1973, 1978, 1984, 2011 by Biblica, Inc.® Used by permission. All rights reserved worldwide.

Scripture marked NKJV taken from the New King James Version®, Copyright © 1982 by Thomas Nelson, Inc. Used by permission. All rights reserved.

Scripture marked TPT taken from The Passion Translation®, Copyright © 2017 by BroadStreet Publishing® Group, LLC. Used by permission. All rights reserved. thePassionTranslation.com

This is a work of fiction. Names, characters, places, and incidents are either the product of the author's imagination or used fictitiously, and any resemblance to actual persons, living or dead, businesses, companies, events, or locales is entirely coincidental.

ISBN - ISBN: 9798450799841

Cover Design by Edgar Winter: edgarwinter@gmail.com

DEDICATION

This book is dedicated to my dearest friend and the love of my life, Ray Chassie.

You and the Holy Spirit have been my greatest encouragers.

You always direct me to look upward towards the Father.

May the Lord continue to bless our marriage and our destiny.

Thank you God, for my three amazing adult children,

Steven, Scott, and Shannon.

You have each been a hand-chosen friend from the Lord to me.

To all my friends who have helped me on my journey

towards the heart of God, *thank you.*

How much more delightful it is to walk closer to God with all of you.

ENDORSEMENTS

Forever Friend is not your typical children's book... and it's a breath of fresh air. Janice weaves deep faith-based themes into a unique and engaging story that children will delight in and be captivated by. Get ready for your child to go on an adventure; and take it with them!
Forever Friend is perfect for reading as a family and using it as a springboard to delve into meaningful conversation together.
Make your way through the invigorating pages with Samuel, the main protagonist as he embarks on a fantastic journey!

Benjamin A. Dietrich
Leader & Visionary of Shekinah Church, Ann Arbor
Author & Public Speaker

Forever friend is a beautifully written and riveting story.
It is seen through the eyes of the young boy Samuel, who discovers the friendship of the One who loves him completely and eternally.
This book is an inspiring tale of the adventures of Samuel and his friends, their courage, and their boldness in the fight for freedom.
It is a biblically based story for the entire family to enjoy, with great spiritual insight woven throughout its pages.
Forever Friend is truly an exceptional and enjoyable book and was a pleasure to read. Great job!

Faith Marie Baczko
President of Headstone Ministries
Author & Public Speaker

CONTENTS

Chapter 1	Faith	13
Chapter 2	The Father's House	19
Chapter 3	First Fruit	35
Chapter 4	Rest	45
Chapter 5	Beginning of the Harvest	53
Chapter 6	The Offering	63
Chapter 7	The Struggle	69
Chapter 8	New Ground	79
Chapter 9	A Decision	87
Chapter 10	Worshipper, Arise!	101
Chapter 11	Divine Encounter	115
Chapter 12	The Third Day	135
Chapter 13	Deceit	147
Chapter 14	The Choice	159
Chapter 15	The Unveiling	183
Chapter 16	The Battle Plan	197
Chapter 17	The Agreement	211
Chapter 18	Fearless	227
Chapter 19	Holy Beginning	247

INTRODUCTION

When the Lord spoke to me and asked me to write a story with him, I never imaged the amazing quest we would go on together. I feel honored and privileged to be the first person to hear this unique story. God would speak into my imagination and as I listened to the Father, I would write exactly what was given. I did not know what the manuscript would contain or where the Lord was leading me. But I loved every moment of my adventure with my heavenly Father.

It was mostly in my quiet times sitting in my garden, pen in hand and clean white paper ready, that the Lord would whisper to me portions of *Forever Friend*. Sometimes the story would come to me quickly as if the Lord was waiting for me! Other times I patiently waited to receive the next chapter. I would sit in my garden expectantly, knowing the Father would come, anticipating what would happen next within the pages of *Forever Friend*. I would ask the Lord, "Where are we going today? What is about to unfold? How will this all come together?"

On other occasions, often during worship, the Lord would capture me up into a vision and show me the next event to be written. The breathtakingly beautiful horse Dunamis appeared to me in a vision. As I held onto his muscular neck, we soared swiftly through the heavenlies in perfect oneness. An event that took my breath away!

Once I had begun writing, I noticed God was giving me scriptures within the dialogue of the characters. Excitedly, I would search the scripture out, always amazed at how perfectly the scripture fit within the pages of *Forever Friend*. Truly God's good and perfect gift (James 1:17).

There were several times I thought God and I were finished writing the story. Then God would ask me to add another layer to *Forever Friend*. The story came to me in many layers. The first layer came in the form of a book. God had asked me to insert His names within the story. After the Lord spoke this to me, a book titled **Majesty, Promises Revealed in The Names of God** by Life Outreach

INTRODUCTION

International, mysteriously arrived on my doorstep. God directed me to the names He wanted added and where and how to place them within the story.

The last layer to *Forever Friend* was the world of Beelzebub. I questioned God about adding this dimension, —yes, I did question God. My Father gently guided me and encouraged me to share some of my own visions and experiences with the darker realm of the spirit world. The Lord explained to me exactly how I was to expose the enemies' camp.

At the end of each chapter, the Lord gave me *Questions to Contemplate*. I pray these questions will ignite a wonder and questioning within all members of the family, sparking deep conversation. Many of the questions ask for an opinion, rather than searching out facts. The open-ended questions have been designed to allow parents or caregivers an opportunity to discover where your child is spiritually; what they are feeling and thinking about God, the world, and themselves. The questions purposely vary in depth to accommodate readers of various age groups.

When you open the pages of *Forever Friend,* whether you are a child or an adult; your soul will be unlocked as you venture into another dimension. Allow your imagination to be stirred and your faith to soar. *Forever Friend* is a world where truth and the spiritual realm have united. This is not just another adventure story; this is training, teaching, equipping, and preparing future warriors to choose a side and fight to gain territory. It is time for, **Your kingdom come, your will be done, on earth as it is in heaven! Matthew 6:10 NIV**

MY PRAYER

It is my prayer that *Forever Friend* stirs up in you a fresh,
inquisitive thirst for the knowledge of God,
a deep hunger for His written word,
and a longing to come closer to His presence.

"...the Lord spoke to Moses face to face, as a man speaks to his friend."
Exodus 33:11 NKJ

May you hear the Father speaking to you as a friend and may you come to
know Holy Spirit as your own personal
Forever Friend.

Chapter One

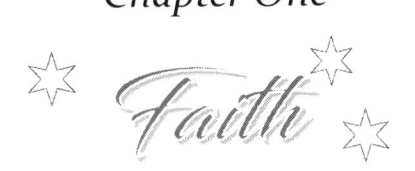

Faith

Samuel squeezed his mother's hand tightly as he gazed up at the enormous flight of stairs leading him to his mysterious Father. Samuel had never met his Father. No one in his tribe had seen his Father face to face, though everyone knew of Him. All the people had great respect for Samuel's mysterious Father, their King.

As Samuel began to climb the stairs, an uneasiness arose inside him. He continued to climb the numerous marble stairs, but his apprehension only grew. Samuel looked towards the top of the stairs. The majestic structure of the Tabernacle stood towering over the small child. The massive structure didn't seem as beautiful as his mother had claimed. It was intimidating to Samuel.

The uneasiness became a large knot inside the child's stomach. Samuel wondered if he would be able to remain obedient to his mother—and more importantly, to his Father's plans for his life. He clung to his mother's hand tightly as they continued to climb the many stairs to the Tabernacle.

Hannah felt the pressure of her son's hand in hers. She knew her son was beginning to question her decision, but she was confident. She began to sing as they continued up the steps. Her voice was soothing to Samuel. "My heart rejoices in the Father! Oh, how the Father has strengthened me!"[1]

FAITH

The tune was melodious. Samuel's mother would often sing this song as she went about her day. He looked up at his mom as she sang, her face shining with a brilliance he hadn't noticed before. Hannah smiled down at her only child as she gently moved her long dark curls away from her eyes. Samuel had been a treasured gift from the Father, and now she was offering him back as a tribute. She had made a promise before the child was born to set him apart for the Father, their King.[2]

Samuel knew about this promise. He also knew he would miss his mom. He would miss everything about her. Especially the times when his mother would race towards him laughing, pick him up, and swing him around singing, "You are the Father's special one, precious one, my little one!" Samuel sighed loudly. He would miss her laughter and their fun games. The knot grew tighter in his tummy.

Samuel stopped. There were only two more steps. He looked across the large marble platform landing and saw the immense wooden door of the Tabernacle. Huge golden pillars stood on each side of the door. Samuel looked up at his mother.

Hannah knelt on the top step. She bent her head down, hiding her face beneath her folded arms, and began talking softly. Samuel listened to his mother's words, though she was speaking in her secret language. Samuel's mom spoke like this often throughout her day. Samuel liked to listen to the unusual words. Very few people in his tribe could talk in the secret language, though they always liked to listen to Hannah's words. After some time, Hannah looked up at her son and smiled. "Your Father waits for you on the other side of that door." Hannah tilted her head towards the alluring structure.

Samuel looked at the large door and then back at his mother. He sat on the top stair and reached for her hand. She began to speak softly again in the secret language. Samuel looked out over the valley. He could see so far from the top of the steps. The colourful banners which surrounded his tribe were moving in the wind. *This won't be too bad,* Samuel thought to himself. *I'll be able to watch everyone from here. This might be an amazing adventure.* His attitude was slowly changing from apprehension to excitement and wonder. The tightness in his stomach began to loosen slightly.

Samuel heard his mother's words becoming louder. *I wonder what my Father looks like,* Samuel thought. *Do I look like Him? Is He big and strong and powerful like the soldiers?* Samuel's mind began to race into the unknown. He tried to imagine what the Tabernacle might look like inside. *Hmmm, will I sleep with walls around me? No more tent to live in with the dusty wind creeping into my bed at night.*

Samuel's mind was still contemplating what might happen when he felt his mother's hand caress his head. He looked up at her and smiled.

"I will come back and visit you this day next year. I promise!" She smiled. "I'll bring you a birthday gift. Today you are five! Oh my! A young man, ready for your Father's teachings to begin. Ah, you will change so much in one year!" She continued to smile at him as she looked down at his tiny hand clenched tightly inside hers. "A mother knows her son's needs, and I will bring you a needed gift in a year."[3] Hannah gazed into her son's eyes. This was an extremely difficult decision—the hardest decision she had ever made. She smiled down at her son. *Yes,* she thought, *I will follow through on my important promise.* Hannah would not hesitate in releasing her only son to his Father, the King. Hannah knew this experience would be life-changing for Samuel. She knew he would spend the rest of his life serving the Father. Over time, he would come to know the Father in a way that most people in his tribe had never experienced. Samuel would build a deep loving relationship with his Father, the King. This was a bittersweet decision. This was the right decision.

Samuel knew his mother would return next year, and he knew she'd have exactly what he needed. He was confident in his mother and in her decisions, though he realized how much she loved him, and how difficult this was for her.

The boy turned and gazed at the large, solid door. He noticed the beautiful gold handle on the massive wooden door. No one he knew had ever lived in the Tabernacle. He thought about being the first to live inside the massive, stately structure. His journey suddenly didn't seem so frightening. The knot in his tummy had disappeared, and Samuel's curiosity was rising inside of him.

"Samuel," his mother spoke softly, "are you ready to enter your Father's house?"

Samuel nodded yes. Hannah placed her hands on the sides of Samuel's face. She kissed him on his forehead and then looked into his eyes. "Remember, you are a gift from your Father.[4] You will be a gift to all who know you. You will learn much from your Father. In time, you will be able to share much wisdom with others. Be obedient, my son. I am so proud of you, my chosen,[5] precious one." Hannah wrapped her arms tightly around her child. For a long time, they remained in their embrace, rocking slowly back and forth on the top of the stairs. Then Hannah leaned down and kissed her son on the forehead. She looked at him once more, smiled, and slowly descended from the top of the stairs.

Samuel watched as his mother walked down the path. He could hear her speaking softly in her secret language. He watched and strained his eyes until her presence became a small dot. Then she disappeared altogether into the horizon.

Samuel stood up and placed his hands on his hips as he studied the massive, spectacular door. As the young boy stood there, gazing at the structure before him, he suddenly felt taller, stronger, more like a soldier than a boy. *This is strange—maybe I grew!* he thought in amazement. *If just sitting here a few minutes makes me feel like this,* Samuel giggled to himself, *just think of my mother's surprise when she sees me next year!*

Samuel continued looking at the massive structure that stood between him and his future with his mysterious Father, the King. The boy scrutinized the large gold latch and the detail of the engraving above the door. *Wow! This is more magnificent than anything I imagined. I wonder what it will look like on the inside?*

Samuel walked towards the entrance of the noble structure with confidence and boldness.[6] What would he behold on the other side of the solid door? Samuel wasn't sure, but he did know that once he had entered his Father's house, his life would be changed forever.

Questions to Contemplate

1. The author titled this chapter "Faith." What do you think faith is? Hebrews 11:6 says that:

    "It is impossible to please God without faith. Anyone who wants to come to him must believe that God exists and that he rewards those who sincerely seek him." The scripture promises us that God will reward us as we seek Him. What might God reward you with as you seek Him?

2. Hannah left her son Samuel on the steps of the Tabernacle without hesitation. Why do you think she was able to freely give up her son?

3. Why didn't Samuel's mother open the door to the tabernacle for Samuel? Why did Samuel need to open this door for himself?

4. What do you think Samuel's mother was saying in her secret language?

5. Samuel believed that "once he had entered his Father's house, his life would be changed forever." How might Samuel's life change after he enters the Tabernacle?

6. What gift do you think Hannah will give to her son Samuel in a year?

7. Do you think Samuel grew as he sat on his Father's steps? Do you feel you grow as you come closer to God?

8. Hannah tells Samuel he is a gift from the Father, chosen and precious. Do you feel this is true of you?

The Passion Translation (TPT) of the Bible tells us in Psalm 127:3, *"Children are God's love-gift; they are heaven's generous reward."* The Amplified Bible (AMP) tells us, *"...children are a heritage and gift from the Lord. The fruit of the womb a reward."*

No matter how you feel, know that you are a gift from the Lord!

---

[1] 1 Samuel 2:1: "Then Hannah prayed: 'My heart rejoices in the Lord! The Lord has made me strong.'"

[2] 1 Samuel 1:28: "Now I am giving him to the Lord, and he will belong to the Lord his whole life."

[3] 1 Samuel 2:18–19: "But Samuel, though he was only a boy, served the Lord. He wore a linen garment like that of a priest. Each year his mother made a small coat for him and brought it to him when she came with her husband for the sacrifice."

[4] Psalm 127:3: "Children are a gift from the Lord; they are a reward from him."

[5] John 15:16: "You didn't choose me. *I chose you.* I appointed you to go and produce lasting fruit...." (emphasis added).

[6] Hebrews 4:16: *"So let us come boldly to the throne of our gracious God.* There we will receive his mercy, and we will find grace to help us when we need it most" (emphasis added).

Chapter Two
The Father's House

Samuel's hand seemed so small compared to the golden latch. It took both of his hands to move its heavy arm. The weighty arm of the latch made a loud groaning sound as Samuel moved it slowly out of the way. *When was the last time someone tried to enter the Tabernacle?* Samuel wondered. The boy studied the massive door for a moment, trying to devise a strategy enabling him to enter the alluring building. Samuel smiled as he confidently put his left foot against the doorframe. His right foot was planted firmly on the ground. The boy grabbed hold of the golden latch and pulled with all his might. Samuel managed to move the heavy door open a few centimeters. *This is hard work!* Samuel thought to himself.

Undeterred, the young boy braced his foot again on the door frame. Samuel pulled the door with all his strength but got nowhere this time. He stopped and examined the door. *It shouldn't be this hard to move,* he thought. Samuel pondered the situation. *Is something, or someone, stopping me from going through the door?*

Samuel looked out towards the horizon. There was no trace of his mother or anyone else. He was alone, or so it seemed—but Samuel knew his mysterious Father lived on the other side of the door. He was determined to get into the Tabernacle and finally meet his Father. Again, he put his foot on the door frame and pulled with all the might he could muster.

THE FATHER'S HOUSE

As Samuel was pulling on the door, he looked up and examined the words inscribed on the top of the doorframe. He didn't understand what the words said—they were in a language he couldn't read. Samuel continued to pull hard on the door with his foot braced against the solid doorframe. The door still wouldn't budge. Something was working against him, keeping the door shut.

Determination rose up inside of Samuel. "No way, whoever you are, this is my Father's house and I have a right to enter. You cannot and will not stop me!" Samuel breathed in deeply and looked around him. He felt better having yelled into the air. The words had poured out of him unexpectedly. Even though he saw no one, he realized speaking out gave him a feeling of empowerment. He felt in control of the situation.

"Father," Samuel said aloud with a pleading voice, "I do want to meet you; I do want to enter your house."[1] He put his foot again on the door frame and pulled. He was mustering up more strength, more determination with each attempt.

The young boy gave a heavy sigh, took a deep breath in, and tried once more to open the large wooden door. "Father! I'm coming in!" Samuel stated as he continued to pull. This time there was no invisible force fighting against him. The door was still very heavy, but it began to move open slightly. Samuel kept pulling until he knew there was enough space for him to squeeze through the opening. He took a deep breath in and pressed himself quickly through the narrow space.

At last, he was through. He'd made it into his Father's house! Samuel leaned back against the massive wooden door, his struggle finally over. The young boy stared in amazement as he absorbed his surroundings.

The walls of the structure towered up, almost unendingly. They were formed out of humongous white stones laid one upon the other. The lower stones of the walls were adorned with every type of jewel, all of them sparkling brilliantly. The first one Samuel saw was a dark red jasper; then he noticed a large deep blue sapphire stone. Samuel counted the precious stones on the walls. There were twelve different gems in total embedded in the walls.[2] The jewels were different sizes and colours, all larger than he was. The colours in the jewels sparkled brightly, creating a rainbow of colour throughout the immense room.

The room was completely empty, except for the rainbow of colours, which seemed to be dancing in the large empty space. The floor appeared to be a sea of glass, sparkling like crystal.[3] Gold sparkles seemed to be glistening just above the floor.

When Samuel looked up at the ceiling, he saw the night sky—only there were more stars than he had ever seen in his whole lifetime. The stars were brilliant. Each one took its turn to be the most radiant.

The boy stared in total amazement. He had never seen such a spectacular sight. Day and night seemed to be mixing together. Samuel stretched his arms out and twirled around, trying to take in all the beauty surrounding him. "O Father! A single day in your Tabernacle is better than a thousand days anywhere else in the world!"[4] exclaimed the young boy.

He took a deep breath in and continued to gaze at his surroundings. The stars and the dancing colours were moving in rhythm with each other. It seemed like the colours and stars were alive and performing just for him.

Samuel looked past the moving colours and saw an exquisite blue, purple, and scarlet curtain embroidered with large gold cherubim.[5] He'd seen cherubim on the armour of the soldiers' shields, and his mother had explained the creatures' importance.

The boy studied the unusual, embroidered creatures. The large cherubim on the curtain looked like lions with the huge, oversized wings of an eagle on each side of their massive bodies. They were exactly like the creatures etched onto the warriors' shields. "Mythical creatures that never existed," the warriors had told young Samuel.

Yet his mother would smile and say, "Someday you will know great and mighty things about your Father and His kingdom. Then you can decide for yourself what is real and what is mythical."

Wow! That must be where my Father is, behind the curtain, Samuel thought. Slowly, gingerly he put his foot on top of the glass floor. The glass sea moved like waves were crashing beneath him, yet the top layer remained solid for Samuel to walk upon. Cautiously he began to make his way across the moving glass floor, through the dancing lights and golden sparkles.

As Samuel moved towards the large curtain, he felt a change happening inside of him. He felt emptied of any cares or concerns. He was no longer cautious or apprehensive. He felt the emptiness being filled with joy, excitement, and expectation.[6] But expectation for what? *What could be more magnificent than all of this?* he wondered.

Samuel began to laugh loudly as he continued to walk—the dancing colours were tickling him as he walked through them. His whole body was beginning to tingle. "My Father's house is fun!" he said out loud. The boy began to twirl around and around, his arms outstretched as a kaleidoscope of colours and stars twirled around him. The golden sparkles from the floor were dancing all about, creating a golden vortex in the air above him.

As Samuel twirled around, he began to hear a new and interesting sound. It started as a faint hum and grew in intensity and depth as his twirls moved him closer to the magnificent curtain. The sound became a series of hums and groans,[7] whines and beats, and all different kinds of noise, which created the most unique and exhilarating celebration.

FOREVER FRIEND

It wasn't like the music which Samuel had often heard in his tribe. This was an indescribable sound, as if all the elements of the earth were singing to Samuel. Rain, wind, thunder, birds, insects, beasts, all earthly noises creating an audible sound together, in a unique rhythm and beat.

Samuel began to twirl around faster as the sound increased in its intensity. Samuel heard himself laughing loudly. This was greater than any of the festivities he had enjoyed on the feast days of his tribe.[8]

Suddenly the colours froze. Then they all retreated back into the jewels they had come from. The beautiful noise ceased. Samuel looked around him. *What made the colours and sound disappear?* he wondered.

A large emerald green jewel on the wall began to dazzle brilliantly. The jewel began to radiate beams of gold and white light. It became so radiant that Samuel hid his eyes behind his hands. He could feel a warm glow from the stone. Then Samuel heard a voice—a man's voice. The voice was deep, yet gentle. "Welcome to your Father's house."

Samuel slowly moved his hands from his eyes and peered into a warm amber glow. As his eyes adjusted to the glow, a shape appeared out of the light. Samuel rubbed his eyes and looked again. As his eyes slowly focused, Samuel saw the most peculiar man—a man who looked like nobody he'd ever seen.[9]

Samuel gasped. The man laughed. His laughter filled the great room and echoed off the walls. The dancing lights and sound resumed their display, and the stars danced into a new formation of brightness and splendour. Samuel laughed too as he began to twirl around in the lights and colours. *What a great place I'm in,* Samuel thought.

"Oh, Father! The one thing I ask, the one thing I seek, is to live in your house, your wonderful Tabernacle, all the days of my life!"[10] exclaimed the young boy loudly. Samuel kept twirling round and round as he gazed up at the starry night sky above him. Then the boy suddenly stopped his movement and gazed into the face of the peculiar man.

Samuel smiled. "You must be my Father," the child stated confidently. "May I live here with you, all the days of my life?"

The man grinned. "I am not your great and magnificent Father, the King," he chuckled loudly. "I am Ezekiel. I am one of your Father's many trusted friends." The tall man looked down upon the boy and released another little chuckle. "The choice to live here, young Samuel, fully depends on you."

Samuel continued to smile, straining his neck slightly as he gazed way up at the interesting older man, who smiled back down upon Samuel. A big broad grin filled the face of his Father's trusted friend. Suddenly the man began to chuckle again. At first it was a little chuckle, but it soon erupted into a hearty laugh. Samuel was quickly overcome with laughter too. Again the young boy twirled around in delight.

Samuel stopped and examined the peculiar man. Ezekiel was extremely tall and slender. He was much taller than any of the men in Samuel's tribe. He had dark brown skin which sparkled with gold flecks. His eyes were emerald, green. They, too, seemed to sparkle. Ezekiel had a beautiful smile and a booming belly laugh, which was contagious. His hair was dark brown—very long, and woven into many fine braids. Each braid had a gold strand running through it, along with various golden beads, shining gemstones, and crystals. Some of his long braids almost reached to the floor, while others were shorter. He wore a majestic cape of many colours. The cape was woven with fine linen and silk and shimmered as he moved, as if the colours were alive. He had golden sandals on his feet. Ezekiel carried a large sceptre, which rose above the tall man's head. It too was golden, inlaid with silver and crystal sparkles. Way up at the top of the sceptre, a huge red sapphire shimmered. The sapphire appeared to be alive—it changed shape and colour randomly on its own, though always returning to brilliant deep red.

"Can I see my Father now?" Samuel asked excitedly. "Does my Father live behind that great curtain?" The boy turned and pointed towards the extraordinary curtain with the large golden cherubim.

"You will see your Father when you are ready for Him, but that won't be for some time. We have much to do to prepare you for your Father. When the Father becomes your *Adonai*, then you will be able to meet him." The tall man laughed loudly. The colours on his cape began to move, creating different patterns. Ezekiel placed his large hand gently on the boy's shoulder as he studied the curtain for a moment. "Exquisite, isn't it?" The peculiar man smiled down at Samuel.

"Yes," Samuel answered, disappointed he wasn't ready to meet his Father. He wondered what the word *Adonai* meant. He'd never heard that word before.

The two continued to stare at the tapestry. "Samuel, you must never touch or go beyond the thick curtain." The man's gentle voice took on a commanding voice of authority. "You must make a solemn promise now, out loud, to never lay your hands upon the curtain or go past it.

"What?!" said Samuel, very disappointed. There was something intriguing about the drapery. *What is behind the veil?* Samuel wondered. *It must be something amazing if I'm not allowed near it*, he thought, continuing to study the huge golden cherubim and their detailed wings.

Ezekiel smiled down at Samuel. "Don't worry, I will let you know when you're ready to go beyond the curtain."

The boy let out a heavy sigh. Samuel felt drawn to this part of the Tabernacle. It was more than curiosity. He believed there was something behind the veil—something more amazing than all the unique things he had already encountered.

Ezekiel knew Samuel was inquisitive, enticed by whatever might be beyond the exquisite tapestry. "To learn, you must love discipline."[11] Ezekiel chuckled deeply as he shook his head. The beads on his braids made a soft tinkling sound. The peculiar man gently tapped Samuel on his shoulder. "There will be much for you to learn here in your Father's house, Samuel. Much to discover, explore, and inquire about." Ezekiel gazed down at the child, who had his eyes fixed on the detailed embroidery of the curtain. Ezekiel admired the intricate design for awhile along with him. He knew everything about the curtain was compelling.

"What happens if I go beyond the curtain?" Samuel asked. He was thinking his Father's house had too many rules, and he was disappointed he wouldn't meet his Father today.

"If you walk in obedience to all the Father has commanded of you, you will live and prosper and prolong your days in this land. A land you will someday possess."[12] Ezekiel grinned.

"Obedience, though often hard to accomplish, leads to righteousness.[13] Such a wonderful quality." Ezekiel continued to examine the magnificent curtain. "Obedience to your Father displays your love for Him."[14] Ezekiel smiled down at the young boy.

"Up to now you have only heard about your great Father. It is difficult to love someone you have only heard about." The peculiar man smiled broadly. "But—you have now chosen to get to know your Father personally!" The tall man continued to smile as he nodded his head in approval of Samuel's decision. The gems and crystals in his hair moved gently, creating a lovely sound. "Oh, how your love for your Father will now begin to grow." The tall man giggled.

"Being obedient to your Father's wishes, even when you don't understand, will prove you are beginning to love and more importantly, trust your magnificent Father." Ezekiel began to chuckle. "Actions do speak louder than words. Especially when the actions come at a cost."

Samuel exhaled loudly. "Okay." The boy released another huge sigh. "I promise never to touch the blue curtain or go beyond it."

"Good," said Ezekiel, as he smiled at the young boy and released a loud chuckle, which echoed across the room. "You are acquiring a willing and obedient heart already! Come with me. I have much to show you!" Ezekiel said excitedly, as his cape displayed a wild pattern of moving colours.

Ezekiel moved past Samuel and crossed the great room. Samuel followed him as the dancing lights once again continued their performance. Samuel turned back and looked again at the great thick blue, purple, and scarlet curtain with its amazing gold embroidered cherubim that towered over the boy. *I wonder who made this huge curtain,* Samuel thought. *There must be something incredible on the other side!*

"Hmm," said Samuel out loud, his curiosity growing. *Could my Father live on the other side of the curtain? Could I be this close to my Father and not know it?* Samuel continued to stare at the large, golden cherubim that were delicately embroidered on the thick curtain. Samuel wanted to stretch out his hand to touch the golden tapestry of the unusual lion-like creatures, but he dared not.

Ezekiel stood in front of the wall, his back to the small boy. Another large red sapphire gleamed brilliantly. Samuel was still studying the tapestry with the huge, exquisite cherubim when he noticed a portion of the thick curtain move. Quickly Samuel glanced at the movement. His eyes caught sight of a very long golden-brown tube moving slowly across the floor. The moving object was partially on Samuel's side of the curtain. At first Samuel thought it could be a snake, but at the end of the moving object were many long black, brown, and golden hairs. The object moved as if it was attached to something and was being pulled along. It didn't slither like a snake. Whatever it was, it moved slowly under the curtain, and then was gone from sight.

Samuel was about to ask Ezekiel about the moving object when he saw the tall man touch the large red sapphire, which instantly radiated warmth and a brilliant auburn light. Samuel closed his eyes because the light was so intense.

Immediately, the young boy felt a cool breeze on his face. Samuel opened his eyes and found himself outside on a balcony with Ezekiel. Now he was overlooking an exquisite garden. Beautiful trees loaded with fruit were planted throughout the garden. The fruit on the trees were the same brilliant colours as the rubies on the wall of His Father's house. Each fruit seemed to take its turn to shimmer brightly. A glorious, sparkling river flowed through the garden.

Far off in the distance, Samuel could see the tents and banners of his tribe. He wondered if his mother was home now. He suddenly missed her.

"You have responsibilities to learn, young Samuel.[15] When your mother comes back in a year, she will scarcely recognize you. You will have grown so much. She will be back, though, and your time will go by quickly. You have many things to be trained up in," said Ezekiel.

Samuel wasn't so sure this was such a good idea. He missed his mom, and hadn't seen his Father yet. He wondered what responsibilities he would be given. After all, he had just turned five that very day.

Ezekiel looked down at the boy and grinned. He seemed to know that Samuel was having second thoughts about living in his Father's house.

"There's a friend waiting for you in the garden," Ezekiel said as he continued to smile at the child.

"A friend!" Samuel had thought he would be the only child in his Father's house. "Wow, can I meet my friend?"

"Of course," said Ezekiel. He waved his hands above his head and a cloud appeared. They became immersed in the mist.

As the cloud slowly disappeared, Samuel found himself in the middle of the garden beside the beautiful sparkling river. The water glistened. Samuel rubbed his eyes. It seemed like the water had crystals bouncing off the surface of the sparkling river. *I have so much to learn about this place,* Samuel thought to himself, *and now I have a friend to share my adventure with.* Samuel smiled. He'd made the right decision to enter his Father's house. Now he could begin a deepening relationship with his Father. Possibly his Father could become his *Adonai*—whatever that meant. He would have to ask Ezekiel about this new word.

* * *

The Father looked down upon Samuel from His throne room. His face smiled with favour[16] upon the child and the decisions he was making.

* * *

Deep under the ground, a battle was raging against the King. The enemy of the Father was planning a siege. The evil beast Beelzebub[17] demanded victory. The large scaly monster stormed through the dark cavern, his gigantic tail with its many spikes swaying back and forth. The tail hammered the cavern walls, causing rocks to splinter from the impact and come crashing onto the slimy rock floor. "We need to remobilize! Argh!" The creature hissed, his deep voice echoing throughout the cavern. The beast spat saliva throughout the dark cave as he stormed back and forth, devising an attack on the King.

Hiding against the damp walls of the cavern, the little Spittles looked at one another and then stared back at their enraged beastly master. The master had commissioned sixty-six of his little evil vapour puffs to keep the boy Samuel from entering the Tabernacle. The Spittles had failed their assignment.

The little creatures had no body, only a black formless head with either beady yellow or squinty red eyes. The vapours all had a small mouth which could only speak evil. Dangling beneath each vapour of evil was a small tail that manoeuvred the Spittles through the atmosphere.

"You fools! You useless, good-for-nothing fools! Why did you leave the Tabernacle door? I told you, don't let him into the Tabernacle! Can't I trust you idiot Spittles to do anything right?!" Beelzebub spit the words out through clenched teeth as he continued marching through the dreary cave deep beneath the ground. A loud, echoing explosion was heard with each step of the creature's massive body. A horde of flies buzzed around his head.

"There were sixty-six of you! There was only one weak, helpless child!" Beelzebub let out a loud groan as smoke spumed from his ears.

"Oh great evil one!" A Spittle slowly left the damp wall and came closer to the morbid, fuming beast. "We were all pushing hard against the door to the Tabernacle, trying to keep it shut," the Spittle began to stammer. "Bbbuuutttt...."

"Spit it out!" demanded Beelzebub.

"But the child called out to his Father for help. We had no choice but to leave."

The large scaly tail of the monster slashed across the damp cavern as Beelzebub abruptly turned in rage at the Spittle who'd spoken. The small vapour of discouragement was instantly slammed into the slimy cavern wall. All the other Spittles moved out of the angry creature's way.

A roar was heard as smoke, fire, and a putrid smell erupted from the mouth of the evil master, Beelzebub.

"That is precisely why you were to discourage him from even trying! Let alone speaking out! Never, never let humans call to their Father for help! You must gag them with hopelessness before they desire to cry out. You were to make him feel scared, helpless, and too frightened to move forward into the unknown! Arghhhh! The child was to cling to his mother and return home, defeated. Defeated! Where is that little scumbag, Defeated?" The evil beast searched the cavern walls for the puff of vapour named Defeated.

More smoke billowed out of the beast's pores, creating a steam which sizzled as it dripped on the cold, damp cavern floor. "The child was to give up in fear... *fear!*" The master screamed the word out as a loud roar. Beelzebub suddenly reached towards the cavern wall and snatched the vapour named Fear by its throat. Slowly he drew the Spittle close to his face as steam continued to erupt from his ears, nose, and the large horns on top of his grotesque head. The horde of flies hovered around the beast's large head, lingering in the steam that was secreted.

"You, Fear, were told to hold Samuel back from venturing into the unknown!" More noxious gases emerged from the enraged creature. Now even the horn spikes on his huge, scaly tail released putrid fumes. The sizzling could be heard throughout all the chambers beneath the ground. All the underworld knew that the beast Beelzebub was once again enraged. "If Discouragement didn't succeed, Fear, you were to fall upon the little brat." Beelzebub threw the Spittle against the cavern wall. The Spittle slid down the wet wall of the cavern and rested on the damp floor.

Fear slowly arose from the floor of the cavern and moved consciously through the smelly air towards the beast. "Oh, great one, I heard the mother singing praises to the Father. Then she began to speak in her secret language and I didn't know what plan she was devising.[18] I can never get close to the humans with praise or that dreadful secret language." The vapour of Fear quickly moved back from Beelzebub, unsure of the consequences for having spoken.

"Useless! Scum! You are all worthless! Why do I even bother to tell you any of my magnificent schemes? Must I do everything myself? I have others to terrorize! A child, I sent you against a mere child. Sixty-six of you couldn't defeat a small, five-year-old child who has not yet been trained up in the ways of the Father!"[19]

"Arghhhhhhh, now Samuel is sheltered inside the Tabernacle. We must wait for our next opportunity to paralyze the brat. I want you to be ever vigilant, watching the boy. Don't take your eyes off the Tabernacle. Let me know the moment he looks like he is vulnerable. We will have another opportunity to attack. *Heh, heh, heh*—we always get to repeat our missions."

With a fiery blast from its eyes and mouth, the evil creature disappeared into a deeper cavern, the horde of flies following. Beelzebub's evil laughter echoed through the chambers and tunnels. The lingering foul smell reminded the vapour puff Spittles of their failure to discourage and defeat the child, Samuel.

Questions to Contemplate

1. Samuel said he had the right to enter the Tabernacle. Why does he have this right?
2. Do you think Samuel was able to change his situation by speaking out loud?

3. Ezekiel never told Samuel what would happen if he touched or went behind the curtain. What do you think might happen to Samuel if he explored this forbidden area?

4. What do you think Samuel saw moving under the curtain?

5. The word *Adonai* means my great Lord, master, owner, and ruler. Why do you think the Father must be Samuel's *Adonai* before the boy can meet Him?

6. Samuel doesn't meet his Father in the Tabernacle; do you think the Father was in the Tabernacle? Explain where you think the Father was.

7. Who do you think Beelzebub might be? What do you think a Spittle could be?

---

[1] Romans 10:13: "Everyone who calls on the name of the Lord will be saved."

[2] Revelation 21:19–20: "The wall of the city was built on foundation stones inlaid with twelve precious stones: the first was jasper, the second sapphire, the third agate, the fourth emerald, the fifth onyx, the sixth carnelian [ruby], the seventh chrysolite, the eighth beryl, the ninth topaz, the tenth chrysoprase (turquoise) , the eleventh jacinth, the twelfth amethyst."

[3] Revelation 4:6: "In front of the throne was a shiny sea of glass, sparkling like crystal."

[4] Psalm 84:10: "A single day in your courts is better than a thousand anywhere else!"

[5] Exodus 26:31: "For the inside of the Tabernacle, make a special curtain of finely woven linen. Decorate it with blue, purple, and scarlet thread and with skillfully embroidered cherubim."

[6] Philippians 4:4: "Rejoice in the Lord always: and again I say, Rejoice" (KJV).

[7] Romans 8:22: "…we know that all creation has been groaning as in the pains of childbirth right up to the present time."

[8] Psalm 65:4: "What festivities await us inside your holy Temple."

THE FATHER'S HOUSE

[9] 1 Peter 2:9: "But ye are a chosen generation, a royal priesthood, an holy nation, *a peculiar people*: that ye should shew forth the praises of him who hath called you out of darkness into his marvellous light…" (KJV, emphasis added).

[10] Psalm 27:4: "The one thing I ask of the Lord—the thing I seek most—is to live in the house of the Lord all the days of my life, delighting in the Lord's perfections and meditating in his Temple."

[11] Proverbs 12:1: "To learn, you must love discipline; it is stupid to hate correction."

[12] Deuteronomy 5:33: "Stay on the path that the Lord your God has commanded you to follow. Then you will live long and prosperous lives in the land you are about to enter and occupy."

[13] Romans 6:16: "Do you not know that when you continually offer yourselves to someone to do his will, you are the slaves of the one whom you obey, either [slaves] of sin, which leads to death, or of *obedience, which leads to righteousness [right standing with God]?*" (AMP, emphasis added).

[14] 1 Samuel 15:22: "'Tell me,' Samuel said. 'Does the Lord really want sacrifices and offerings? No! He doesn't want your sacrifices. *He wants you to obey him*'" (CEV, emphasis added).

[15] Genesis 1:26: "Then God said, 'Let us make human beings in our image, to be like us. They will reign over the fish in the sea, the birds in the sky….'"

[16] Psalm 67:1: "May God be merciful and bless us. May his face smile with favor on us."

[17] Matthew 12:24: "Now when the Pharisees heard *it* they said, 'This *fellow* does not cast out demons except by Beelzebub, the ruler of the demons'" (NKJV).

[18] Romans 8:26–27: "And the Holy Spirit helps us in our weakness. For example, we don't even know what God wants us to pray for. But the Holy Spirit prays for us with groanings that cannot be expressed in words. And the *Father who knows all hearts knows what the Spirit is saying*, for the Spirit pleads for us believers in harmony with God's own will" (emphasis added).

[19] Proverbs 22:6: "Train up a child in the way he should go, And when he is old he will not depart from it" (NKJV).

Chapter Three
First Fruit

Samuel followed Ezekiel beside the sparkling water. As Samuel gazed at the dazzling water, he realized there were actual crystals bouncing across the top of the moving river.

"Wow! My Father's Garden is amazing!" the child exclaimed. Samuel had entered into a land that was completely different from anything he had ever seen or heard about.

"Where does this water come from?" he asked Ezekiel.

"The river flows from your Father's house.[1] The water feeds the garden. It will be your responsibility to pick the fruit on the trees as they ripen. You will place the fruit in a basket and bring it to the giving altar. Each tree ripens on a different day, and there will be a new crop every month, without fail. The fruit will be for food, and the leaves for healing.[2] Both the fruit and the leaves on the trees are very special. Each leaf knows when it is needed for healing." Ezekiel reached way up, gently touched a delicate leaf, and smiled. "The leaves from these trees will never fall on the ground, and they will never turn brown and dry up like the leaves you saw in your tribe." The tall man looked down at Samuel and winked. "This is where you are needed, young Samuel. It will be your responsibility to watch for any leaves that may be needed for healing, along with picking the ripened fruit. The leaves that are to be released from the tree will glow with an incandescent brilliance. Then they will wait for you to arrive with the golden plate." As Ezekiel spoke, he waved his hand upward and a beautiful golden plate appeared in his outstretched hand. The man chuckled as he examined the plate. "Beautiful, isn't it?" Samuel nodded his head in agreement. "The leaves will all land upon this golden plate. You will then bring them to the giving altar. Another day, I will tell you more about the fruit and the qualities they hold. Today we will search for the healing leaf." Samuel could hardly believe his eyes as he gazed upon the golden plate that had mysteriously appeared. Everything in his Father's land was new and astonishing.

"There's a leaf!" Ezekiel said, with excitement in his gentle voice. He pointed towards a beautiful emerald green and crimson red tree. The fruit on the tree was large and round, with beautiful shiny amber skin. One leaf on the tree was glowing brilliantly.

"These leaves look like the giant tailfeathers of a rooster," Samuel stated as he closely studied the tree.

The glowing leaf suddenly released from the tree and slowly drifted upon the gentle breeze. The leaf landed softly on the golden plate which was in Ezekiel's outstretched hand. Ezekiel smiled and held the leaf like a precious treasure.

"When you catch a leaf, you must hold it with great care and attentiveness. Always thank the tree for giving you its leaf or its fruit. It is very important to be thankful." Ezekiel said words to the tree in a language Samuel didn't understand as the peculiar man delicately positioned the unique leaf on the golden plate. "Would you like to bring this leaf to the altar, Samuel?"

"Sure!" Samuel responded. "I'll be very careful with it, I promise," he answered with enthusiasm.

Ezekiel smiled and handed the boy the plate with the large feather leaf. Together, the two strolled under the canopy of the trees. The gentle breeze continued to blow softly on their faces. Carried on the breeze was the sweet perfume of the garden.

"What kind of trees are these?" Samuel asked. "Why are they all different? Each one has a different coloured fruit and unique leaves." Samuel reached up and gently touched one of the leaves on a tree as they continued to saunter through the lush garden. Oil from the leaf caressed the boy's hand, and was quickly absorbed into his skin. The leaf was pink and furry. "The trees in my tribe look nothing like this," Samuel stated as he looked down upon his hands. The boy smiled as he noticed his dry, cracked hand was now silky smooth. "You are very observant. There are many different trees all producing rare fruit."

"Why?" Samuel asked.

Ezekiel chuckled. He was enjoying the inquisitive child's company. "We have many different needs and appetites." Ezekiel explained. "When people are feeling sorrowful, they need to eat from the tree of joy. They may be so distressed that they need the oil of joy, which is extracted from the leaf of this tree. Someone may feel impatient and need a soothing tea made from the leaf of the patience tree. Its fruit is crimson, with golden dots. This fruit will soothe the most irritated, stressed-out person. My favourite is the fruit of righteousness, from the tree of life. It wins souls and produces wisdom.[3] The fruit tastes sweeter than honey! You will eventually learn all the qualities of the fruit trees and their leaves. There are many[4] trees in the garden. In time, you will come to know them all. Hmmmmm..." Ezekiel thought. "Along with the tree of life, there is the tree that holds the fruit of salvation. It is another favourite of mine! Oh my, my, my, the cherished fruit of salvation is a number one pick! It tastes, ah, let me think now, hmmm... indescribable, and oh yes, filling!"[5] Ezekiel licked his lips. His hearty laughter echoed through the garden. He made a funny smacking sound with his mouth and chuckled like he was being tickled. The unusual man rubbed his belly with his hands. "Ummm, yes, so filling and yummy!"

Samuel laughed too. He thought Ezekiel was funny, like a big kid. Samuel was glad to be in the company of such a delightful man. The pair continued on their journey through the garden, enjoying the tapestry of smells, sights, and sounds.

"There are many varieties of trees in your Father's garden," Ezekiel explained as he gently moved a low-growing tree branch out of his way. "Some trees aren't as plentiful, but they do pack a powerful punch when you eat their fruit."[6] As the tall man began to giggle, the gems woven into his braids made a lovely tinkling sound. "Much to learn, young Samuel, but not all in one day." Ezekiel gently tapped the boy on his head as he continued to chuckle. "Yes, one day at a time." The man laughed again and then began to hum a lovely little melody.

"Here we are at the giving altar," Ezekiel informed Samuel.

In front of Samuel stood a wide, tall wall. It was made from a single glistening pearl. The very top of the wall was formed out of solid gold, which created a thick mantle. Red and purple sapphires were inlaid around the top edge of the wall. There was a golden braided rope wrapped around the altar, just under the red and purple sapphires. The foundation of the altar was built upon deep red sapphires, which sparkled brilliantly in the sunshine.

"You will always place the fruit and leaves on the very top of the altar. I believe you will need some help to reach the top," Ezekiel said as he looked down upon the boy.

"Unbelievable!" Samuel stated slowly as he looked upon the magnificent structure. "It looks more like a large wall than an altar," he exclaimed. The boy's little hands gently caressed the pearl and inlaid jewels. "This is much more beautiful than the altar in my tribe!" Samuel continued to run his hand across the length of the long altar. Once he reached the end, the young boy turned and walked back towards Ezekiel, continuing to touch the iridescent pearl wall. Samuel stopped next to the tall man and gazed into the large red sapphire base. His tiny fingers gently moving across the shimmering gem. "Amazing!" said Samuel as he saw his reflection in the dazzling red stone. As the boy looked at his brilliant red reflection, he made funny faces. "The altar in my tribe is just a pile of rough old stones. It's made from rocks found throughout the desert wasteland. It looks nothing like this!"

Ezekiel laughed—a sound that was now like thunder as it echoed throughout the garden. "Ruach will enjoy having you for a friend. It has been a while since we enjoyed having a young boy with us. Ruach, Samuel is here." Ezekiel smiled as he looked all around. "Ruach," Ezekiel called out louder, "Samuel could use your help." Ezekiel smiled down at the boy and winked.

"Ruach," the man said gently, "we invite you to come!" The peculiar man nodded his head slowly and grinned. "Yes, we invite you to come," Ezekiel said once more as he continued to look about the garden.

Samuel suddenly felt something warm and soft against his leg. The young boy looked down and saw a spotless white ram. The ram looked up at Samuel with large, sparkling, brilliant blue eyes. "Awwww! A ram! I've heard about them, but I've never seen one till now. The soldiers in my tribe spoke about large, strong rams high in the mountains. They told me rams had short, creamy wool, grungy and scraggly in the winter months." Samuel laughed. "Amazing— look at the long, snow-white wool of my Father's ram. You're so beautiful!" Samuel said as he gazed at the delightful creature. "Can I touch the ram?"

"Ruach is your Forever Friend. He has been waiting for you to arrive at your Father's house." Ezekiel looked lovingly at the ram. "Of course you

FIRST FRUIT

can touch and caress your Forever Friend. It will be an embrace you will always remember."

Samuel knelt down and put his arms gently around the ram. "He likes me, I know he does!" Samuel said as the little ram cuddled securely in his arms.

"He loves you very much. Ruach will never leave you. He will guide you in all truth.[7] Ruach is young like you, Samuel. He is just now starting to mature. His horns have begun to bud on his forehead. He will be a strong and courageous ram, sturdy and true. It is very important you allow Ruach to direct your ways and guide you in the things of truth. He will also be of great comfort to you."[8] Ezekiel looked down at the child embracing his new Forever Friend. "*Great* comfort," he repeated, stressing the word "great."

Samuel continued to caress the ram's beautiful wool. It felt soft and silky. The ends of each long strand of wool had a silver tip which sparkled like crystal. Samuel continued touching his beautiful friend; his heart was filled with joy.[9] No one he knew had a friend like this—a Forever Friend.

"Okay, Ruach," said Ezekiel, "it's time to help Samuel place the leaf of love on the giving altar."

"This is the leaf of love," Samuel said in amazement. He looked down at the leaf on the golden plate. The colour of the leaf had turned from greens and reds to a dazzling iridescent glass leaf. It seemed to be pulsating as a soft red hue was forming around the unusual delicate leaf.

Ezekiel smiled at Samuel. "Ruach will help raise you up.[10] Place yourself on his back and you will be at the perfect height to place the plate on the top of the altar."

"Won't I hurt Ruach? I would never want to hurt him!" Samuel said defensively, proclaiming his loyalty to his new friend.

FOREVER FRIEND

"No, Samuel." Ezekiel chuckled loudly. "Ruach is your sturdy companion. He is here to guide[11] and help you.[12] He will always lead you in the right direction. Always trust and lean on Ruach with all your heart. Don't depend on your own understanding. Seek your new Forever Friend in all you do, and he will show you which path to take."[13]

Samuel watched as Ruach moved from Samuel's side to the pearl giving altar. Ruach looked over at Samuel, blinked his twinkling blue eyes, and waited patiently. Samuel couldn't help but smile down at his wonderful new Forever Friend. Ruach's brilliant eyes continued to gaze at Samuel, and his extremely long black eyelashes blinked lovingly up at the young boy.

Samuel looked up again at the unique wall. He was a little hesitant. The young boy moved slowly towards his new Forever Friend. With the plate held carefully in one hand, Samuel placed one foot on Ruach's back. Ruach didn't move. Samuel placed his other foot on the ram's back. He took a moment to gain his balance. Then the boy reached up high over his head with the precious leaf. With his hands held high, Samuel slid the golden plate, which held the pulsating love leaf, onto the giving altar. He quickly jumped backwards off the ram's back and landed solidly on the ground.

The ram came over to Samuel and snuggled up to the side of Samuel's leg. "That wasn't too hard for you, Ruach?" Samuel asked his new friend. Ruach looked up at Samuel and shook his head back and forth as if saying no. "What, he understands me?!" Samuel exclaimed, totally astonished.

"All your Father's creatures understand us, Samuel," said Ezekiel. "You have much to learn and do here with your Father." The tall, gentle man chuckled. Laughter could be heard throughout the lush garden.

"Now, I will show you where you will sleep." Ezekiel led Samuel back towards the Tabernacle.

What will happen to the love leaf? Samuel wondered. *What's on the other side of the giving altar? I do have so much to learn,* he thought, with excitement building inside him. He touched the head of his new friend Ruach, who was walking closely by his side. Samuel enjoyed the feel of the silky wool. The three ventured together towards the Father's house. The cool air of the evening was beginning to settle on the garden.

The Father was nearby, watching. He smiled upon them. He was delighted in the progress Samuel was making. The Father began to hum a new melody as He continued to watch the threesome.[14]

Questions to Contemplate

1. Why do you think the first leaf given to Samuel was the leaf of love?

2. If you could have a Forever Friend, what would your Forever Friend look like? Can you draw a picture of your Forever Friend?

3. What qualities would you like your Forever Friend to have? Why would you choose those qualities?

4. Why do you think the altar is referred to as "the giving altar"?

5. Who do you think the Father is?

FOREVER FRIEND

[1] Psalm 46:4 "*There* is a river whose streams shall make glad the city of God the holy *place* of the tabernacle of the Most High." (NKJV)

[2] Ezekiel 47:12: "Fruit trees of all kinds will grow along both sides of the river. The leaves of these trees will never turn brown and fall, and there will always be fruit on their branches. There will be a new crop every month, for they are watered by the river flowing from the Temple. The fruit will be for food and the leaves for healing."

[3] Proverbs 11:30: "The fruit of the righteous *is a* tree of life, And he who wins souls is wise" (NKJV, emphasis in original).

[4] Galatians 5:22–23: "But the fruit of the Spirit [the result of His presence within us] is love [unselfish concern for others], joy, [inner] peace, patience [not the ability to wait, but how we act while waiting], kindness, goodness, faithfulness, gentleness, self-control. Against such things there is no law" (AMP).

[5] Philippians 1:11: "May you always be filled with the fruit of your salvation."

[6] 1 Corinthians 12:8–11: "To one is given through the [Holy] Spirit [the power to speak] the message of wisdom, and to another [the power to express] the word of knowledge *and* understanding according to the same Spirit; to another [wonder-working] faith [is given] by the same [Holy] Spirit, and to another the [extraordinary] gifts of healings by the one Spirit; and to another the working of miracles, and to another prophecy [foretelling the future, speaking a new message from God to the people], and to another discernment of spirits [the ability to distinguish sound, godly doctrine from the deceptive doctrine of man-made religions and cults], to another *various* kinds of [unknown] tongues, and to another interpretation of tongues. All these things [the gifts, the achievements, the abilities, the empowering] are brought about by one and the same [Holy] Spirit, distributing to each one individually just as He chooses" (AMP, emphasis in original).

[7] John 14:15–17: "If you love me, obey my commandments. *And I will ask the Father, and he will give you another Advocate, who will never leave you. He is the Holy Spirit, who leads into all truth.* The world cannot receive him, because it isn't looking for him and doesn't recognize him. But you know him, because he lives with you now and later will be in you" (emphasis added).

[8] John 14:16: "And I will pray the Father, and he shall give you another Comforter, that he may abide with you forever" (KJV).

[9] 1 Thessalonians 1:6: "So you received the message with joy from the Holy Spirit...."

[10] Ephesians 3:16: "I pray that from his glorious, unlimited resources he will empower you with inner strength through his Spirit."

[11] John 16:13: "When the Spirit of truth comes, he will guide you into all truth."

[12] Romans 8:26: "And the Holy Spirit helps us in our weakness."

[13] Proverbs 3:5–6: "Trust in the Lord with all your heart; do not depend on your own understanding. Seek his will in all you do, *and he will show you which path to take*" (emphasis added).

[14] Zephaniah 3:17: "For the Lord your God is living among you. He is a mighty savior. He will take delight in you with gladness. With his love, he will calm all your fears. *He will rejoice over you with joyful songs"* (emphasis added).

Chapter Four

Rest

Ezekiel stopped at the base of the Tabernacle. The structure towered over them. The lower part of the Tabernacle was built out of large granite stones. Ezekiel placed his hand on one of the large stones. He then knocked on the stone as if knocking on a door. The majestic man waited a moment as he gently rubbed his hand.

"Hmmm," said Ezekiel as he raised his eyebrow. He looked down on the ground, picked up a small round stone, and banged it against one of the large stones in the wall. Again, Ezekiel said "hmmm," only louder. Ezekiel looked down at Samuel and winked. "Sometimes you just have to keep knocking!"[1] The peculiar man chuckled to himself.

Ezekiel banged the smaller stone several more times against the large rock. Suddenly, a rumbling sound could be heard. Ezekiel chuckled again and put the smaller rock back down on the ground. The rumbling sound grew louder and louder. Samuel couldn't believe his eyes as he witnessed a large chunk of the rock wall crumble into dust, creating a large opening into the Tabernacle for Ezekiel and Samuel to walk through.

"This is your room, Samuel," said Ezekiel as he stepped over the fine dust and into the newly created space. Samuel followed Ezekiel into a splendid chamber, then he turned around and looked at the opening he had just walked through. Ezekiel clapped his hands three times and the dust rose up and returned to stone. Samuel went to touch the rock, when the entire wall changed form again. Now it turned into a huge window. Samuel could feel the cold, rough texture of the stone under his fingers, but he couldn't see any stone in front of him.

The young boy was puzzled. Then Samuel realized he could see right through the stone wall and look out at the lush garden. The doorway had turned into a see-through wall!

"How can this be?" Samuel asked Ezekiel.

"Your Father wants you to keep a watchful eye on his garden at all times.[2] You can now see through the rocks."

"Wow! Why can't I see in this direction?" Samuel asked pointing to the opposite wall. Ezekiel laughed loudly. What a pleasure it was to have a curious child with him in the Tabernacle. "The garden isn't in that direction. Your eyes and thoughts need to be focused on the garden."

"Is this a pearl?" asked Samuel, running his hand along the beautiful, smooth, shimmering walls.

"The walls are pearl-coated. The actual pearl is here." Ezekiel pointed to a large round ball.

"Amazing," said Samuel.

"All you need to rest[3] is here, Samuel." Ezekiel bent way down and touched the large, shimmering pearl. A bed of the softest down grew from it. The down feathers were the same creamy white colour as the pearl. On the feathers appeared a blanket of gold with sparkling red threads running through it. The pearl itself became a cushiony pillow.

"I've never slept in anything like this before. In my mother's tent, I have a mat on the floor and a colourful blanket my mother made from wool."

Ezekiel grinned. "Your Father's house is filled with riches yet to be discovered. I will leave you with this fruit to eat for tonight." Ezekiel reached inside his colourful cape and pulled out a shiny oval fruit. Ezekiel held the beautiful fruit up high and examined it. The fruit had intricate markings of blue and purple swirls on its shiny surface.

The peculiar man smiled at the piece of fruit. "The entire fruit is edible," Ezekiel said as he leaned way down and placed the fruit into Samuel's small hands.

Samuel looked at the shimmering fruit. He could see his face reflected in the oval gift.

"Awesome! What's this fruit called?" asked Samuel. When he looked up, Ezekiel was gone.

Samuel felt Ruach rub up against his leg, and then the ram leaped onto Samuel's new bed. The down bed seemed to bounce under him. Feathers flew up into the air and gently floated around the ram. Ruach curled up, put his head on his legs, and rested. His brilliant blue eyes looked lovingly up at Samuel. A couple of the feathers were still slowly floating towards the bed. Ruach batted his long lashes as his large blue eyes beamed at the boy.

Samuel laughed. *That looks like fun.* He ran and jumped onto his bed. Ruach flew up into the air as Samuel landed. Samuel laughed. He and Ruach bounced on the bed together. The pearly feathers appeared to be dancing around the two new friends. Samuel laughed as Ruach's long, white, silky wool with the silver tips rose and fell in slow motion as the ram bounced up and down on the bed. Samuel finally fell into the bed and lay there for a moment, looking at the beautiful pearl ceiling.

Samuel remembered the fruit and began to eat it hungrily. It was sweet and juicy. It tasted better than any fruit he had ever eaten. "Are you hungry, Ruach?" Samuel gave the remainder of the fruit to the ram. The young boy's tummy was full, and he was becoming tired. Samuel looked out at the garden. The sun had almost set. It was now dusk. Samuel could see the first star sparkle in the evening sky. He wondered if there were fewer stars in his Father's Tabernacle ceiling. *Is the Tabernacle a keeping place for all the stars during the day?* he wondered.

Samuel rested his head on his pearl pillow. He was remembering his day and all the treasures he had discovered. Ruach nestled up next to him on the bed. Samuel stroked the soft, silken wool of his new Forever Friend.

"Ruach, I need to thank my Father, the King, for this very special day. Today is the beginning of a new adventure for me—and you too! I'm so excited. You are my Forever Friend. Do you know what that means? We will be together forever!"

Samuel said the words he had heard others in his tribe say nightly to the King. He didn't give the words much thought—Samuel knew them all by heart. He was so proud he could recite them. Most of the boys his age still struggled to remember all the words. There were lots of words to remember.

When the young boy was finished, he noticed Ruach was still gazing at him, as if there was more he should be saying. Samuel thought and then added, "Thank you, Father. Thank you for this incredible day. Thank you for my new Forever Friend, Ruach, and for Ezekiel." Samuel thought for a moment. "Thank you for my mom and all my friends in my tribe."

Ruach blinked his big blue eyes, his long black lashes moving slowly up and down. Samuel smiled. A warmth entered into his heart. He thought a while longer and then added, "Father, I look forward to meeting You. I can't wait to get to know You." Ruach nuzzled up closer against the young boy and rested his head on Samuel's chest. Samuel smiled down at his new Forever Friend. He liked how he felt after saying his own unique prayer to the Father. The ram closed his beautiful blue eyes and released a gentle sigh. Samuel continued to stroke the luxurious wool of his new, treasured friend. The young five-year-old boy's eyes quickly grew heavy, and he fell into a sweet sleep.[4]

*　*　*

The large, hideous creature Beelzebub stormed through the tunnels deep under the earth. The horde of flies tried to keep up with the beast as they buzzed noisily around his head. The little Spittles who served the vile beast knew their master was rising from the darkness. The bashing of his tail, which loosened rocks from the tunnel walls, was a warning that the ominous creature was on the prowl. Beelzebub left a trail of destruction everywhere he went.

As the vapours of evil heard their master approaching, they quickly moved into the dark shadows of the cavern walls. No one willingly moved into the presence of the beast—to do so would be to risk an uncertain fate.

Beelzebub emerged from the narrow tunnel into the large underground cavern. He was wringing his long scrawny fingers as he paced back and forth in the cavern. Suddenly Beelzebub snatched an evil vapour puff from the dark shadow and drew it to his face. With his long, jagged fingernail, he scratched at the black vapour. "Where, where is the brat now?" Beelzebub demanded to know, taking his long claw-like fingernail and raising the chin of the evil Spittle who was clenched in his grip. "I told you to keep an ever-watchful eye on the mortal. Where is he?" yelled the beast as he continued to choke the puff of vapour.

"The child," the Spittle squeaked out, "Samuel is still in the shelter of the Tabernacle."[5] The beady yellow eyes of the Spittle began to pop out of its head.

"Argh!" Beelzebub threw the vapour into the damp wall of the cavern. "Useless creatures! Why do I tolerate you? Inform me when the brat begins to move towards the outskirts of the Tabernacle. I will be devising a plot against the little germ. Be ready to attack the child."

Beelzebub blew fire from his mouth and stormed into another tunnel that led deeper into the depths of the earth. A noxious gas remained in the cavern, settling slowly on the damp floor. The Spittles quickly moved through the winding passageways towards the surface of the earth.

The vapour puffs peered out through the cracks of the planet's surface. The Spittles with beady yellow eyes scrutinized the horizon. The red-eyed Spittles all fixed their gazes upon the Tabernacle, searching relentlessly for any signs of movement outside the protected home of the Father.

Questions to Contemplate

1. The ram was a gift to Samuel to help guide and direct him and to be his Forever Friend. Can you think of someone else God gives us to help guide and direct us?

2. Do you think of this person as your Forever Friend?

3. Would you like to sleep in a room like Samuel was given? What would your favourite part of the room be?

4. Why does Samuel's Father want him to keep a watchful eye on the garden?

5. Samuel's prayer to his Father the king changed from being one of remembrance and repetition to a prayer of fellowship from his heart. How do you pray? Do you repeat the same words every night, or do you talk to God as a friend?

FOREVER FRIEND

---

[1] Matthew 7:7: "Keep on asking, and you will receive what you ask for. *Keep on seeking, and you will find. Keep on knocking, and the door will be opened to you.* For everyone who asks, receives. Everyone who seeks, finds. And to everyone who knocks, the door will be opened" (emphasis added).

[2] Genesis 2:15: "The Lord God placed the man in the Garden of Eden to tend and watch over it."

[3] Hebrews 4:3: "For only we who believe can enter his rest."

[4] Proverbs 3:24: "When you lie down, you will not be afraid; when you lie down, your sleep will be sweet" (NIV).

[5] Psalm 27:1: "The Lord is my light and my salvation—so why should I be afraid? The Lord is my fortress, protecting me from danger, so why should I tremble?"

Chapter Five

Beginning of the Harvest

Samuel felt the warmth of the morning sun on his cheeks. Casually, he moved his arm to stretch, and as he did, his fingers touched the soft, silken wool of his new Forever Friend. Samuel slowly opened his eyes and looked out past the see-through stone wall and into the garden. The colours on the trees seemed to be exploding with splendour. The sun was shining brightly. A magnificent new day was calling to Samuel.

The small ram, feeling the movement of the little boy, nuzzled up closer to him, resting his head on the boy's chest. Samuel continued to run his fingers through the silken wool of the ram. "Ruach, our day has begun. We have fruit and leaves to collect for my Father. I want him to be proud of me! Maybe today I'll be ready to meet my Father!"

Ruach blinked his blue eyes at the sound of Samuel's words. The ram jumped out of the bed, thrilled to begin the day. Samuel stood up and stretched his arms high above his head. As the boy stretched, the little ram rubbed up beside his legs. Samuel bent down and roughly hugged the ram, who eagerly wiggled into Samuel's arms. The boy laughed.

Samuel suddenly found himself lying on his back on the floor as the ram nudged his soft, woolly head into Samuel's neck. "Ruach, you're tickling me!" Samuel giggled. The two played together on the floor for awhile.

Samuel smiled at his Forever Friend, who now rested on top of Samuel's tummy. The ram had burrowed his head securely under Samuel's chin, attempting to get as close as possible to the child.[1]

Samuel cuddled the ram and looked out to the garden. "Ruach, I really want my Father to be proud of us. Will you be my forever helper and friend?" The ram shook his head yes and snuggled up even closer to Samuel's face. "I'm so happy to have a friend like you, Ruach."

Samuel got up and began to think about how he was going to leave his see-through room. There appeared to be no real door. As Samuel stood studying the top of the unusual clear door, Ruach simply sauntered through the see-through door, turned, and waited for Samuel. "What?!" the child exclaimed as he noticed his Forever Friend waiting in the lush garden. "How did you do that, Ruach?"

The ram smiled at Samuel as he stood in the flourishing garden and blinked his twinkly blue eyes. The boy remembered the words of his peculiar friend Ezekiel. He had told Samuel the ram would always show him the correct path.

Samuel closed his eyes and cautiously stepped forward, knowing there was an invisible stone wall in front of him. After several steps, the boy opened his eyes. He realized he could simply walk right through the see-through wall! Ruach leaned against Samuel's legs. Samuel was astonished at how he had entered the garden. He turned and looked at his room, but all he could see was the large stone wall of his Father's Tabernacle. "Incredible!" Samuel said out loud. "My Father's house is full of mysteries."

Samuel looked all around. The air was fresh and crisp, and a gentle breeze was blowing. Today was a new day for Samuel—a new beginning. Samuel's heart was filled with joy and his mind was filled with curiosity. Everything he saw and touched was unique and thrilling. His new world was a wonder constantly unfolding. "Oh Father!" Samuel said out loud, "let me know and understand the mysteries and secrets of your Kingdom."[2]

Samuel and Ruach strolled through the garden together. The ram stayed close to Samuel's side. The boy could smell the sweet fragrance from the blossoms on the trees. *This will be a great day!* Samuel thought to himself. The ram looked up at Samuel and smiled knowingly.

"Which fruit do I pick, Ruach? How do I know when they are ripe for picking?"

The ram brushed his head into the side of Samuel's leg. Then the ram ran off among the trees. Ruach's long white wool with silver tips moved up and down in rhythm with the ram.

"Wait, Ruach," Samuel called out. Samuel chased after his friend and found the ram lying beneath a magnificent tree. *Wow,* thought Samuel, *that tree is gigantic!*

"Is the fruit ripe for picking, Ruach?" Samuel asked.

The ram nodded his head.

"Okay. I need to get started." Samuel reached up to pick a fruit, but it wouldn't come free from the tree. "Are you sure this tree is ready to be harvested?"

The ram stood up and placed himself under a large, lower limb of the tree and looked upwards towards the branch.

"Do I need to climb the tree, Ruach?"

The ram shook its head yes.

"Great, I love to climb. I am one of the best tree climbers in my tribe. The soldiers always asked me to climb a tree and scout out for enemies."

Samuel climbed onto the ram's back. This time he wasn't worried about hurting his new friend. He knew Ruach was strong, and he trusted the ram to steady him. Samuel pulled himself up onto the large limb of the tree. He smiled down at Ruach, who was waiting below the large limb. The boy continued to climb the large tree, stopping to pull on the different fruit.

The fruit which had a purple shimmer to them were the ones which the tree released to his grasp. Samuel placed the fruit carefully inside his shirt. As he climbed higher into the giant tree, he gazed out, far across the countryside. There in the distance he could see the tents of his tribe. Samuel wondered what his mother was doing. He knew she would be so proud of him.

Samuel surveyed the tree. All the fruit with the shimmering purple tone had been picked. "Okay Ruach, I'm coming down. Get ready to be my sturdy step." The boy climbed skillfully down the tree without squishing any of the fruit tucked inside his shirt.

"Here I come, Ruach." Samuel lowered himself from the limb of the tree onto the ram's back. Then he jumped off the ram onto the ground. "There, one tree harvested. Which tree is next?"

Ruach walked behind the tree and used his head to push a basket toward Samuel. "Where did this come from, Ruach?"

"From me!" a gentle, deep voice spoke to the two friends. Samuel turned around quickly to see Ezekiel standing behind him. "Well done, Samuel—well done!"[3] The peculiar man began to clap his hands. "You did a magnificent job harvesting the fruit for your Father. You've quickly learned which fruit were ripe for picking. Not one of the ripened fruit was forgotten or bruised. Now you can place them in the giving basket. The basket can be strapped to Ruach's back, and he will carry the fruit for you. Allow him to always choose the trees you harvest from. He is wise. Ruach always knows which trees are ready for picking." Ezekiel grinned down at the young boy. "Samuel, you are learning and growing quickly in your Father's garden." The peculiar man gently placed his hand on the boy's head and rubbed his hair. Then he leaned way down and whispered into the boy's ear. "Did you thank the tree for releasing its fruit to you?" Ezekiel stood up and chuckled.

Samuel's eyes widened. "Oh, right! Thank you for the fruit..."—Samuel paused and giggled— "...tree!" he added. The two chuckled.

"Good job, good job." Ezekiel grinned. "So tell me, Samuel, how did you sleep last night?"

"Great! I love my bed and my room."

"Your Father laughed as He watched you and Ruach jumping on the bed. You gave Him such joy!"

"My Father saw me? How? He wasn't with us when we were jumping on the bed!" Samuel said, astonished.

"Your Father sees everyone, at all times. He watches over all His children. The Father looks down from His throne and sees each and every person. From His throne room, He observes all who live on the earth."[4] Ezekiel smiled down at the young boy. He bent his knees so he was closer to Samuel's height. Ezekiel gently put his finger on Samuel's heart. "He is the one who made your heart, so the Father understands everything you do."[5] Ezekiel stood up, towering over the small boy. The friend of his Father released his booming laughter. "Your Father smiles on you. You are the apple of His eye."[6]

"Is my Father proud of me?" Samuel's heart began to beat loudly in his chest. He wanted his Father to be proud of him.

The tall man continued to chuckle. "Yes, Samuel, your Father is very proud of you. But more than that, He loves you with an everlasting love.[7]

A love which can never be broken or taken away from you. Never! Don't concern yourself with whether you make your Father proud or not. Doing tasks for your Father doesn't change His magnificent love for you." Ezekiel once more bent down towards the small boy. He put his sparkling golden-brown face close to Samuel's and looked into the child's eyes. "He loves you because you are His child, His offspring, His son.[8] That and that alone is why He loves you." The man continued to stare into the boy's eyes, the jewels on his long braids glistening in the sunshine.

Samuel knew he would have to think about all this. In his tribe, most people liked you when you pleased them or did all your chores in the perfect order that the tribal leader requested. There were so many rules Samuel had to remember and obey in his tribe. Ezekiel was now telling him that his Father loved him simply because he was His child. Was it possible that nothing Samuel did could make his Father love him more or less? This was a new thought for Samuel. The boy looked towards the immense Tabernacle, which towered over the trees a distance away. He still had an intense desire to please his Father. *Why?* he wondered. *To prove myself?* He would have to think on this.

"When will I get to see my Father?" Samuel asked with a huge sigh.

Ezekiel grinned, stood up, and looked lovingly at the boy. "Soon. You must be hungry. You can eat any ripened fruit whenever you want. The water in the river is for you to drink. All you need to nourish yourself can be found in the fruit and in the water. Watch for the illuminating leaves during your day's adventure. Oh! And remember to thank the tree for giving you its leaf or any fruit. I will see you later today. Have fun, you two!"

Ezekiel bent his tall body down and touched the ram gently. He smiled at the young friends and walked away, singing loudly in a strange but beautiful language. Samuel watched Ezekiel as he wandered among the exotic trees until eventually the man could no longer be seen or heard.

"Are you hungry, Ruach? Which fruit should we eat this morning?" The ram hurried off and Samuel followed, laughing. The ram was bouncing as he ran, and his wool was once again moving up and down. It all seemed so spectacular to Samuel.

Ruach stopped beside an odd-looking tree. It was smaller than most of the trees in the garden, and its fruit were bumpy with fluorescent yellow and dark blue swirls. Samuel reached up and pulled a piece of fruit from the tree. The young boy took a bite. Juices squirted out from the fruit and ran down Samuel's face. "Mmmmm," he said. "This fruit is delicious and sweet!" Samuel reached for another one and gave it to his clever friend. Ruach motioned towards the tree. Samuel thought a moment and then remembered he was to always thank the trees for releasing their fruit or leaves to him. "Oh, so sorry, I forgot to say thank you, tree." The child took another large bite of the delicious fruit. "Mmmmm... this is so yummy! Thank you for this delicious fruit, Mr. Tree!" Samuel giggled. It felt funny having to talk to a tree.

Ruach nodded his head in approval and quickly ate the mouth-watering fruit. "Ruach, this fruit is so delicious!" Samuel stated. The two ate several more of the colourful fruit, as Samuel continued to thank the tree for its provision. The juices from the fruit were running down Samuel's chin as he licked his fingers. Samuel looked over and noticed the sparkling water.

"Let's clean all the juice off of ourselves, Ruach." Samuel's hands were still sticky. They raced to the water's edge and splashed around in the water. Samuel cautiously moved deeper into the river. Once chest deep in the water, he began to swim. The water was refreshing. The crystals bouncing on top of the water would bounce near Samuel's face and create splashes. The splashes tickled the young boy's face and nose.

Samuel enjoyed swimming in the water. The current wasn't too strong. Samuel floated on his back and let the gentle flow carry him downstream. The sun was shining brightly overhead. *What a glorious day.* Samuel thought to himself as he floated on the gentle current of the water. Ruach ran on the shoreline, keeping a close eye on the boy.

After a time, Samuel ventured to the water's edge and found some interesting stones. He picked them up and examined them. *These are different from the stones where my tribe lives,* Samuel thought. The stones were sparkling with gold dust, and were as smooth as glass. There were different colours and patterns on each one. None of the stones were the same. They were nothing like the dusty, jagged, gray stones around his tribe. The young boy threw a few of the stones across the water and watched them skip. The stones seemed to hop across the water for a great distance. Then they would rest on top of the water for awhile, eventually sinking as a little bubble rose up into the atmosphere. The bubble would float on the wind, changing colours and finally bursting, releasing a small fireworks display. Samuel was mesmerized by all the unusual activity. Everything in his Father's world was amazing.

After awhile, the two friends rested by the river's bank. Samuel was in awe of all the beauty he found in his Father's garden. The boy felt at peace in the new lush world of his Father. He relaxed as a gentle breeze and the sunshine began to dry his clothes.

As Samuel rested on his back by the river's edge, he looked down and noticed the size of his feet. The boy quickly sat up and examined his hands. "Unbelievable!" he proclaimed out loud, "I think I've grown!" Samuel stood up as he continued to examine himself. He knew he was bigger.

Samuel smiled. "We have work...." The boy's voice cracked. He cleared his throat.

"...work to do. Let's go, Ruach." The breakfast break was over. The warm sun and breeze had completely dried Samuel's clothes. Samuel smiled as he looked towards the Tabernacle. Harvesting was important work for a young man who still had a burning desire to please his Father.

Questions to Contemplate

1. Why do you think it is important for Samuel to please his Father? Is this important to the Father?
2. Samuel wants to understand the mysteries of his Father's Kingdom. What mysteries do you think he will discover?
3. Why do you think Samuel is growing so quickly?
4. Ezekiel walked away from Samuel and Ruach singing in a beautiful but strange language. What do you think this language is? Could it be the same language that Samuel's mother spoke?

---

[1] 1 Corinthians 3:16: "Don't you realize that all of you together are the temple of God and that the Spirit of God lives in you?"

[2] Mark 4:11: "You are permitted to understand the secret of the Kingdom of God."

[3] Matthew 25:21: "Well done, my good and faithful servant."

[4] Psalm 33:13–14: "The Lord looks down from heaven and sees the whole human race. From his throne he observes all who live on the earth."

[5] Psalm 33:15: "He made their hearts, so he understands everything they do."

[6] Psalm 17:8: "Keep me as the apple of your eye; hide me in the shadow of your wings" (NIV).

[7] Jeremiah 31:3: "I have loved you, my people, with an everlasting love. With unfailing love I have drawn you to myself."

[8] 1 John 3:1: "See how very much our Father loves us, for he calls us his children, and that is what we are!"

Chapter Six
The Offering

Samuel and Ruach walked together in the spectacular garden. Samuel spotted large butterflies dancing among the treetops. The sun seemed to sparkle on their brightly coloured wings, creating a trail of fine gold dust in the air. The two walked back to the tree Samuel had harvested. The ram stood steadily by the giving basket as Samuel placed the basket, filled with fruit, on the young ram's back. Samuel tied it securely, being careful that it wasn't too tight for his Forever Friend.

"Okay Ruach, it's time to take the basket to the altar. Is the basket too heavy for you?" The ram shook his head no. The two walked down through the trees towards the altar. As they walked, Samuel saw many more insects and interesting animals in his Father's garden. Samuel's keen eyes noticed a large yellow insect scurrying up one of the tree trunks. He stopped and watched as the insect opened up a pair of fiery red wings and disappeared into the canopy of the tree. As Samuel was staring at the treetop, he spotted a small bird with magnificent fluorescent blue, green, and red tail feathers. The bird had a long, ivory beak and was darting in and around the blossoms on the tree.

Ruach knew all about the garden and its creatures. The young ram butted his head into the back of the boy's legs, behind his kneecaps. Samuel fell to the ground. "Hey!" he yelled as he began to laugh.

THE OFFERING

Ruach took off through the trees with the basket of fruit. "Okay, I get it—no time to explore, we have fruit to harvest. Hey, wait for me Ruach!" Samuel chased after the ram, who was very fast, even though he carried the heavy basket.

Samuel stopped, out of breath, beside the altar. Ruach was already resting beside the altar wall, in the cool shade of the large structure. Samuel slid down beside the ram and relaxed, his back up against the wall of the altar. The shade and gentle breeze felt refreshing.

As the two rested, Samuel noticed another brightly coloured bird darting in and out of a nearby tree. Samuel observed the bird for awhile. The creatures in his Father's garden were unlike any he had ever seen before. They were fascinating to watch.

After a brief rest, Samuel stood up and looked at the altar. "Ruach, why must we place the fruit on top of the altar? It would be so much easier if we just left it here on the ground. The altar is so high."

Ruach stood up. The ram walked around in a small circle and then looked up towards the top of the altar. The ram shook his head no. "Okay, Ruach, we'll place the fruit on top of the altar, but this will be no easy task for you or for me!"

Samuel untied the basket from the ram's back. The fruit was heavy. Samuel placed the basket on the ground and looked over at his Forever Friend, who was standing patiently by the altar wall. "Ruach, this fruit is very heavy, and I don't want to bruise it. I'll have to step on your back for each piece of fruit and place them on the altar one at a time. This will take awhile. Will you be okay?" The ram nodded his head in agreement.

Samuel carefully took the first beautiful piece of fruit out of the basket and stepped upon the ram's back. He reached his arms upwards and was able to gently place the fruit on the altar. Samuel was grateful for his amazing growth spurt. Reaching the top of the altar was so much easier than it had been the day before.

Standing on his Forever Friend's back, Samuel could see out across the top of the altar, his nose barely peeking over the top of the structure. Samuel realized outside the garden was a vast, barren, desert landscape. It was very similar to the land around the boy's tribe.

Samuel repeatedly stepped onto Ruach's back, placing each piece of fruit gently on the top of the altar. When all the fruit had been placed in a row, Samuel lay down on the ground beneath a large tree and rested. Ruach lay down beside him. The adolescent reached out his hand and touched his Forever Friend gently. Samuel ran his fingers through the fine, silken wool on Ruach's back. "Maybe tomorrow I won't need to use you as a step. I'm growing so quickly. Yesterday I couldn't see over the wall, and today I can!"

Samuel sat up and looked towards the top of the altar, expecting to find all the fruit sitting neatly in a row, just as he had placed it. To Samuel's astonishment, he couldn't see any fruit on top of the altar.

"What?!" Samuel shouted in confusion. "Where is my Father's fruit?" He stood up quickly and moved backwards, hoping to get a better view of the top of the altar. Still, no fruit could be seen. "No way!" the boy exclaimed loudly.

Samuel ran over to a nearby tree and quickly began to climb up. He looked again at the altar top, clearly seeing there was no fruit. "How can this be, Ruach? I took great care to place the fruit exactly as Ezekiel had asked me. Where did it go?" Samuel came down from the tree. He was disappointed and baffled by the sudden disappearance of the precious fruit he had so carefully gathered and delicately placed on top of the altar.

Samuel sat on the ground, crossed his legs, and thought about his dilemma. Ruach came and lay beside the boy, putting his head on Samuel's lap. As Samuel sat trying to figure out what to do, feeling responsible for the safety of the fruit, a tear fell from his eye. The teardrop was captured in Ruach's silken wool.[1]

Ruach looked up at Samuel. "I didn't want to disappoint my Father, and now I've lost his precious fruit. Ruach, please help me understand what happened."

The blue eyes of the little ram looked up into the soul of the young boy. Ruach was stirred with compassion. He stood up and walked over to the altar wall. The ram then peeked around the corner of the wall. Ruach looked back at Samuel. The boy cautiously got up and followed the ram. The two were now peering around the wall of the altar, their feet still inside the garden. Samuel stood still, in total shock when he saw what was behind the altar wall.

* * *

The evil Spittles were peeking out of the cracks of the earth. Their little tails curled up in expectation. The boy was venturing closer into the world, and away from the sanctuary of the Father. The Spittles knew it wouldn't be long till they would be able to approach the boy again and ambush his destiny. The tails of the evil vapours continued to twist and turn in expectation as their beady eyes stared, looking upon the King's son, Samuel.

Questions to Contemplate

1. Did you ever have a dilemma? Did you ask anyone for help?
2. Will God help us in our dilemmas?
3. Why is Ruach able to have and show compassion towards Samuel?
4. Who do you think Ruach is? The definition of *ruach* in *Strong's Concordance* is breath, wind, or spirit.[2]
5. What do you think Samuel will find behind the altar?

---

[1] Psalm 56:8: "You keep track of all my sorrows. You have collected all my tears in your bottle. You have recorded each one in your book."

[2] "7307. ruach," *Bible Hub* (https://biblehub.com/hebrew/7307.htm).

Chapter Seven
The Struggle

Samuel remained frozen, watching in horror as an older boy placed the last of the fruit into a golden sack. The robust boy stood up and threw the heavy sack over his shoulder. As the older boy turned to begin his journey away from the altar, he stopped, unable to move, glancing at Samuel in shock.

Samuel suddenly bolted towards the older boy in an attempt to retrieve his Father's fruit. As Samuel pounced, Ruach darted between the two boys. The ram's thick, soft wool cushioned the two boys from impacting.

Samuel found himself face down in the dirt. The other boy was lying on his back, his arms wrapped securely around the sack full of fruit. The mysterious boy had managed to keep the fruit from being squished. Samuel quickly stood to his feet and glared down at the boy.

"Give me back my Father's fruit!" demanded Samuel.

Ruach stood between the two boys. Samuel reached down to take the fruit in the sack from the intruder. The boy quickly sprang to his feet in defense, still clutching the sack.

A loud cry was heard from above the boys. A sudden wind burst forth, and a large eagle swooped down and landed between the boys. The eagle towered over them. The immense eagle and the ram looked at each other, and then stood back-to-back and gazed at the boys.

Samuel was confused. *Why did Ruach stop me from retrieving my Father's fruit? Ruach should be fighting along with me!* Samuel thought. "Why are you stealing my Father's fruit?" demanded Samuel.

"It's my responsibility to take this fruit to the people. Who... who are you? What are you doing here?" the mystery boy asked.

"My name is Samuel. This is my Father's house." Samuel pounded on his chest as he amplified the words *my Father*, "This is His garden and His fruit. Give me back the fruit." Samuel stared intensely at the confronting boy. "Now!" he yelled in frustration.

The boy scratched his head and looked down at his feet, puzzled. He continued to scratch his head as he looked up at the eagle and then over to the ram. "Ruach, does this boy speak truth?"

The ram nodded yes.

"Well, we have much to explain to our new friend then," continued the boy.

"I am not your friend." Samuel boldly declared. "Anyone who would steal from my Father is not my friend!" Samuel glared at the older boy. He could feel his teeth grinding and his entire body stiffening up, fists clenched.

"Ruach, you will have to help him," the intruder stated. "Samuel... you said your name was Samuel. Do you trust Ruach?"

"I did," Samuel quickly glanced over at his Forever Friend. "I did before he stopped me from taking back the fruit you stole!" Samuel shook his head at Ruach and squished up his face, questioning why his friend had kept him from tackling the thief.

"Ruach, we need the fruit of peace," the mystery boy stated. Samuel stood in disbelief as his Forever Friend followed the directions of the intruder. Ruach returned shortly with a deep blue and white fruit resting gently in his opened mouth. Ruach dropped the fruit between the two boys' feet. The eagle let out a loud cry which pierced Samuel's ears. Samuel covered his ears with his hands and closed his eyes for a moment. When he looked again at the fruit, it had multiplied.[1] Now there were two identical pieces of fruit lying on the ground.

The mystery boy bent down, picked up one of the pieces of fruit, and began to eat. Samuel suddenly had grumblings in his tummy, and felt extremely thirsty. Samuel glared over at his supposed Forever Friend, wondering what was going on. Ruach batted his large blue eyes at him, the long lashes moving slowly up and down. The young boy's thirst was increasing. His throat suddenly became very dry. Reluctantly, Samuel picked up the other piece of fruit and began to eat. A calm came over him as he munched away. His soul was no longer agitated. His thirst was gone. He seemed to relax.

Samuel's curiosity grew, and he wanted to know more about this boy who had so much knowledge of his Father's garden. The mystery boy knew about the fruit and the qualities they possessed. More amazingly, he knew Ruach's name and had Samuel's Forever Friend's trust. *How could this be?* Samuel wondered.

Samuel sat down on the ground beside the altar. He was no longer agitated by all that had happened so quickly. Ruach came over to Samuel and curled up beside him. The ram put his head under Samuel's arm and nudged the bottom of the boy's hand with his soft face. Samuel laughed and began to scratch the top of the ram's head. "You're not acting like a traitor now!" The ram looked up at the boy, its intensely blue eyes shining. The ram seemed to be asking for forgiveness and understanding rather than judgement. Samuel's heart softened.

THE STRUGGLE

Samuel looked up at the intruder. "Who are you?"

"I am one of the Father's Prophets. I have come from Mount Zion. The Father has commissioned the prophets to come to Him daily. When fruit or leaves from the garden are placed on the top of the altar, we are entrusted to take the precious substance and distribute it to the Father's people in Zion. My name is Shear-Jashub."

Samuel studied the intruder. He looked much older than Samuel, possibly sixteen or seventeen. He had dark brown hair and golden-brown eyes that seemed to glisten. The mystery boy was not only bigger than Samuel he had muscular arms protruding from under his shirt. Samuel looked down at the ram, and was almost glad his Forever Friend had intercepted the impact of the two boys. Samuel knew he would have been hurt if they'd collided.

Samuel was trying to decide if he should allow Shear-Jashub to leave with the fruit when Ruach suddenly jumped up and began making odd noises. The ram dug his front hooves into the soil. The ram's head was down, and seemed to be banging into something. Over and over again the ram said, "Baaad, baad, bad, bad."

Samuel stood up and looked out into the distance. All he could see was the desert sand and the far-off jagged mountain range.

Shear-Jashub turned and looked into the distance, too. "What is it, Ruach? What is bad out there?"

Ruach began to run forward with his head down, then stopped abruptly and pawed at the ground. Then the ram went into tight little circles. He kept rushing out into the desert and stopping abruptly. All the time, the ram was saying "baaad."

"I've never seen Ruach do this before," Samuel stated.

"Your Forever Friend has keen senses. He knows when danger is nearby. He is alerting us to something we cannot see."[2] Shear-Jashub turned to the large eagle. "Gimel, go and return with knowledge." The eagle instantly opened its wings, revealing its incredible size. Making a loud shrill sound, the bird set to flight. The wind that burst forth from the bird sent Samuel falling backwards, only to land softly on top of Ruach, who had darted behind him as the bird opened its wings.

Shear-Jashub burst into laughter as he witnessed the event. "You can't stand behind Gimel when he begins his flight. No one can stand against his wind. You will learn more about my Forever Friend. He was a gift to me from the Father, just as Ruach was to you."

The two boys looked up into the sky as the large eagle flew off into the distance. The piercing cry from the creature softened as it soared further away. The large eagle quickly became a small dot in the blue sky.

"How often do you come to get fruit from my Father's garden?" Samuel asked.

"When I am summoned by the Father, I come. Only the Father knows the needs of His people."[3]

"Where did you say you take the fruit?"

"I take the fruit to Mount Zion," Shear-Jashub responded, his keen eyes staring into the sky, probing for Gimel's return.

"How long does it take you to travel from the Father's Tabernacle to Mount Zion?"

"That depends on Beelzebub. His presence makes it more difficult to bring the fruit to the people." The mystery boy shook his head in disgust. "Ack! Beelzebub!" The boy spit out the name. "You must know, we always deliver the fruit. The only thing that changes is the duration of time it takes to get to Zion. Beelzebub is a constant threat. He is unrelenting in his attacks." The mystery boy looked at Samuel and grinned. "I always give him a good fight. The victory can never be his."

Samuel was a little confused. Things seemed to be unravelling at a speed he could barely keep up with. Samuel looked out into the distance. He could no longer see the eagle. Ruach was still making the "bad, bad, bad" sound and digging his hooves into the soil. Samuel wondered if this Beelzebub was upsetting his Forever Friend. He remembered the words Ezekiel spoke earlier. *Always trust your Forever Friend. He will always help you step in the right direction.* Obviously, something in the desert was troubling Ruach—but what? The only thing Samuel could see was the far-off mountain range with its jagged peaks.

Ruach came over to Samuel, who was now standing beside the altar wall, staring at the distant mountain range. The ram began to nudge his friend back behind the altar. Samuel looked down at the ram, and pushed him away from his leg as he continued to search for an enemy. Ruach kept pushing Samuel to move behind the altar wall, but the young boy was refusing to be guided by his Forever Friend.

Samuel felt he need more time to determine what was happening. The words of Ezekiel once more came back into his mind: **"Always** *allow Ruach to guide and lead you."*

Samuel planted his feet firmly beside the altar wall. He needed more time on his own to decipher what was happening. After he solved what was occurring, he would follow Ruach's lead and move back into the garden. *After all,* he thought, *I'm only a footstep away from the garden. What harm could occur standing here?*

* * *

Meanwhile, deep under the earth in a world of darkness and dread, the evil plot to destroy the Father's Kingdom was advancing. The large beast paced back and forth, his red eyes glaring. Fire spit out of his mouth. His massive tail banged loudly, creating a booming echo through the deep dark cavern. The little Spittles stayed close to the cold damp walls of the cavern. They knew Beelzebub's rage could erupt at any moment. No one was safe from his deadly wrath.

"First you let the child through the door into the Tabernacle. Now he has begun to learn! Acquiring knowledge! I told you: never let that happen. Knowledge of the Father is one of our worst setbacks![4] What good are you stupid things? Useless, rotten, incompetent creatures! Why do I allow you near my great presence?"

Smoke blew out from the top of Beelzebub's head through his grotesque horns. The damp cavern was suddenly sizzling hot and filled with a pungent odour. The small, bodiless Spittles gagged from the foul, thick, toxic air.

"Have you been watching? I want all eyes on the Tabernacle and the garden!" roared the vile beast. "As soon as Samuel gets anywhere near the edge of his Father's garden, I want to know." The tail of the morbid beast whipped through the air, catching two Spittles off guard. They were walloped against the cavern wall. The small black creatures of vapour slowly rose.

"Get out of my way!" demanded Beelzebub. "What good are you? What good are any of you? You are all useless imbeciles!" Beelzebub snorted black smoke from his nose. The room, which already smelled terrible, became engulfed in more noxious smoke and a vile stench, making it unbearable to breathe. An odour of death arose, with the smoke choking the smaller Spittles.

THE STRUGGLE

Suddenly a whooshing sound was heard, and then a splash. A Spittle plummeted into the inner cavern chamber through a small tunnel which had been carved out for easy, direct access for the vapours.

"Your kingship, Lord of all evil, the child has stepped foot outside the garden," the vapour spoke quickly.

A loud squeaky cry was heard from the small Spittles as Beelzebub released more noxious gas and fire. "It's about time!" roared the creature. "Get out of my way!" Beelzebub flew upward through a large tunnel. Rocks fell away from the sides of the tunnel as the beast stormed towards the earth's surface. The horde of flies which were always circling around Beelzebub's head buzzed around the rocks and quickly followed after the beast.

Nearing the earth's crust, he slowed his speed. Slyly, he poked his head up from a rocky outcrop in the mountain range. He cunningly watched from a distance, his fiery red eyes glowing.

Then the evil creature lowered himself back down into the mountain cavern. "Finally, vengeance is mine! All mine!" The beast laughed at the thought of destroying the child. "I will do it without mercy! Yes—slowly! Ha ha ha!" Beelzebub laughed as his red eyes glowed out through another chamber in the rock face. He didn't want to lose sight of his target. "First I will take everything from him! Yes! Everything of importance. After I have stolen everything, I will destroy him completely. Ha ha ha!" The creature's hideous laughter filled the caverns. "This will be so easy and enjoyable!" Again the evil beast roared, his laughter hissing out clouds of rancid smoke and flames. The Spittles had to be careful where they stood, or they would disappear forever in a vapour of fire.

"To watch the Father's child suffer will be such pleasure! Oh yes!" The tail of the beast flung back and forth, banging new holes in the cavern walls. Rocks flew in all directions. No one was ever safe around Beelzebub!

The creature stopped. He thought a moment. A grim, sneaky smirk appeared on his face. "Or better yet, I could tempt the child. Aha! I could tempt the innocent mortal into sin. Oh, alluring, lingering sin. How rewarding for me when they take my bait. What pleasure for me to lure them in!" The creature laughed, gasping out the smell of death from his belly, which birthed a new horde of flies. "Not only do I claim the tasty humans, I get to then slowly suck the life out of them. Mwahaha—suck the life out of them forever!" Evil laughter echoed throughout the cavern. "How I love this war!" Beelzebub's laughter shook the ground for miles. The beast was on the prowl.[5]

Questions to Contemplate

1. Shear-Jashub asked Samuel if he trusted Ruach. Do you think Samuel should trust his Forever Friend?

2. What do you think the fruit of peace tastes like?

3. Gimel is the third letter in the Hebrew alphabet. One of its meanings is "to lift up." Would you like to have a giant eagle as your Forever Friend? Where would you like the eagle to take you?

4. Samuel is trying to figure out what is happening rather than depending on his Forever Friend Ruach's prompting to move back into the garden. Do you think Samuel should listen to Ruach?

5. Shear-Jashub tells Samuel he is a prophet. A prophet is someone inspired by God through the Holy Spirit to deliver God's message. Do you know anyone who is a prophet? Would you like to be a prophet?

THE STRUGGLE

---

[1] 1 Peter 1:2b: "Grace to you and peace be multiplied" (NKJV).

[2] Ephesians 6:12: "For we are not fighting against flesh-and-blood enemies, but against evil rulers and authorities of the unseen world, against mighty powers in this dark world, and against evil spirits in the heavenly places."

[3] Matthew 6:8: "…for your Father knows exactly what you need even before you ask him!"

[4] Hosea 4:6: "…my people are destroyed from lack of knowledge" (NIV).

[5] 1 Peter 5:8: "Stay alert! Watch out for your great enemy, the devil. He prowls around like a roaring lion, looking for someone to devour."

Chapter Eight

New Ground

Shear-Jashub continued scrutinizing the distant horizon. His hand was above his eyes, which helped shield his view from the glare of the sun. The young warrior was holding tightly to the golden sack of fruit, which was securely tucked under his arm, close to his chest.

Ruach was becoming more creative with drawing Samuel back into the garden. The ram had bitten onto Samuel's pants and was now trying to pull him back towards the wall. But Samuel was intently interested in what could be lurking around unseen.

"Samuel, should anything occur that isn't normal, I want you to run quickly into the Tabernacle. You will always be safe in the Father's Tabernacle. The Father is *Jehovah-Jireh*, our provider, our protector. He will provide safety for you."[1] Shear-Jashub reached over and placed his hand on Samuels shoulder. "Will you promise to do this?"

Shear-Jashub's voice had a sense of urgency. Samuel looked over at the older boy who seemed to be positioned in a warrior's ready stance. Samuel thought to himself, *If anything unusual happens! What has been usual?* The normal life he'd led had ended the day his mother had told Samuel she was bringing him to his Father's house; to live with and serve his Father.

NEW GROUND

No one he knew had ever been given away to a Father they had never met. This was now the second day, and Samuel still hadn't met his mysterious Father, though he had an intense desire to be with him. Samuel grinned. His normal life had surely ended.

Samuel thought about the days in his tribe, and the excitement he was experiencing now. The boy realized how rewarding and accelerated his life had suddenly become. While he'd lived a simple life in his tribe, he and all the people didn't really know the Father, their King. They had lots of rules to follow which they thought would bring them closer to pleasing and knowing the King. Yet Samuel had never felt close to Him. He never felt like he knew his mysterious Father. And he definitely didn't understand Him or His ways. Here, in the Tabernacle, he was quickly learning all about his Father's glorious Kingdom. And more amazingly, learning about his Father's love for him. Now Samuel had a purpose; he had a vision.[2] The boy had acquired a determination he'd never experienced before—a determination to know and understand, to search out, and explore more of his Father's wondrous ways. In a matter of a day and a half, Samuel's life had completely changed.

Samuel looked over at Shear-Jashub in his warrior pose, the sack now securely fastened to his back. His arms were out as if he held an invisible shield and a spear. The older boy reminded Samuel of the soldiers in his tribe. Ruach kept his grip on Samuel's pants and continued tugging.

"Samuel, promise me you will go to the Tabernacle!" Shear-Jashub was yelling urgently at Samuel while looking out into the parched landscape.

Before Samuel could answer Shear-Jashub, the young boy looked up and noticed the mountain range was now a short distance from them. Samuel turned towards the altar, which was still directly behind him. *How can this be?* Samuel wondered. *We haven't moved.* Instantly, a black cloud came from the mountain, along with a blast of fire. The blast was so close that Samuel didn't merely see it—he could feel the intense heat from the flames.

"Go to the Tabernacle!" Shear-Jashub ordered. Samuel could only hear the young man's voice. The thick smoke had wrapped the boys like a blanket. Samuel was shrouded in a black cloak of smoke, unable to see anything—not even his own hands and feet. The smoke quickly began to suffocate him. The dark smoke was accompanied by a putrid smell. As the boy struggled for air, he tried to feel for the pearl wall of the altar, but he could feel nothing behind him. A large knot tightened within his stomach. Samuel was becoming afraid. Panic was choking him on the inside, just as the black smoke was strangling him.

Abruptly, Samuel heard a loud burst of rushing water. It sounded like he was standing beside a large waterfall. Instantly a blast of water fell onto Samuel, and he was washed away in what seemed to be a sudden river. The boy found himself now swimming in a strong current that was bringing him to an unknown destination. The water propelled the child along, fast and furious, until slowly the smoke began to clear away.

As the black smoke diminished, the current began to slow down slightly. Samuel found himself floating on the water. Regaining his breath, and now able to see more clearly, Samuel realized he was riding on a current of water through the desert. Samuel looked over the water, and far in the distance, he could vaguely make out the form of the pearl altar.

Samuel was unable to swim against the strong current. He was now drifting further and further away from his beloved garden. With all the strength Samuel had left in his body, he cried out, "Ruach!" Where had his wonderful Forever Friend disappeared to? His mind was racing. Where was Shear-Jashub? Samuel was able to keep himself afloat as he looked up into the clear, sun-filled sky. There was no trace of Gimel. *Where did everyone go?* he wondered.

NEW GROUND

The water was still moving quickly. Samuel wasn't sure how much longer he'd be able to stay afloat. He realized there was roughly six feet of water on each side of him. Samuel tried to swim towards the edge of the water through the current, but the powerful torrent of water was relentless. The boy was held captive in the center of the stream. Samuel again looked around to see if any of the others were nearby, but he could see no one.

As Samuel's strength slowly faded, he slipped under the water. Somewhere deep inside of the young boy a burst of energy came forth, and he propelled himself above the water and gasped for air. Samuel looked up to the clear blue sky. "Father" Samuel cried, "I wanted to make you proud of me. I wanted to know you! I am so sorry. I have failed you." With little strength left, Samuel once again sank under the moving water. The boy looked up and could see the surface of the water as he descended into the depths.

Samuel refocused, clutching onto life. New inner strength emerged, and he kicked his way up towards the surface of the water. He gasped for breath as he emerged.

As Samuel's face came out of the water, he looked around to see if anyone was nearby to help him. All he could see was the fast-moving water and the endless sand of the desert. Samuel again tried to swim against the current, which held him prisoner in the centre of the stream. "Help me, Father!"[3] was all he could say, softly with his last breath. Again, Samuel sank under the water. This time the boy had no energy left in his body to emerge into freedom. The crystal blue sky disappeared in a blur.

A sudden jolt startled Samuel. He could feel a strong force pulling him up out of the water, although his body had no energy to move. The child was limp and helpless, but somehow moving in the right direction. Samuel was being raised out of the water, but how? As Samuel's head emerged, he breathed in the sweet air of life.

FOREVER FRIEND

Amazingly, Samuel kept rising out of the water. Now he was above the water and climbing higher into the air. A loud, shrill scream sounded from behind and above Samuel. As Samuel soared higher, he knew Shear-Jashub's eagle, Gimel, had saved him from a watery death.[4]

The eagle's sharp talons had scooped up Samuel without injuring him. Gimel had skillfully grabbed only Samuel's shirt. The two now flew high above the desert. After a short flight, the eagle glided to a gentle stop and released Samuel onto the flat top of a lofty rock tower. The eagle then soared back over the desert. Gimel was searching with keen eyesight, his majestic head moving slowly back and forth. The Forever Friend returned to the rock tower, slowly coming to a stop near Samuel.

Samuel lay on the towering rock, still exhausted. The boy only had enough strength left to look at the noble eagle and quietly whisper, "Thank you." Gimel moved closer to the exhausted child and released another loud shrill. The powerful eagle stood guard over Samuel as the boy rested on the high ground.[5]

* * *

"You fools!" Beelzebub spat out fire from his mouth as he talked. "You sleazeballs; you useless, good-for-nothing imbeciles! I should spit death fire at all of you pathetic Spittles. Never can I depend on you! Must I do everything myself!? I have others to torture. Others to seduce into sin and corruption. A child! You couldn't destroy a child!" Beelzebub paced throughout the deep cavern. The Spittles all remained close to the damp walls, fearing for their existence. The mission to seize the child had failed.

One of the Spittles slowly approached. "We have spotted the child on a rock tower. He is resting."

"Is he by himself?" the evil beast Beelzebub questioned.

"No, oh evil one; the eagle is standing watch over him." The Spittle cowered back to the slimy wall.

Beelzebub turned quickly around; his scaly tail flung in the direction of the Spittle. One of the spikes on the evil creature's tail caught the small demon and threw him into the wall. "What good is that! Useless, all useless! I cannot approach the eagle. Argh!" Noxious gas and fire was once more released into the atmosphere. "Have you listened to the mother? Is she still making that offensive noise?" Beelzebub asked another Spittle, who had been commissioned to hover over the mother.

The Spittle slowly nodded its head yes as it backed up towards the damp cave wall.

Another angry roar rose up from Beelzebub. "The eagle is working with the mother in agreement! How can I get anywhere near them when they are working together?! We will wait. The child will grow weary with what is happening." Beelzebub rubbed his scrawny hands together. "Hover around in the darkness. Bring a dampening chill into the atmosphere. Yes! A cold, daunting cloud of dismay." The evil creature Beelzebub began to bellow for Dismay. All the Spittles cleared the room for the large beastly cloud of Dismay to arrive.

Questions to Contemplate

1. Why do you think it is always safe in the Tabernacle? Who keeps the Tabernacle safe?

2. What do you think moved: Samuel, the altar, or the mountain range?

3. Can you guess who caused the abrupt waterfall?

4. Why do you think Samuel felt he had failed his Father? Do you think he really did?

5. What do you think happened to Shear-Jashub and Ruach?

6. Why would an agreement between Samuel's mother and the eagle Gimel hinder Beelzebub from capturing Samuel?

---

[1] Proverbs 18:10: "The name of the Lord is a strong tower; The righteous run to it and are safe" (NKJV).

[2] Proverbs 29:18: "Where there is no vision, the people perish…" (KJV).

[3] Matthew 14:30: "But when he saw the wind boisterous, he was afraid; and beginning to sink, he cried, saying, Lord, save me" (KJV).

[4] Isaiah 43:1a–2: "Do not be afraid, for I have ransomed you. I have called you by name, you are mine. When you go through deep waters, I will be with you. When you go through rivers of difficulty, you will not drown."

[5] Psalm 27:5: "For he will conceal me there when troubles come; he will hide me in his sanctuary. *He will place me out of reach on a high rock*" (emphasis added).

Chapter Nine

A Decision

When Samuel woke, it was dusk. Shear-Jashub's eagle was still standing guard beside him. Samuel shivered in the damp air. The boy looked upwards at the giant bird. Samuel was amazed—not only by Gimel's immense size, but by the beauty and stately royalty of the elegant creature. The eagle let out a powerful loud scream and then moved closer towards Samuel, beckoning the boy to climb onto its back.

Samuel was unsure. He was still exhausted from the current of water which had almost drowned him. The damp, cold air hovered all around Samuel. The boy began to shiver.

Gimel slowly moved closer to Samuel. The giant eagle gently wrapped its wings around the boy and released a loud shriek. Samuel felt warmth and energy surge into his exhausted body. The eagle sheltered the boy awhile longer with its wings, and then moved away from him slightly. Then Gimel again beckoned the boy to get on its back.

The warmth and energy from Gimel continued to move though the boy's body, reviving him. Samuel looked up at the majestic bird and nodded his head in agreement. Cautiously, he stood behind the large bird. The eagle gently used its beak and guided Samuel onto its back. Samuel fastened his arms around Gimel's neck, as the bird extended its immense wings. The eagle moved to the edge of the rock tower and waited. Samuel felt a small wind on his face, coming from the desert below. That was all

A DECISION

that Gimel needed to fall forward into the current. The invisible channel of air slowly lifted the two of them upwards.

Samuel, now restored, laughed as he soared with the eagle over the desert. He noticed the water, still flowing swiftly, carving a new river through the wasteland. Samuel wondered where this mighty force of water had come from. Then he remembered the smoke and the moving mountain. Samuel surveyed the desert to see if he could spot either. The sun was now setting, so Samuel was unable to see much. His eyes continued to scout the land in search of his beloved Forever Friend and Shear-Jashub. The only thing he could make out was a small red glow in the horizon. He kept his eyes on the glow, wondering what it could be.

* * *

Dismay dropped slowly into the den of despair. The Spittles were pushed back against the damp walls as the creepy cloud creature continued to emerge into the den. "Your evilness," the large dark cloud said gloomily, "the eagle is now flying with the child on his back!"

"Argh! Where is the eagle taking the child?" Beelzebub roared as smoke filled the area. "I... I don't know." All the little Spittles moved quickly away from the cloudy creature. "Again! Must I do everything myself? The eagle will probably bring the child to Shear-Jashub. Spittles, go hover around in the night. Try to cause division. See if you can do anything right for once! Cause a fight, discord, rebellion. Yes—Rebellion!" A large Spittle came forth from the damp wall at the sound of his name. "Do not disappoint me. Bring Confusion and Indecision, too. Where have they been hiding?"

Two Spittles quickly appeared. Beelzebub slowly approached them. An evil grin was on the beast's face. His long, thin fingers touched each of the Spittles' throats. The sharp claws slowly lifted the faces of the shaking creatures. Flies buzzed all around the Spittles' faces. The beast drew the vapours closer to his mouth and coughed out more irritating flies as he kept his long claw under the Spittles' chins.

"Mwahahaha! You will both do nicely. Go with Rebellion and cause a division between the two boys. We will wear them down.[1] Do not let the children become friends! That would be a disaster. Keep them at war with each other! Yes—they must stay at odds with each other. Slowly but surely, the child Samuel will fall into my clutches. Don't let up. Ha ha ha! Go!"

Confusion, Indecision, and Rebellion flew up through the chamber's hole and entered the twilight sky. The three vapours looked at each other and instantly disappeared into the atmosphere. A damp chill covered the land as Dismay was sent to linger around the earth's crust.

* * *

The sun was setting quickly, creating a magnificent sunset. Samuel remembered how his mother loved to watch the sun setting at night. She would remind Samuel, "God paints us a beautiful picture each evening, to remind us that tomorrow will be another day filled with blessings, wonders and treasures."[2] She would wink at him, smile, and add, "It is our job to seek out the hidden treasures each day. What treasure will you find tomorrow?" she would question Samuel. He was warmed by the thought of his mother.

The young boy sighed. The night air was beginning to chill him again. Samuel thought of the glow he'd spotted, wondering if it was a fire. He thought about the times he would sit by the evening fires in his tribe, listening to the soldiers talk. Samuel's face was tucked into the eagle's feathers as he tried to keep himself warm. His eyes were getting heavy. He had experienced another incredible day. The boy's head was now completely tucked into the eagle's feathers as he began to doze off.

A DECISION

Suddenly, Samuel felt a jolt. He popped his head up from the back of the eagle. They had landed on the ground near a fire, and Shear-Jashub was standing nearby. Shear-Jashub looked over at Samuel and began to laugh. Samuel was visibly surprised when he raised his head up and noticed where he was. The younger boy still had a sleepy look of bewilderment on his face.

Samuel slid off the back of Gimel, only to be bumped to the ground and then pounced on by Ruach. The ram licked the face of his friend and cuddled his head into the boy's neck. "Hey, what's this?" Samuel stated as he examined his Forever Friend. "Your horns have grown, Ruach!" It was true—the small horn buds on the ram's head had grown. Ruach was now proudly displaying two large, brown horns on top of his head.

"Samuel, Ruach did a great job warning us of danger. His horns increase as he defends us," Shear-Jashub knowingly stated.

As Samuel was cuddling Ruach, he looked over at Shear-Jashub, who was keeping warm by the fire. "How is it you know so much about my Forever Friend? And now that I think about it, you know about the garden, the fruit trees, my Father?" Samuel shook his head as he stood up. "How did you get here?" Samuel turned around, his arms outstretched, and looked about. "What happened to all of us? Where are we?"

"Whoa, slow down! That's a lot of questions. First, I think you need to have some of this fruit. It will restore your strength." Shear-Jashub reached into his golden sack and pulled out a round piece of fruit. He examined the piece, smiled, and threw it towards Samuel, who raised his arm and caught the fruit in his hand. "Come and sit by the fire, and I will tell you all that I know. We are safe—" the boy paused, "—for now." The seasoned warrior looked cautiously out into the desert wasteland. "We will spend the night here."

FOREVER FRIEND

Samuel sat by the fire. Ruach lodged up behind his back and lay down. Samuel placed his back up against his Forever Friend, who made a cozy pillow. He bit into the fruit. It tasted delicious.

"We are safe for now," Shear-Jashub restated. "Tomorrow we will rise early and begin our journey to Mount Zion. Gimel will guard by air, and Ruach will continue to guard on the ground, watching for our enemy."

The little Spittles nodded their heads as they floated in the darkness, moving towards Samuel and Shear-Jashub. They had arrived just in time. The vapours cautiously moved towards Samuel, keeping a watchful eye on the eagle and the ram. Confusion began to whisper into the ear of the younger boy.

"Enemy—what enemy?" Samuel asked as he hungrily ate the fruit Shear-Jashub had given him. "The only thing that tried to hurt me was a crazy gush of water that came from... where did the water come from? I was nearly drowned!" Samuel took another bite of his fruit and thought a moment. "Hey, how is it you and Ruach escaped and I got caught in the water current?" Samuel continued to eat his fruit, making smacking noises as he sucked in the tasty juices. "I don't get this. All of you are here, safe and dry. Not me! I got caught in a crazy downpour of water and washed into a raging river—I practically drowned—and look at you!" Samuel greedily took another large bite of the fruit. "You're all perfectly fine! Argh!" He let out a sound of frustration. "The only enemy I have," Samuel stated in between more bites of the mouth-watering fruit, "is confusion! I don't understand any of this." The young boy threw the large pit from his fruit into the fire and rubbed his arms vigorously for warmth. The pit began to sizzle in the fire, releasing colourful flames. Samuel let out a loud yawn as the warmth from the fire comforted him.

"Well, confusion is an enemy. Beelzebub is also our enemy. He controls confusion. Ruach was quick to notice his sneak attack on us."

A DECISION

"Beelzebub? Wait, I remember you mentioned that name when I first met you. Tell me more about this Beelzebub." Samuel said, looking up from the mesmerizing fire.

"He is the enemy of your Father and all your Father's people. He will try to hide in the world around us. He is a master of disguise. He is total evil and darkness. There is nothing good in him.[3] His goal is to stop the fruit of the garden from being placed in the hands of the people. He will stop at nothing to get the fruit that has been harvested. The Father is training up His people with the produce from the garden. That is why Beelzebub hates it when we deliver anything to the King's people. The fruit and leaves from the Father's garden are a powerful source of life, truth, and marvellous qualities that the people can feed upon." Shear-Jashub sat down beside the fire. "The people hunger for the food from the Father. It is vital the food never dry up or cease being supplied."

"Wait a minute! Ezekiel never told me to watch for an enemy. I didn't know there was one! Why wasn't I told to protect the garden?" Samuel questioned.

"Aaaaah, Ezekiel! How is he? I haven't seen him for awhile. Don't you just love his belly laugh? It's contagious!" Shear-Jashub started to giggle as he looked over at Samuel. The younger warrior had a frown on his face, and his eyebrows were furrowed. Shear-Jashub let out a loud sigh. "Okay, where do I begin? The garden itself is safe," Shear-Jashub said. "The garden is under the protection of your Father. Your Father is greater and mightier than Beelzebub.[4]

While you were in the garden, all was well. You made the mistake of stepping outside the garden. You were on the outside wall of the altar. Outside your Father's home, evil exists.[5] Ruach noticed the mountain range was closing in on us, but Ruach also instinctively knew the mountain range was really Beelzebub. He can become whatever he wants to. He is skilful in deceit."[6] The older boy rubbed his hands together by the fire.

"I'm still confused. The mountain never hurt me. The water did. I almost drowned." Ruach moved his head under Samuel's arm and nestled closer to the boy. Samuel wiggled himself up against the ram, glad that his Forever Friend had grown slightly in size. The ram continued to support the boy as he leaned back.

"The water was actually a gift from your Father. You should be grateful for His help."

"I almost drowned! Did I mention that?" Samuel shouted. He was puzzled at Shear-Jashub's lack of concern over what had happened to him. As the boy thought back on all that had transpired that day, he shook his head in total disbelief. Nothing about his Father's world seem to make sense. It was all so confusing.

The little vapour puffs who were circling around the boys smirked mischievously after Samuel's frustrated shout. Confusion quietly snickered an evil laugh. He was proud of his accomplishment and boastfully moved his head up and down, pleased that he had infiltrated the child's thoughts and emotions.

"I almost drowned," Samuel muttered under his breath, still shaken by the experience and wondering why this didn't concern the older boy.

"Yep, you mentioned that several times. Now listen carefully to what I'm about to tell you," Shear-Jashub said, moving on from Samuel's water experience and trying to remain calm.

Indecision moved slowly over to Samuel and began to speak into one of the boy's ears as Confusion continued its constant rant in Samuel's opposite ear. Rebellion floated in the outer darkness, keeping a watchful

A DECISION

eye on the Forever Friends. He cycled round and round unseen, releasing a heavy spirit of selfishness through his small tail.

Samuel blinked his eyes. They were beginning to get heavier and heavier. It had been a long, troubling day. Samuel didn't feel like arguing with Shear-Jashub. He was becoming weary. He just wanted to understand this new world he had entered.

Shear-Jashub was now pacing back and forth by the fire. He was trying to gather the right words to explain to Samuel what was truth and what was deception. The young man sighed and began, "Beelzebub was the mountain range. The smoke came from his intense hatred towards good. Beelzebub tried to suffocate you with his hatred. The fire would have quickly engulfed you, had it not been for the river, suddenly supplied by your Father. The water washed us away from the presence of evil quickly. Beelzebub cannot stand anything created by your Father's hands to help us. You need to always remember: whatever the Father does, or creates, is greater than anything Beelzebub attempts to do. The Father is greater!" Shear-Jashub grinned as he looked down at Samuel, who was cuddled up next to Ruach. "Always remember, Beelzebub can't create anything. Only the Father can create! Beelzebub imitates the Father; he twists things all up." The older boy looked out into the darkness and sighed, thinking about all the Father had created. After a few minutes he continued. "The water not only took us out of the presence of Beelzebub—the evil creature didn't know what direction we were going in."

The three vapours gathered together in the darkness. They waited patiently for a time. Rebellion smirked and shrewdly approached the weary boy. The vile creature began to whisper into Samuel's mind. "You were all alone. No one cares for you. You were abandoned." The vapour repeated the word "abandoned" several more times, letting the word echo slowly around Samuel's mind. "Abandoned! Abandoned!" The Spittle held back an evil cackle. The vile creature was enjoying its taunting. An evil growl was quietly suppressed as it added a new word to its lies. "Forgotten—yes, forgotten. You were forgotten!" The evil vapour emphasized the word slowly. "No one understands you. Shear-Jashub is your enemy—your enemy—enemy!" The Spittle pronounced the word slowly and held back evil laughter, not wanting to give his position away to the protective Forever Friends.

"Beelzebub didn't know where you were headed," Shear-Jashub stated again, trying to make his point clear for Samuel to understand.

"Neither did I!" Samuel shook his head and tried to understand what Shear-Jashub was saying. "Okay, why did I go under the water several times if this was help from my Father? Where was His helping hand? I didn't see my Father, or anyone else for that matter!" Samuel sat up, no longer leaning back on his Forever Friend.

Shear-Jashub let out a deep breath as he looked over at Samuel. He scratched his head and thought a moment. "Did you cry out after you went under the water?"

"Yes, I was desperate. Don't you get this?" Samuel placed his head in his hands and looked down at his lap. Both boys were becoming frustrated.

The vapour puffs smirked at each other. They knew they were making a difference, impacting the boys' thinking and emotions.

"Samuel, listen to me. Your Father can only help us when we ask for His help. When you cried out to your Father, He immediately[7] sent Gimel to release you from the current. Your Father will only let you endure what He knows you are capable of enduring. What you go through will strengthen you for future battles against Beelzebub."[8]

"No way! No way! I'm not fighting anything again. I'm out of this mess!" Samuel quickly stood up and began to pace back and forth by the

A DECISION

fire. He looked out into the vast wasteland of darkness. The boy shook his head and sat back down, leaning once more into his Forever Friend.

"We're all in a battle, all of us, all the time." Shear-Jashub's voice was rising louder. He looked over at the young boy sitting defiantly by the fire. Samuel's legs and arms were crossed and his head was down. Shear-Jashub felt compassion rising up within his heart for the younger boy. Samuel's physical body was growing quickly, and his mind was trying to absorb all the new information.

Shear-Jashub spoke inside his head to his Father. *Father, help me to choose the perfect words to give insight and understanding to Samuel.* Again, the older boy spoke, only this time with strength and wisdom from the Father. "We are all in a battle, all of us, all the time." Shear-Jashub's voice was calm now. "The choice isn't being in or out of the battle. The choice is whether or not you pick up your armour and fight." Shear-Jashub warmed his hands by the fire. "There are no neutral players in this war. There is no middle ground to stand on, Samuel. No one can watch on the sidelines—no spectators! We are all, every one of us, in the battle. Whether we like it or not." Shear-Jashub paused, looking over at the tired, discouraged boy. "The real question is...." The older boy waited, getting the attention of Samuel, who eventually looked up from the fire. "...whose side are you on?"[9] No one spoke for awhile. The crackling of the fire was the only sound in the dark night. The older warrior sat down near his Forever Friend. "Samuel, if you choose not to fight, you have already lost the battle. You will have chosen your side—the side of Beelzebub. He will never win over the Father! Beelzebub is a loser, a defeated foe." Shear-Jashub rubbed his hands over the fire a little longer, allowing the information to settle into Samuel's head and heart. "You don't look like a loser to me."

The older boy shook his head, hoping his words had impacted Samuel. "If you don't want to bring the fruit to the people of Zion, stay here tomorrow. Beelzebub will quickly sniff you out and consume you.[10] I will rise early tomorrow and do the work I have been born to do."[11] Shear-Jashub paused a moment as he looked up into the starry night sky. "Samuel, I would like to have you by my side—" Shear-Jashub smirked, "—if you can keep up with me."

Samuel was too tired to discuss any more of his day. With heavy eyes and now a full belly from the fruit Shear-Jashub had given him, Samuel shook his head, rolled his eyes, and managed a brief response. "Wake me before you leave." The young boy's eyelids were becoming heavier by the second. Samuel could stay awake no longer. He slid into a deep sleep, with his head resting comfortably on his Forever Friend's back.

The three vapours grinned, their little tails slowly twisting and turning in pleasure. Their king, Beelzebub, would finally be pleased. The boys were no longer united. The Spittles slowly departed into the darkness from which they had come. They were clearly pleased with their accomplishments, as they released grim laughter.

Shear-Jashub smiled at his younger friend resting on Ruach. "Oh Father," Shear-Jashub spoke out loud, "Give Samuel the strength and courage he needs to move as a warrior in your Kingdom. This is all so new to him. He has barely spent any time with you in the garden being trained up. Beelzebub has tried to destroy Samuel before you could instruct him in the ways of the Kingdom."[12] Shear-Jashub stayed by the fire, speaking loudly in his own special secret language,[13] knowing tomorrow would be a challenging day for both of the boys.

Then Shear-Jashub thanked the Father and settled himself under his Forever Friend. The golden sack of fruit had been placed gently by the talons of the majestic eagle. Shear-Jashub smiled up at his Forever Friend and began his rest. Gimel stood guard over the boys and the fruit, his keen eyes watching for any signs of danger.

A DECISION

Questions to Contemplate

1. Do you think God hides treasures in our day for us to seek and find? Have you ever found a treasure from God? What did you do with your treasure?
2. Why do you think Shear-Jashub knows so much about Samuel's Forever Friend, Ruach?
3. How do you think Shear-Jashub and Ruach got to the fire unharmed?
4. Samuel didn't see his Father in the water, so he thought his Father wasn't with him. How do you feel about this?
5. Do you think God only lets us endure what we are capable of enduring? Do you think it will make us stronger?
6. The author writes, "The choice isn't being in or out of the battle. The choice is whether or not you pick up your armour and fight." Do you think you live in a battle? What are you battling? Do you have armour to fight with?
7. What is the decision Samuel must make?

---

[1] Daniel 7:25: "And he shall speak great words against the most High, and shall wear out the saints of the most High…" (KJV).

[2] Lamentations 3:23: "Great is his faithfulness; his mercies begin afresh each morning."

[3] Ezekiel 28:15 "You were blameless in your ways From the day you were created Until unrighteousness and evil were found in you. (AMP)

[4] Romans 16:20: "The God of peace will soon crush Satan under your feet."

[5] 1 John 5:19: "We know that we are children of God and that the world around us is under the control of the evil one."

[6] Revelation 12:9: "…Satan, the one deceiving the whole world—was thrown down to the earth with all his angels."

[7] Isaiah 30:19b: "…you will weep no more. How gracious he will be when you cry for help! As soon as he hears, he will answer you" (NIV).

[8] 1 Corinthians 10:13b: "…God is faithful. He will not allow the temptation to be more than you can stand. When you are tempted, he will show you a way out so that you can endure."

[9] Luke 11:23: "He who is not with Me [believing in Me as Lord and Savior] is against Me [*there is no impartial position*]; and he who does not gather with Me [assisting in My ministry] scatters" (AMP, emphasis added).

[10] 1 Peter 5:8: "Stay alert! Watch out for your great enemy, the devil. He prowls around like a roaring lion,

[11] Jeremiah 29:11: "'For I know the plans I have for you,' declares the Lord, 'plans to prosper you and not to harm you, plans to give you hope and a future'" (NIV).

[12] Psalm 32:8: "I will instruct you and teach you in the way you should go; I will counsel you with my loving eye on you" (NIV).

[13] Ephesians 6:18: "Pray in the Spirit at all times and on every occasion. Stay alert and be persistent in your prayers for all believers everywhere."

Chapter Ten

Worshipper Arise!

Thick, dark, black smoke hung everywhere in the intense heat, saturating the air. Samuel could hear people's cries, piercing his heart and soul, but he couldn't see them, couldn't help them. They weren't pleas of help, but of agony, torture, and a slow death.

Then, above all the cries, he heard a whimper, like that of a child. Soft, slow, and heartbreaking. Then the sound of a woman's voice was heard, repeating the same word over and over again. The woman's voice rose above the cries of the people, above the whimper of the child. The woman's voice was suddenly calling his name. "Samuel, Samuel..."

The whimper became louder, clearer, and stronger. Then the woman's propelling cry:

"Samuel, continue your journey. Continue!"

It was a voice he recognized.

"Mother!" he shouted. He hurled himself up and looked around, trying to spot her. He realized it must have been a dream.

"What's wrong?" Shear-Jashub asked as he awoke from his sleep.

"Nothing, nothing," Samuel said, his mind still spinning with the clarity and intensity of the dream. It had seemed so real—unlike any dream he'd ever had before.

He stood shivering by the hot embers of the evening fire. All the while, his mother's voice kept crying out to him in his mind, over and over again.

The boy stared at the fire and tried to reason out what he'd experienced.

"Samuel, tell me about your dream," Shear-Jashub said as he arose from his deep sleep. The older boy rubbed his eyes, breathed in deeply, and tried to stir himself fully awake. "It may help us tomorrow."

"How can a dream help us? And how do you know I had a dream?"

"Samuel, you jumped awake and called out for your mother. Whatever was happening in that dream, it's important. Your Father speaks to us through our dreams. He gives us important clues on how to fight, and can show us what's in our future.[1] I need to know what you saw."

Samuel warmed his hands above the still-glowing fire. "It felt so real, Shear-Jashub. Like I was there with my mom, but I couldn't help her or anyone else. It was like I was paralyzed in the smoke. The smoke was so thick, and I could only hear the people's cries. Shear-Jashub, it was awful. It seemed so real, but it was just a dream. A horrible dream."

"I don't think so, Samuel," the older boy said. "It was from the Father, in warning, in preparation. What else was there?"

Samuel sat down by the embers, enjoying the remaining warmth of the fire. He could still feel himself shaking. "I don't know…"

"Samuel, close your eyes and go back into the dream. I need you to tell me every detail."

He shook his head in disgust. "That's ridiculous. I'm tired. Go back to sleep."

"No, Samuel, close your eyes. This is important. Go back. Was your mother calling for you?"

Samuel closed his eyes, and as soon as he did the dream began replaying itself in his mind. His eyes snapped back open in horror.

"What did you see?" Shear-Jashub asked, coming closer and sitting next to Samuel by the fire. "What did you hear?"

"It's awful. The smoke is so intense; the flames are scorching!"

"Flames—that's new. You didn't say that before. Go on."

"The heat is unbearable. The cries are deafening."

"Go back into your dream." The older boy stood up, wide awake now and trying to understand the message of the dream.

Samuel closed his eyes once more as the images returned. "I can't see through the darkness... there's no water to save us this time." He opened his eyes. "I can hear my mother's voice calling out to me." Samuel looked over at Shear-Jashub. "She is crying out for me to continue...." Samuel paused. "She is calling my name. We have to help them! We can't let them perish."

"I know. The Father is warning us." Shear-Jashub put his hands on his hips as he stared into the fire, trying to devise a plan. "We can't wait till morning. We need to travel now."

"Do you know the way in the dark?" Samuel asked, looking out at the black world beyond the fire.

"No. But I know someone who can see in the dark. Someone who knows the way by heart. We need Shamar."

"Who's Shamar?"

"A warrior, like none you've ever seen before. I'm just not sure how to summon him here."

"Where does this Shamar live?" Samuel asked.

Shear-Jashub, grinned at Samuel. "He lives in the Tabernacle, with the Father."

"I've never seen anyone else in the Tabernacle. Only Ezekiel."

"Trust me, Shamar was there. He honours and guards the Father. He's the greatest of all warriors, and we need him. Samuel, this may seem strange to you, but we need to reach the ears of the Father.[2] We need to cry out in unison—there's power in unity.[3] If we do, the Father may release Shamar to us."

Shear-Jashub took a long, thin log out of the fire. Only one end was burning, so he blew on the smouldering end until flames appeared.

"Here, Samuel—hold this." The older boy passed the branch over to Samuel, then kicked another one out of the fire. This one was slightly longer. The seasoned warrior blew again on the end of the branch to create flames. "We need to dance around the fire and wave our fire poles.

We will paga together. The Father will hear us. I believe the Father will dispatch Shamar to come to our aid. In fact, I know the Father will send him, because He already warned us with your dream."

"Paga?" Samuel asked. "What's a paga?"

"We cry out to the Father in unison. We sing, dance, and praise the Father," Shear-Jashub said as he inspected his fire pole.

"Seriously, Shear-Jashub? I'm a guy, I don't dance!" Samuel looked at the older boy with disgust, turning up his nose and shaking his head.

"Samuel, this isn't just any dance—this is a dance to the Father. This is a cry for help from the deepest part of our hearts! We need to hit the target with our words and praises. Why don't you get this?" Shear-Jashub's thick brown eyebrows furrowed downward.

"I don't know what you're talking about. Hit a target!" Samuel grumbled under his breath. "All of this is new to me, foreign actually, and very, very strange." Samuel shook his head in disgust.

Shear-Jashub looked at the fire. His heart ached for Samuel. How could he help the younger boy understand all that was happening? How could he explain the urgency of their actions? What Samuel said was true. It was all new to him. But somehow Shear-Jashub had to help Samuel understand.

"Samuel, I realize you have never met your Father face to face. I know there is a deep longing inside of you to know Him more fully. I understand many new and unusual things have occurred. I get that this is hard for you to comprehend." Shear-Jashub paused a moment.

"What I do know for certain is that your Father has always been with you. Your Father has watched you grow up.[4] He loves you with an everlasting love.[5] He loves the things you do. Nothing can separate us from His love. Nothing![6] He desires for you to know Him, and He wants you to know Him in an intimate, loving relationship.[7] A relationship that's pure. A relationship even greater than the one you have with your mother." Shear-Jashub blew on the embers of his fire pole, which released sparks in the air.

"Someday, Samuel, you will meet your Father face to face. On that glorious day you will be transformed. You will never be the same again. You will come to know him as *El Shaddai*. The all-sufficient one. The Father who is more than enough to meet all your needs in every circumstance."

The fire began to crackle loudly. Shear-Jashub thought for a moment.

"For now," the older boy continued, "you have to trust me. Trust that all I've said is true. As your relationship with the Father increases, everything will change. You will never doubt or question again. You will obey—not out of duty, but out of the greatest love and desire known to mankind. I can't wait for you to experience all this, Samuel." He grinned. "It will happen."

Shear-Jashub paused and let out a long, loud sigh. "Until then, can you trust me as a friend? Can we paga, in unison? Samuel, this is important: we need Shamar. This is the only way to summon him here to help us. Are you with me?"

Samuel didn't know what to say. He looked into the huge, golden-brown eyes of Shear-Jashub. He seemed so trustworthy. What did Samuel have to lose? Possibly his pride. Yet, no one was around to see him dance. Then his mind went back to his tribe. Only the women would dance at the gatherings. The men banged the drums and made war calls. The mightiest warriors held their spears and moved them with skill and speed, pretending to do battle.

"Samuel, don't copy the behaviour and customs of this world."[8] Shear-Jashub slowly shook his head, looking at the confused younger boy. He shook his head again and looked down at his feet for a moment. "Samuel," the older boy said gently, "I wish you could understand the Father's will for you, which is good and pleasing—and more importantly, absolutely perfect."[9]

Samuel let out a loud sigh. His memory then raced back to his terrifying dream. Once again he heard the screams of the people and the plea from his mother to help. That was enough to turn his heart and to release his pride. "Okay, I'll paga... you start first."

Shear-Jashub looked over at Samuel. He couldn't help but grin. Samuel was choosing his destiny. He was now thinking of others. He was moving towards the Father's heart, and was quickly being propelled into a warrior. The smirk that first appeared on Shear-Jashub's face now grew into a huge smile. He wanted to run over to Samuel and give him a big bear hug. Shear-Jashub admired the younger boy for a minute more, and then began his dance. There was no time for playing, and they were no longer boys. They were becoming young men—warriors with a war to fight. The war of all wars!

Shear-Jashub took his wooden fire pole and began to wave it through the air. He moved in amazing gestures. The sand beneath his feet began to fly all around him. As Samuel watched in amazement, he thought his new friend looked more like a warrior then a girl dancing. Shear-Jashub's moves were jerky and strong. His words, though unknown to Samuel, were masculine and loud. This was different from the dances he'd seen in his tribe. Shear-Jashub's dance seemed to speak of power and strength. There appeared to be a purpose to his movements.

Samuel watched for a few more seconds, and then he began to imitate his older friend. Once he was able to move in a jerky fashion similar to Shear-Jashub, he began to shout out loud, "Father, we need Shamar. Father, please send us Shamar to help us fight for your people." Samuel kept moving and shouting around the fire.

Ruach was moving alongside Samuel. The ram kept looking up at Samuel as he danced around the fire.

After a short time, Samuel began to feel a change come over him. He felt strong and capable. All the fear, apprehension, and confusion were leaving his mind and body. Samuel was enjoying the dance, and he could feel his body being powered up. His shouting was releasing something into the atmosphere. He knew this—he felt this—yet it didn't make any sense to him. But that didn't seem to matter; he was enjoying the thrill of the dance!

Now Samuel's words changed. Instead of asking the Father for help, Samuel was thanking the Father for bringing him help. He was thanking the Father as if Shamar was already present.

The boys continued their dance, creating a path around the fire. Samuel was completely immersed in the dance as he jumped, stamped, and moved in unusual gestures. Sand from the boy's feet was flying everywhere.

"Mighty warriors, we are ready for battle." A deep, booming voice echoed in the darkness. Samuel froze.

Shear-Jashub let out a huge scream of joy. "Shamar! You're here!" The older boy leaped into the air, only to land on a large, tawny brown animal. A loud roar was heard, as the animal lifted his huge head to reveal a massive lion's face. Shear-Jashub buried his head in the lion's mane. His arms wrapped around a portion of the creature's huge neck. "Oh, how I've missed you."

The unique beast seemed to smile at the boy. He rubbed his majestic head gently against the young warrior's face. Then the mighty beast, which towered over them, stood back and spoke again, his deep voice booming through the atmosphere. "Shear-Jashub, we need to move quickly. Mount Zion is in danger. The people of Zion need to continually feed upon the powerful fruits and leaves from the Father's garden. Without its rich truths and anointing, the people will grow weak." The giant creature released a loud roar as he opened a display of many large wings.

Shamar walked over towards Samuel, who was standing still, frozen beside the fire. The unique creature's wings were folded against his body. The boy looked up at the beast. "So, I get to meet the valiant son of the Father! You have changed since I saw you in the Tabernacle." As Shamar said this, he flicked his tail near the boy's face. Samuel saw the long, round, tawny brown tail with gold, black, and brown hairs at the end. Then he remembered the movement under the curtain in the Tabernacle, and the object he'd seen moving about.

"You—you were behind the curtain. I saw your tail!"

"You did. You are very observant. A quality your Father has given to you. You will need to continue sharpening that skill. Ruach will help you. Now quickly, put out the fire. Only bring your fire poles. We must advance at once."

Shear-Jashub instantly took his foot and began kicking sand onto the fire. Samuel joined in to help, but kept a watchful eye on the large beast. He was fascinated with the creature. *Wait till I tell the soldiers in my tribe that I've seen an actual cherubim! They do exist and they are more amazing than they look on a curtain or on the shields of the warriors' armour!* Samuel continued to kick the sand onto the fire while studying Shamar. He snickered. *Mythical creature, ha—wait till I tell them all about this!*

"Shamar, it is done," exclaimed Shear-Jashub. He stood at attention, awaiting his next set of commands. The golden sack of fruit was slung over his shoulder, and his arm was securely encircling the precious treasure.

"Quickly, place yourselves on my back. Ruach will have to travel in the clutches of Gimel. Keep your fire poles behind my wings, and all will be well. Come; there's no time to waste." Shear-Jashub quickly mounted Shamar.

Samuel cautiously approached the massive talking lion. Shear-Jashub put his hand out to Samuel. Samuel locked his arm with Shear-Jashub's, and he was pulled onto the back of the enormous creature.

"Samuel, use one arm to hold on tightly and place the fire pole behind you with your opposite hand." Shear-Jashub instructed the younger boy. Samuel carefully moved his fire pole so as not to catch anyone on fire. "We are ready Shamar," Shear-Jashub stated. "The battle is ours for the Father!"

The creature pounced up into the air. Its beautiful wings unfolded and began to move, displaying magnificent colour, as if the wings were a sparkling display of the northern lights. Samuel noticed there were six iridescent wings—three on each side of the creature—carrying the boys upward, over the desert, and into the night.

Samuel could see nothing below—only darkness. He looked up into the night sky and observed all the stars. He thought about the stars in the ceiling of his Father's Tabernacle. Now he began to wonder if there actually *was* a ceiling in the Tabernacle. As Samuel stared at the stars, his eyes once more began to get heavy and he felt himself drifting off to sleep, holding tightly to the huge, regal creature.

* * *

Confusion, Indecision, and Rebellion smirked at one another as they prepared to enter the small tunnel crack which led to Beelzebub's chamber of doom. They slowly dropped, one at a time, deeper into the pit. Their vapour heads swelled slightly with pride over their accomplishment.

Beelzebub was eagerly awaiting them. Steam was rising from his head and ears, and the flies were hovering all around him. "You imbeciles! Useless, good for nothing... *uhhhhhh!*" The beast couldn't contain his anger as fire erupted from his mouth. "You left the children unattended! How many times do I have to repeat myself? Never stop bombarding the mortals with lies! Confusion, you failed again. Reellion, you didn't even attempt to destroy the child!"

Beelzebub quickly grabbed the throat of Indecision with his spindly hands. "Why didn't you remain with the child? Why? You are to constantly wear the mortal down with unrelenting whispers!" Beelzebub threw the Spittle into the wall.

Rebellion slowly began to speak. "The ram and eagle were too close. I thought..."

"Thought?! You are not to think. You are to do what I tell you. After you left and took your time sauntering back here, the children united! *United!!!* This is why you need to remain and continue your unrelenting attacks! Confusion, where are you?" the beast demanded through clenched teeth.

Confusion slowly moved away from the damp, dark wall where it had been nervously hovering. "Here, your lordship."

"Next time I send you, accomplish your assignment or all of you will be no more. You are all just vapour. I can destroy you at any moment. Useless, rotten beings. Division, division between two boys is all I demanded. Is that too hard for you? Morons, imbeciles—you all disgust me!" The creature lunged at the Spittles, and then stormed off into a deeper chamber, his footsteps causing the inner cavern to shake. "I must do everything myself!" The creature grumbled through his yellow clenched teeth. "I can't be in two places at once. Rrrrrr...." The beast growled in frustration. "I need to devise a new plan. The fruit can't get to the people of Zion. They have already been fed too much of the powerful fruit and leaves. Arghhhhh! Two messily children have become such a threat to my overall plan of seizing the Father's Kingdom."

The creature continued to growl and grumble as he went deeper into his tomb of evil, devising a diabolical plan to overthrow the world of the Father. A large plume of fire erupted from the grotesque horns on top of his head. The fire blew all the way into the cavern where the Spittles remained. "I will have to take care of the little brat myself! Mughhhhhhhh!"

the beast bellowed. More fire erupted as the creature continued to steam over the situation.

The Spittles all remained by the damp wall as the evil beast left the chamber, murmuring and growling. A putrid, gagging odour remained to remind the small demon vapours of their failure.

Questions to Contemplate

1. Do you think God can talk to us in dreams? Has this happened to you?
2. How did the dance change Samuel's thinking?
3. Do you ever dance, sing, and pray to God? How do you feel after this activity?
4. Can you draw a picture of yourself singing and dancing for God? This is called worship.
5. Do you think worship is a dance anyone can participate in?
6. The word *paga* taken from *Strong's Concordance* (#6293) means "to encounter, meet, reach, make intercession, to hit the mark, or hit the target."[10] What target do you think Shear-Jashub and Samuel are trying to hit?
7. The author writes, "You are very observant. A quality your Father has given to you." What qualities has God given you?
8. *Shamar* in *Strong's Concordance* (#8104) means "to watch, observe, pay attention, guard."[11] What do you think Shamar is watching out for? Who do you think he is guarding?

FOREVER FRIEND

[1] Job 33:15–16: "In a dream, a vision of the night [one may hear God's voice], When deep sleep falls on men while slumbering upon the bed, Then He opens the ears of men and seals their instruction…" (AMP).

[2] 1 Peter 3:12: "The eyes of the Lord watch over those who do right, and his ears are open to their prayers."

[3] Genesis 11:6b: "The people are united, and they all speak the same language. After this, nothing they set out to do will be impossible for them!"

[4] Jeremiah 1:5: "I knew you before I formed you in your mother's womb."

[5] Jeremiah 31:3: "I have loved you, my people, with an everlasting love. With unfailing love I have drawn you to myself."

[6] Romans 8:38–39: "And I am convinced that nothing can ever separate us from God's love. Neither death nor life, neither angels nor demons, neither our fears for today nor our worries about tomorrow—not even the powers of hell can separate us from God's love. No power in the sky above or in the earth below—indeed, nothing in all creation will ever be able to separate us from the love of God that is revealed in Christ Jesus our Lord."

[7] Deuteronomy 4:29b: "And if you search for him with all your heart and soul, you will find him."

[8] Romans 12:2a: "Don't copy the behavior and customs of this world, but let God transform you into a new person by changing the way you think."

[9] Romans 12:2b: "Then you will learn to know God's will for you, which is good and pleasing and perfect."

[10] 6293. paga," *Bible Hub* (https://biblehub.com/hebrew/6293.htm).*Bible Hub* (https://biblehub.com/hebrew/6293.htm).

[11] "8104. shamar," *Bible Hub* (https://biblehub.com/hebrew/8104.htm).

Chapter Eleven

Divine Encounter

Samuel awoke to a piercing scream. Gimel was calling over and over again through the night air. The sharp shriek of the eagle gave Samuel shivers down his spine. He gripped Shamar's tawny fur tightly.

"Gimel is alerting us to something. What can you see, Shamar?" Shear-Jashub's voice had a sense of urgency.

Shamar's deep voice boomed. "I don't see anything. It's what I smell that concerns me. Can you smell it? Beelzebub is nearby. I can smell his stench!" Shamar's voice seemed to echo in the darkness with disgust.

Samuel looked around, trying to observe any unusual activity. The boy moved his fire pole, which was still glowing, in an effort to aid himself. He noticed they were travelling through a mountain range. Shamar was skillfully maneuvering through the high ravines of the mountains. The night sky was slowly giving way to the morning dawn. Samuel could see how close the jagged edges of the rock faces were to them as they flew quickly through the narrow pass.

The young boy closed his eyes, thinking it was better not to look. He tightened his grip on Shamar's fur. Both of his hands were now clinging to the fur of the majestic beast, and his fire pole was tucked securely under his armpit.

"Oh Father," Samuel whispered, "We need to reach the people. We need to bring them your fruit."

Samuel heard another screaming cry from Gimel. Then a heavy black cloud of smoke descended upon the group. They could feel the thick smoke layering upon their skin. The smoke was accompanied by an awful, pungent smell. Samuel struggled to breathe as he held tightly onto Shamar. The disgusting odour made the young warrior want to gag.

As Samuel was struggling to breathe through the smoke, something solid struck him on his shoulder. The tight grip Samuel had on Shamar's fur was jarred. Samuel let go of the great beast and fell off its back.

Samuel could feel himself falling downward. He tried to right himself as he plummeted, hoping he could land on his feet, but the speed at which he was descending, and the pull of gravity were against him. As he struggled, trying to right himself in the air, he lost his grip on his fire pole. A second before he was to hit a cliff edge, Samuel felt Gimel swoop by him. The giant eagle pushed Samuel away from impacting a jagged rock that was jutting out from the cliff.

Samuel continued to fall towards the ground. The black smoke was clearing the closer he came to the ground. Gimel flew towards him for another rescue. This time, the great eagle lost its grip on Ruach, who had been travelling in the clutches of the bird. Now Ruach and Samuel were both plummeting towards earth, and about to impact the ground.

Samuel landed with a loud thud on top of Ruach. The ram looked up at Samuel, blinking his large blue eyes. Both were sprawled out on a dry desert floor.

Samuel jumped to his feet. "Ruach, are you alright?" The ram shook his head yes and rose to his feet. "Great! We have to get out of here. Beelzebub is somewhere nearby. We need to stay alert." Samuel noticed his fire pole by the wall of the ravine. The wind from the fall had snuffed out the fire.

Samuel looked all around. He caught a glimmer of the sun beginning to rise. "Which way should we go, Ruach? Do you know the way to the people?"

The ram lifted himself up on his two back legs and began to sniff the air. Ruach did this for a while, until he finally seemed satisfied which way they should move. Ruach took off quickly, with Samuel running closely behind.

Samuel looked up between the sides of the gorge as he ran. The fall had been great. There was no sign of Shamar, Shear-Jashub, or Gimel. "We are on our own, Ruach. We can do this," Samuel yelled as the two raced through the narrow ravine. He knew he had to encourage himself. His words became a powerful source of energy.

After a while, the boy began panting as he ran. Samuel had developed an ache in his side, and the feeling was becoming intense. "Ruach," Samuel gasped, "stop! I have to catch my breath." Samuel stopped and bent over, trying to breathe.

The ram stopped and came back to Samuel. "I have to catch my breath, Ruach." Samuel fell to his knees on the ground. He gripped his stomach, trying to subdue the pain. "I just need a minute."

The ram nestled up close and placed his head near Samuel's face, breathing gently towards the tired boy. The two rested for a few minutes. Then Ruach began to sniff the air again. The ram stood up quickly, still investigating the air. Samuel looked at his friend.

"What is it? Do you smell something?" Samuel looked around himself as the ram continued to sniff the air. From Ruach's behaviour, Samuel knew something was definitely nearby. The sun was slowly rising, allowing Samuel to see where they were. He searched the sky, squinting as he looked into the rising sun. He was hoping to see Shamar or Gimel, so his running would be over.

The ram cautiously walked deeper into the narrow gorge. The path took a sudden turn. It was around the turn that Ruach found a small cave entrance. The ram waited outside of the cave for Samuel.

Samuel slowly made his way over to Ruach. He was still out of breath, and his side continued to hurt. The ram had positioned himself in front of the cave entrance, blocking Samuel from entering.

Samuel thought he heard a sound. He pivoted his head and listened.

"Ruach, is there something inside the cave?" Samuel looked all around. There was nothing but enormous cliffs on both sides of him. The cliffs went up hundreds of feet. There was no vegetation, only rock and dust. *What could possibly be in this cavern?* Samuel wondered.

Curiosity began to lure Samuel. He pushed past Ruach and took a few steps into the cave. Quickly, Ruach moved in front of Samuel and tried to push his friend out of the cave. The Forever Friend shook his head back and forth to gesture *no!*

Samuel stood still and peered into the darkness. Curiosity began to rise inside his mind.

As his eyes adjusted to the dark, he saw what his faithful friend had smelled.

Lying on the ground of the cave was a horse. The horse was glistening white.[1] Samuel could almost make out its size—there was just enough morning light coming into the cave. The horse raised up its head and looked at Samuel, but the animal remained lying on the ground and made a quiet neighing sound. "Is the horse hurt, Ruach? Why is it just lying

FOREVER FRIEND

here in this cavern?" Samuel asked. He couldn't understand why a horse would be hiding in a forlorn mountain cave.

Samuel moved slowly towards the horse. Ruach bit onto a piece of Samuel's clothing and began to pull him from the cave. Samuel stood defiantly as he heard a buzzing sound. A fly flew by his head and then buzzed in front of his face. Samuel shooed the fly with his hand and continued to peer into the darkness, trying to understand the mystery of the white horse. The horse gave a gentle nicker. Its face seemed to beckon the boy closer. Samuel was about to move forward when more flies moved about his face and around his head. One fly tried to enter Samuel's ear. Irritated, Samuel began to swat at the flies. The flies were a nuisance, distracting him from his thinking.

Samuel suddenly smelled a nauseating scent. He asked himself, *Where have I smelled this horrible odour before?* Samuel stood very still, trying to decipher all that his eyes and his senses were taking in as the flies continued to buzz around his head. An uneasiness arose inside of Samuel. *Something is not right!* Samuel thought to himself.

Ruach quickly moved in front of Samuel and began to push him backwards out of the cave. Samuel was slowly moving backwards as he looked at the horse. "Ruach, it appears injured. Should we help?" he asked. Despite his feelings of uncertainty, the young boy was thinking of his side ache and all the running he had done. If Samuel could help the horse to health, he wouldn't have to walk to Mount Zion. *This could be a good thing,* thought Samuel.

The horse now had flies hovering all around it, besides the flies darting near Samuel's face. *Where are all these pesky flies coming from?* Samuel wondered as he continually batted at them. At the same time, Ruach was persistent, pushing the boy backwards with his horns now digging uncomfortably into the boy's tummy. Samuel was becoming irritated at Ruach, who wasn't giving him enough time to think through this predicament. The hovering flies were adding to his irritation. Ruach quickly stopped pushing Samuel out of the cave, turned abruptly and looked at the horse. Standing defiantly between Samuel and the horse, Ruach announced loudly, "Bad, bad Beelzebub!"

At the speaking of his name, the horse transformed into a gigantic black beast. The grotesque monster stood up to reveal its immense size, and roared at the two young friends. Samuel stood still, shocked at the transformation that had taken place in front of his eyes. The beast's head had instantly grown five times larger. Its body swelled up, revealing its enormous strength.[2] The monstrous creature glared at Samuel with red, penetrating eyes[3] and opened its mouth, revealing rows of sharp, fearsome teeth.[4] The gruesome creature spat out fire and sparks of red-hot coals. Black smoke streamed from its nostrils.[5] The smell from the creature was overwhelming, and the cave was now completely engulfed with smoke.

Samuel stood frozen for a moment, unable to move as he witnessed the lame white horse transform into an ugly, monstrous, fire-breathing creature. Ruach's body pushed backwards against Samuel, releasing him from his frozen state of fear. The mighty ram stood between Samuel and the frightening monster. Samuel, able to move now, bolted out of the cave. As he ran, he felt a strong gush of wind go by his head. Samuel realized the rush of air had come from Ruach, who had been violently propelled into the air. Beelzebub had intended to strike Samuel with the ram but had slightly missed his target.

The ram hit the adjacent rock face outside the cave, smashing headfirst into the stone wall. One of Ruach's horns was knocked from his head. A small pool of white cream lay beside the ram's horn.

Samuel screamed. *"No, Ruach!"*

The ram slowly looked up at the boy and beckoned towards the horn. Samuel tried to gather the ram in his arms, but the ram shook his head. Again, Ruach beckoned Samuel to the horn lying on the ground nearby. Samuel remembered the warriors in his tribe using rams' horns to sound the alarm.

Samuel quickly grabbed the horn. The youth stood defiantly, looking towards the cave entrance. The monster emerged, blasting his way out of the small cave opening. Large rocks were spumed outward as the creature roared, violently lunging towards the boy.

The hideous creature continued to release its frightful scream as its unveiled identity was now seen in dawn's light. Beelzebub looked upwards towards the rising sun and shrieked. Instantly the flies hovered closely over the grotesques creature's eyes, blocking out some of the irritating sunlight. Samuel could clearly see the sharp glassy black scales[6] which covered the creature as an impenetrable armour.[7] The beast had two large horns on its sinister head which spat sparks of fire and sizzling stream. Again, the evil beast blew dense smoke and spat out fire. The creature's repulsive mouth remained open, revealing its many rows of razor sharp yellow and brown teeth. The beast then emitted a low, menacing, eerie growl as it slowly stalked towards Samuel. The evil beast's spindly arms with scrawny hands and claw-like fingernails were reaching out towards Samuel, preparing to scratch and claw at him. The heat from the fire of the monster's breath could be felt on Samuels skin. The blast of fire came within inches of touching the boy's stomach. Samuel breathed in deeply as he stood frozen against the large rock wall. He looked down at the flame as he continued to breathe in, trying not to let the blast of the fire burn him up. His legs trembled in fear.

Samuel had nowhere to go. He was pinned against the towering rock wall.

The Spittle named Discouragement had accompanied Beelzebub on this attack. The vapour quickly moved into position and began his unending lies, eager to work with his master. "You are doomed, doomed,

doomed! This is the end for you! You have nothing to fight with. *Nothing to defend yourself with!* You're frozen in fear. You're ours! Helpless! Hopelessly, helpless, hopeless!" the vapour repeated.

Then the words of Shear-Jashub came into Samuel's remembrance. "You must choose a side. There are no spectators." Ruach pushed up against the boy's leg and motioned to the ram's horn in Samuel's trembling hand. Ruach once more rubbed himself up against the child. Fear began to dissipate. The boy quickly took a deep breath in, and with all the zeal and courage the young warrior could summon, he blew through Ruach's horn.

As the horn blasted a penetrating sound, the smoke and fire once more came towards them from the beast's mouth. The powerful sound from the horn was amplified within the smoke. The two elements, evil and purity, mingled together in the air. Then the fire, smoke, and putrid smell violently retreated towards the evil monster. Beelzebub was thrown off guard and swayed backwards, trying to stabilize himself with his tail. Samuel stood in awe as he watched the blackened air move backwards towards Beelzebub.

Again, the boy stood steadfast and blew his horn. This time Samuel noticed the sound of the horn was building an impenetrable invisible wall, blocking any smoke, fire or odour from moving towards Samuel or Ruach. Beelzebub let out a horrifying cry. Once again, Samuel blew though his ram's horn. The gruesome beast let out another terrifying scream and flew off, up and out of the gorge. The smoke settled like a dirty blanket on the ground.

Samuel looked up into the sky. He could see the giant, black winged beast departing. Its serpentine tail with large sharp spikes was moving back and forth as if to direct the movement of the detestable creature's flight. The two small bat-like wings moved quickly up and down, trying to raise the humongous Beelzebub into the air. The cloud of flies trailed behind the dreadful, scaly beast.

* * *

As Beelzebub flew away from the powerful noise of the ram's horn, he captured Discouragement in mid-flight. Beelzebub's scrawny hands were clenched around the vapour's tail as the beast drew the Spittle towards his fire-breathing mouth. "Discouragement, stay with the boy. Whisper lies repeatedly into his mind. Do not let up this time! Wear the mortal down."

The beast threw the vapour towards the earth as the giant smelly creature retreated into the depths of darkness.

* * *

Ruach put his head against his friend's leg. Samuel looked down at the ram. His head was bleeding where the horn had broken off. "Ruach, you saved me!" Samuel rested on the ground, placed his face in his Forever Friend's silky wool, and began to sob. He kept his hand on the opened wound, trying to stop the bleeding. Samuel cried for what felt like a long time, his tears moistening Ruach's silken wool. He ached inside his heart.

The vapour of Discouragement wasted no time as it began its bombardment of lies. The evil puff grinned as it hovered close to the boy's ear. "Useless. Failure. Worthless. You're a disappointing child." The vapour held back from releasing an evil laugh as it watched the child sob. Discouragement knew it was impacting the child's thoughts.

The vapour moved beside the child's beating heart. "That's correct—you're a complete failure. Your mother will be so crushed. You've disappointed her again. All you can do is fail. Why do you even try?"

The vapour continued to circle around the boy's head. "Look—you can't even take care of your Forever Friend. It's all because of you that Rauch is hurt. He will never forgive you. Your precious Forever Friend will die out here in this wilderness. It will all be your fault." The vapour smiled at the effects his words were having on the pathetic child.

"What good am I, Ruach? I can't help the people of Zion. I can't even stay on the back of a lion," Samuel sobbed. "I'm useless, no good for anything. Now you're missing your horn and you're bleeding. We're in the middle of nowhere. I can't do anything brave and strong. What good will I be to my Father?"

Ruach nuzzled in closer to the child. His big blue eyes looked forgivingly up at Samuel.

Samuel continued to sob. His heart felt like it was being ripped into tiny pieces.

The small vapour was enjoying its taunting. "Your usefulness is over. Go crawl into the cave. No one wants to see you again. No one cares for you. Disappear. That will make everything better. That is where you belong. Alone, so you won't hurt anyone else. You want to be alone." The vapour grinned as an even more diabolical thought came to it. "You don't even want to be with Ruach anymore. That's right. Leave that useless, broken-down ram on its own. Go crawl into the cave and be by yourself. You want to be alone. All alone! All alone!" The Spittle slowly repeated the words over and over again. Discouragement took pleasure at watching the child become more and more pitiful.

Samuel sat on the ground amidst the remaining filthy black smoke. He felt his young life was over. He wanted to just disappear. "I should crawl back into the cave," he suddenly stated out loud. Ruach continued to push himself in closer to the boy. The ram continued to warm the boy with his presence, gently rubbing up against the child. He was trying to reassure the boy he was loved.

Discouragement's beady yellow eyes glowed. "Yes, yes, yes, it's all over for you!" the vapour of evil lied.

Samuel felt worthless, empty, lost, wondering why he had ever been born. He was certain all hope for him becoming a warrior was over. His chance to meet and get to know his Father more deeply had been ruined by his own actions. Yet in his heart the burning desire to know and understand his Father grew stronger with each sob. Ruach's face was now buried against Samuel's chest. The ram's big blue eyes were looking steadily up at the sobbing child. All of Samuel's tears were being collected in the soft white wool of his Forever Friend. The ram gently nudged the boy's chest, massaging Samuel's heart with his warmth and love. The stirring of inner worthlessness and a desire to meet the Father mixed together in Samuel's soul.

The Spittle's tail began to curl. The atmosphere suddenly changed. The small vapour started to shake. Discouragement looked upward and saw the gleaming light. Its beady yellow eyes were suddenly blinded. The puff of evil quickly departed the child.

As Samuel cried into his friend's soft, silky wool, a warmth came upon him. The boy lifted his puffy, swollen eyes. There was a bright, warm light in front of him. He didn't feel afraid. He was intrigued by the brilliant warm light. A calm entered over and into the boy. Samuel rubbed his eyes, hoping to see more clearly.

Ruach instantly jumped up to his feet and then bent his front legs as if he was kneeling. The ram lowered his lopsided head to the ground. Then he let out a beautiful sound—a soft soothing "Father" sound. The light slowly came closer to the ram and touched Ruach's head. The ram instantly was healed. The bleeding had stopped. The ram stood to his feet and walked into the beautiful light, which seem to beckon him.

Samuel rubbed his eyes again. *Is this real?* he thought. The ram came out from the warm light, with two majestic horns of gold and silver swirling together upon its head. Ruach had grown in size and was now fully mature. His wool remained like strains of silk, only now it was white mixed with purple, silver, and gold. The little silver crystals at the tip of each strain of wool sparkled brilliantly. Ruach had once again changed. He turned and again knelt before the warm bright light. The ram's face was entranced by the light.

The golden splendour was all around them. Samuel placed his hands on his eyes. The light was too intense for him to look upon.[8]

"Samuel!" He heard his name as if it was floating on the wind. "You have looked for Me wholeheartedly and you have found Me.[9] Your love for your people, your love for Me, burns inside your heart. Your curiosity and deep longing to meet and know your Father have propelled you forward. Your mind and heart are becoming more and more open to My ways. Samuel, you are becoming a mighty warrior. I have longed for this encounter.[10] Your heart's cry has allowed this encounter to happen."

The sound of the wind moved through the narrow gorge. Samuel could feel the fresh air on his face. He breathed in deeply.

"When you come close to Me, I will come close to you."[11] The words were intertwined with the sound of the wind.

"Who are you? What are you? How do you know me? How did you fix Ruach's horn?" Samuel asked. His mind was spinning with so many questions.

"I am your Father. I am *Elohim*.[12] I have watched you since the beginning of time. I know everything about you—more than you know about yourself.[13] You have searched for Me. You have longed for Me. You have shown a willingness to learn and accept new ways. You are beginning to show compassion for others. You are truly a son of Mine. I am proud of you! I have always been proud of you."

"I have failed you, Father. I didn't take care of the fruit. I allowed Ruach to get hurt. I have been unable to help my people. Unable to save my mother!" Samuel felt his unworthiness now more than ever. He was wishing his mother had never taken him to the Tabernacle. Then he could have lived an ordinary life in his tribe. Why did all this have to happen to him? Suddenly, Samuel yearned for his old life.

"Samuel, I know all your thoughts—even before you think them.[14] You see yourself as a failure. I look at you and see a great and mighty warrior. I look into your heart and soul. My son, I see who you are destined to become.

"Samuel, you were destined to live the life of a warrior. It is in you to fight evil. To fight for righteousness. For I have placed inside of you the hatred of evil.[15] I have given you access to truth, righteousness, and love. You have all you need to fight Beelzebub and win. It is all inside of you."

The gentle breeze continued to blow upon the boy's face. "You've had this armour and many weapons ever since you cried out to know me at the tabernacle door. You just did not know how to use them. That is why I have given you Ruach. I also arranged for you to meet Shear-Jashub. He and Ruach are helping you to learn the ways of a warrior. This is how My Kingdom works. One who is trained and fully committed to Me in love will begin to train another."[16]

"Shear-Jashub isn't much older than me. Wouldn't it be better to leave this fight to the men?" Samuel asked. "Like the men in my tribe? Wouldn't they be good? They know all the rules by heart. They practice every day."

"The age of a person means nothing to Me. Their works mean little to me. I look at the heart of a person,[17] young or old. When their heart is right, I will begin their training. Your heart, Samuel, has much love growing in it. Soon your heart will overflow with love, because you are beginning to draw from Me, the source of love.[18] You, Samuel, are a soldier in training. My son, I am raising you up to do a great work."

"Father, help me to be all that You have desired me to be. Let me know Your ways so I can understand You more fully."[19]

"Do not despise these small beginnings, for I rejoice seeing the changes begun in you."[20] With those words, the warm light grew in intensity and the voice on the wind grew louder. "I will call out my name, *Yahweh*, before you. For I show mercy to anyone I choose, and I will show compassion to anyone I choose. Samuel, I choose you."[21]

Suddenly, golden rays of light beams were bouncing all around Samuel. A warm rain began falling on him. The rain poured down—only on Samuel. He was being washed. Samuel opened his arms wide, tilted his head back, and swallowed the warm, nourishing rain. It tingled against his body. He felt immersed in the downpour.

As Samuel stood with his arms wide open, looking upwards, a sound emerged out of his mouth. It was a strange new sound. Samuel couldn't hold it back. It came forth with such force and intensity. The sound was pure energy. Samuel could feel strength rising up the more he allowed the sound to come out of himself. An inner groan was intermingled with the new syllables being released.[22] Now Samuel was almost screaming the newly formed foreign words as they echoed through the ravine. The words erupted into sentences. The marvellous language penetrated the atmosphere.

Then the rain slowly subsided. Samuel looked down at the ground and noticed all the soot and smoke had been washed away. He realized his feet were larger than before. He looked at his hands. They too had grown. Samuel had developed into a young man. He also felt strength and love flowing through his body like never before.

A gentle breeze moved over Samuel's body. His Father's voice was carried on the breeze. "The healing, washing rains have prepared you for My work. You have been bathed in My glory, My goodness. Continue to follow righteousness. Continue to allow Ruach to lead and guide you. I will equip you with another gift and a weapon."

The brilliant light quickly vanished. In its place was a long silver sword. Samuel picked up the weapon and examined its splendour. Exquisitely crafted, it was sharper than any blade Samuel had ever seen.

Beside the sword lay a belt and a shield. Samuel placed the belt around his waist. It fit him perfectly. He then placed the sword carefully inside the leather sheath on the belt. Next, Samuel picked up the shield. He admired its beauty for a long time, his large hands slowly touching and examining the craftsmanship. The shield had different coloured stones embedded on the outside. The shield itself seemed to be made from a very strong material, unknown to Samuel. It was hard and shiny—so shiny Samuel could see himself.

Samuel smiled as he looked at his reflection. He was now a young man. He was indeed a warrior! Would his mother know him? He thought about his Father's words, claiming Samuel had always been a warrior. Samuel would have to think about that some more.

Samuel was smiling at himself in the shield when he heard the whinny of a horse. Samuel jumped around, instantly taking a posture of defense with his shield instinctively before him and his hand on his new sword, ready to retrieve the weapon. Behind Samuel stood a large royal-looking horse. The newly commissioned warrior was unsure. Could this be another trick from Beelzebub?

"This is My gift to you, Samuel," whispered the Father gently. The warrior listened intently. "Dunamis is swift and strong. Dunamis has miraculous power, and will help you withstand any attack from Beelzebub. He knows the way to our people." The soft, still voice of the Father echoed through the ravine and slowly disappeared with the wind.[23]

Samuel stood still in total amazement, marvelling at his magnificent new friend. The horse was larger than any Samuel had seen before. It had fiery red eyes, which were unsettling to Samuel. The horse's body was golden in colour, and golden sparkles seemed to dance off it. The mane and tail were soft curls of white, purple, silver, and golden hair, just like the silken wool of Ruach. The royal creature had huge white feathered wings on each side of its massive, muscular body. The wings appeared to be made of glass or crystals, even though they were covered in feathers. Samuel was almost mesmerized by the glassy, iridescent wings.

The newly commissioned warrior cautiously stared at the horse, who remained perfectly still. Samuel gazed upon the fiery red eyes of Dunamis. The horse's eyes seemed unnerving to the questioning warrior.

Slowly, Samuel walked towards the muscular stallion. "Hi, Dunamis—I'm your new friend Samuel. I won't hurt you. I want to ride with you to Zion, to help my people. My Father said you know the way. You are very smart for a horse." Samuel reached up to the horse's neck and gently stroked the massive animal. Even after Samuel's sudden growth, the creature was immense. The sparkles of gold tingled on his hand.

"Would it help if I kneel down as you mount me?" Dunamis said to Samuel.

Samuel jumped back from the horse in total shock.

Dunamis whinnied as if in laughter. "I didn't mean to startle you, young man. We must catch up to the others. We have no time to waste on formalities." The horse bent its two front legs, looked at Samuel with its fiery red eyes, and waited. The glorious feathered wings were bent backwards slightly, and slowly moving up and down. This movement captured the gold flecks bouncing off the heavenly creature, producing a gentle current of gold dust that swirled around the spectacular being.

Samuel was stunned. "Well, if a lion can talk, I suppose a horse should be able to speak too." Samuel chuckled. Then he noticed the ram's horn on the ground. He quickly grabbed the horn and tucked it under his arm. Samuel held his shield in his hand and mounted the magnificent horse. Gracefully, Dunamis stood up.

Samuel looked over at Ruach, "Will you be able to keep up with us, my Forever Friend?" The ram seemed to smile at Samuel. Hidden within his silken wool, the ram opened two fascinating transparent wings. The wings were clear, but they had veins with deep amber blood flowing through them.

"Wow! You have wings like a giant dragonfly!"

As Samuel said these words, the horse leaped into the air. Samuel grabbed hold of its luxurious flowing mane. Dunamis wasn't jumping—rather, the horse kept moving up towards the rising sun. Samuel looked behind him and admired the glorious wings which cut through the air as they propelled upwards. The feathers glowed individually, putting on a spectacular light show as the companions mounted up higher into the atmosphere.

Samuel looked down at the ground where he had once been. *I will never forget this spot*, Samuel said to himself. *For it was in this ravine between the two steep mountains, in the dry land, that I had an amazing encounter with my Father. It was here a transformation began. I will always remember this place and this time.* Samuel seemed to be sailing, moving effortlessly on Dunamis. The fully mature ram was flying beside them, and they were all heading into a new day, a new dawn.

Questions to Contemplate

1. Samuel had to encourage himself with his words. The author writes, His words became a powerful source of energy. Do you think words can become energy? Who in the Bible is known to encourage himself with his words? Have you ever tried to encourage yourself with words? What was the outcome of your actions?
2. When Samuel blew the ram's horn, the sound moved the smoke, fire, and Beelzebub backwards. What do you think was happening?
3. The Father healed Ruach. Do you think God heals people? Do you know anyone who has been healed?
4. The name *Elohim* means divine majesty and power. (*Strong's Concordance #430*)[24] Yahweh is the proper name of the God of Israel (*Strong's Concordance, #3068*).[25] Do you have a special name for God?
5. If you could talk to the Father face to face, what would you say?
6. What do you think was happening when the rain was falling on Samuel?
7. The Father told Samuel He looks at the heart of a person. What do you think the Father finds in your heart?
8. The word *dunamis* in *Strong's Concordance* (#1411) means "force, miraculous power, and might."[26] The power referenced in Ephesians 1:19–20 is the *dunamis* power of God: *"I also pray that you will understand the incredible greatness of God's power for us who believe him. This is the same mighty power that raised Christ from the dead and seated him in the place of honor at God's right hand in the heavenly realms."* Would you like to ride on a horse with *dunamis* power? What would you and your horse do?

9. Do you think you are a warrior? Do you like to pretend you are a warrior? Draw how you see yourself as a warrior. What weapons would you use?

---

[1] 2 Corinthians 11:14b: "Even Satan disguises himself as an angel of light."

[2] Job 41:12: "I want to emphasize Leviathan's limbs and its enormous strength and graceful form."

[3] Job 41:18: "When it sneezes, it flashes light! Its eyes are like the red of dawn."

[4] Job 41:14: "Who could pry open its jaws? For its teeth are terrible!"

[5] Job 41:19–21: "Lightning leaps from its mouth; flames of fire flash out. Smoke streams from its nostrils like steam from a pot heated over burning rushes. Its breath would kindle coals, for flames shoot from its mouth."

[6] Job 41:30: "Its belly is covered with scales as sharp as glass."

[7] Job 41:13: "Who can strip off its hide, and who can penetrate its double layer of armor?"

[8] Job 37:22: "Out of the north comes golden *splendor* [and people can hardly look on it]; Around God is awesome splendor *and* majesty [far too glorious for man's eyes]" (AMP).

[9] Jeremiah 29:13–14: "'If you look for me wholeheartedly, you will find me. I will be found by you,' says the Lord."

[10] Isaiah 30:18: "Yet the Lord longs to be gracious to you; therefore he will rise up to show you compassion. For the Lord is a God of justice. Blessed are all who wait for him!" (NIV).

[11] James 4:8: "Come close to God, and God will come close to you."

[12] Genesis 1:1: "In the beginning God (Elohim) created [by forming from nothing] the heavens and the earth" (AMP).

[13] Psalm 139:2: "You know my sitting down and my rising up; you understand my thought afar off" (NKJV).

[14] Psalm 139:4: "Before a word is on my tongue you, Lord, know it completely" (NIV).

[15] Romans 12:9b: "Hate what is evil; cling to what is good" (NIV).

[16] Matthew 28:18–20: "Jesus came and told his disciples, 'I have been given all authority in heaven and on earth. Therefore, go and make disciples of all the nations, baptizing them in the name of the Father and the Son and the Holy Spirit. Teach these new disciples to obey all the

commands I have given you. And be sure of this: I am with you always, even to the end of the age.'"

[17] 1 Samuel 16:7: "But the Lord said to Samuel, 'Do not look at his appearance or at the height of his stature, because I have rejected him; for God does not *see* as man sees, since man looks at the outward appearance, but *the Lord looks at the heart*'" (NASB, emphasis added).

[18] 1 John 4:16: "We know how much God loves us, and we have put our trust in his love. God is love, and all who live in love live in God, and God lives in them."

[19] Exodus 33:13: "If it is true that you look favorably on me, let me know your ways so I may understand you more fully and continue to enjoy your favor. And remember that this nation is your very own people."

[20] Zechariah 4:10: "Do not despise these small beginnings, for the Lord rejoices to see the work begin, to see the plumb line in Zerubbabel's hand."

[21] Exodus 33:19: "The Lord replied, 'I will make all my goodness pass before you, and I will call out my name, Yahweh, before you. For I will show mercy to anyone I choose, and I will show compassion to anyone I choose.'"

[22] Romans 8:26–27: "And the Holy Spirit helps us in our weakness. For example, we don't know what God wants us to pray for. But the Holy Spirit prays for us with groanings that cannot be expressed in words. And the Father who knows all hearts knows what the Spirit is saying, for the Spirit pleads for us believers in harmony with God's own will."

[23] 1 Kings 19:12: "And after the earthquake there was a fire, but the Lord was not in the fire. And after the fire there was *the sound of a gentle whisper*" (emphasis added).

[24] 430. Elohim *Bible hub* (https://biblehub.com/hebrew/430.htm).

[25] 3069. Yhvh," *Bible Hub* (https://biblehub.com/hebrew/3069.htm).

[26] "1411. δύναμις (dunamis)," *Bible Hub* (https://biblehub.com/greek/strongs_1411.htm).

Chapter Twelve
The Third Day

Samuel enjoyed the feel of the wind hitting his face as he rode on the back of his new friend. Dunamis's speed was incredible. Samuel looked down at the ground so far away from him. He could see the formations of valleys and canyons. The young warrior sighted a river and wondered if it was the same one his Father had formed to take him out of Beelzebub's path.

Samuel looked back and laughed as he saw Ruach flying through the air, his magnificent dragonfly wings catching the sun's rays and bouncing the golden rays off into the sky. The amber light flowing through Ruach's wings was mixing with the beams of sunlight. As Samuel looked down into the dry desert valley, he noticed that instead of a gray shadow, his Forever Friend was displaying an image on the ground of golden sunlight. Ruach had a permanent smile on his face. His colourful new silky wool was blowing in the wind. There was something so pure and yet powerful[1] about Samuel's Forever Friend. The warrior was grateful to be moving forward with his constant companion Ruach and his powerful new friend Dunamis.

Samuel looked up into the sky. "Thank you, Father! You believed in me when I could only see failure. You have strengthened me! I know I have much still to learn." The young warrior thought about Beelzebub. "I have an enemy who wants to destroy me and our people. Father, teach me how to conquer the evil one!"

THE THIRD DAY

Samuel was immersed in thoughts about his Father when he realized the temperature around him had changed. The air was becoming increasingly hotter. Then, far off in the distance, he saw an intense wall of fire.

"What is that, Dunamis?" Samuel asked.

Flames of red, orange, and yellow were exploding outwards, towards the group. They were awestruck by the spectacle of a scorching blaze erupting before their eyes. Boiling spots kept spewing outward, and the combustion would ignite a ripple effect of gigantic waves of flames. Sparks and embers were being thrown into the air in all directions.

Dunamis and Ruach both hovered in the air as the trio surveyed the situation.

"I'm not sure about the fire. I do know the people of Zion are on the opposite side of those flames," declared Dunamis.

"Are they burning?" Samuel asked.

"We will have to take a closer look. We'll have to go through the fire. It's too immense to go around." The fire wall had no ending, rising to the heavens and extending east to west as far as the eye could see. "Tell me when the temperature is too intense for you."

Samuel gazed ahead at the burning wall of fire. He knew he had a choice to make. Without hesitation, the newly commissioned warrior burst out, "Rend the air!"

Upon the declaration of those words, Dunamis rose up on his strong back legs and whinnied loudly. Gold dust was released from the royal horse as he moved gallantly, his front legs waving into the air.

"I will withstand it!" Samuel said with determination in his heart. He wondered how thick the fire wall would be. Would it go on into infinity?

FOREVER FRIEND

Samuel looked over at Ruach. "Can you endure the flames with us, Ruach?" The ram shook his mighty head up and down in agreement and then lowered his head, readying his gold and silver horns for entrance into the inferno.

"Let's do this!" Samuel hollered. "Rend the air!" he yelled again violently, waving his new sword fearlessly. The trio burst into the wall of flames together. There was no smoke inside the wall of fire. The intense heat hit Samuel. He felt like he was melting into a puddle. *Will I become nothing more than a vapour?* Samuel wondered.

"Father, I call to you for strength! Your arm is endowed with power, your hand is strong![2] Reach down with your powerful arm and strengthen me." Samuel proclaimed the words loudly, knowing the Father would not forsake him. "Train my hands for battle!"[3]

No sooner had Samuel said these words than he realized his clothing was being transformed. He now had a silver suit which encased his body. As Samuel examined his new clothing, he moved the arm holding his shield. A fluorescent light burst forth. Samuel moved his shield in another direction, and lightning seemed to explode from it. Samuel realized the different stones were emitting different lights in the fire. The inferno that had created the armour encasing Samuel had also supercharged the gems on his shield.

Samuel moved his shield around, learning all the qualities of the different stones. Then he remembered the ram's horn. He wondered how that would sound in the fire. Samuel placed the horn to his mouth and blew. Immediately the fire parted, and Dunamis flew skillfully through the opening with Ruach right behind them. The threesome burst forth into a clear blue sky. Samuel turned back around, and there behind him was the immense fire wall.

THE THIRD DAY

"Dunamis, we're through!" yelled Samuel. "I don't think the fire was from Beelzebub. There was no smoke."

Dunamis slowly flew to the ground and landed by a stream with trees, grass, and wildflowers. Ruach descended with them, and quickly went to the stream for a drink. Samuel dismounted his royal friend.

"What was the fire all about, Dunamis? Do you know?" Samuel touched and examined his skin, which now appeared to be wrapped in silver armour. The suit was a texture Samuel had never seen before. It was as if the armour was his own skin, moving with ease and flexibility. The fabric was light, as if he was wearing loose clothing. Yet he could tell that it was strong and refined.

"I believe the fire was from your Father." Dunamis said. "Look at yourself, Samuel. You have changed in appearance again. Your Father always strengthens and purifies us in the fire.[4] I too feel changed and strengthened. Mine may not be an outward change as yours is, but I know I have been imparted with greater gifts."[5]

Ruach came over to Samuel. The ram had entered the stream and was dripping wet. With his mouth, Ruach pulled on the cape hanging from Samuel's back. The ram pulled several times, jerking the warrior.

"What are you doing, Ruach?" Samuel asked. "Ahhhhh, where did this come from?!" he asked in wonder as he looked behind himself at the golden cape he was now wearing. Samuel touched the iridescent garment. "This is magnificent!" He looked down at Ruach and smiled.

The ram bent his head and began to shake the water off. As he shook, small beads bounced onto the ground. Some of the beads flew onto Samuel and bounced off his armour.

"Hey. You're hitting us with pellets." Samuel said as he laughed and moved back from the ram.

FOREVER FRIEND

Ruach stopped shaking, now fully dried and refreshed. Samuel looked at the little sparkling pellets on the ground. "Look, Dunamis—the water droplets resemble diamonds!"

The regal horse pranced over to Samuel and examined the pellets, which were shimmering on the lush green grass. "Ruach has been transformed into a diamond fighting machine!" Dunamis responded. They all laughed as they began to relax in the marvellous surroundings.

Samuel bent down and took a drink from the sparkling-clear water with cupped hands. It reminded him of the river in his Father's garden, though there were no crystals sparkling and bouncing off the top of the water. Samuel looked around at the beautiful lushness of the area.

"Where are we, Dunamis?" The area was tranquil and lush, but not as magnificent as the Father's garden.

"We are close to the mountain of Zion, the perfection of beauty.[6] The land becomes more and more splendid as we get closer. That is, if we get there before Beelzebub."

"Do you think we will find Shear-Jashub, Gimel, and Shamar before we get to Zion?" Samuel questioned.

"If the Father, *Yahweh Shammah,* is with us. We need His presence." The stately horse whinnied. "We need to be carriers of His presence." Dunamis pranced over to the water's edge and took a drink. The golden sparkles bouncing off the horse created a shining dust cloud around him.

The horse lifted up its majestic head. "Once we are all together, in unity, the Father will give us His battle plan."

Samuel thought about what Dunamis had just said. He wondered how they would be carriers of the presence of his Father. Samuel thought back to his encounter with the Father. He instantly became entranced by the memory. As he recalled the splendour of his Father, he felt his heart begin to enlarge.

Suddenly a wonderful burning warmth erupted inside his chest. Then an unearthly heaviness fell upon Samuel. His entire body began to tingle. Samuel looked up at Dunamis with questioning eyes.

"Your Father's presence is upon you now." Dunamis shook his mane wildly as currents of gold dust swirled around his head. "As you move, always focus upon the weighty heaviness and glory you carry. Never take it for granted."

Samuel nodded his head in agreement. As he stood absorbing all that was transpiring, Ruach came and nestled up against his legs. The warrior looked down at his Forever Friend and smiled.

"How much further till we reach Zion?" Samuel asked, trying to focus on his mission.

"I think we should be there in a day's travel. Can you ride for that long?" Dunamis inquired.

"I can ride—it's falling off that gets me into trouble." Samuel laughed and gently touched Ruach, who was still by his side. "You make a great pillow to land on. What would I do without you?"

Samuel's love for his friend was intense. They had journeyed far together in a short amount of time. The pair had also grown up together. Ruach was no longer a young ram, and Samuel was quickly becoming a man. However, he knew he still had the curiosity of a child and a child's heart.[7] These would be good qualities to keep forever. Then Samuel thought about his venture into the cave. He had allowed curiosity to rule over wisdom and Ruach's insistence to leave the cave.

Samuel looked out into the distance. He knew he needed to follow the direction of his Forever Friend more closely. He looked down at the ram still rubbing up against his legs. "Thank you for always guiding me, Ruach. I will be more attentive to your leading in the future."

"You need not look backwards, Samuel, but only to your future. Your fall off Shamar brought you closer to discovering who you are inside. Your entrance into the cave taught you to stay focused on Ruach's leading. You also discovered your enemy and his hatred for all who walk the face of the earth." The horse gave a loud whinny.

"The Father will never waste a hurt. Once we allow the Father into our hearts, He uses our failures and our pain for His glory," Dunamis explained. "The Father will always use our failures for His benefit—but only when we allow the Father's work to begin in us first."

Samuel nodded his head in agreement and then asked the others. "Should we start the next part of our journey?" Dunamis knelt down, and Samuel, with his ram's horn tucked securely under his arm, shield in hand and sword in place, quickly mounted the mighty horse.

Ruach smile at Samuel as he unfurled his beautiful dragonfly wings. The ram's blue eyes were shining brightly.

Samuel grinned at his Forever Friend. "Onward, towards Zion!" Samuel exclaimed. The three flew together towards their destiny, Mount Zion, as Samuel loudly continued to praise his Father.

The Father smiled down on His son Samuel as He flew above them, riding the clouds.[8]

* * *

Deep inside the earth, an eruption of hatred was spewing. Beelzebub was pacing back and forth within a large damp chamber. Steam was being released from the creature's nose and ears as he fumed over the situation. The horde of flies swarmed about Beelzebub's head, creating an eerie buzzing sound.

"Samuel is stronger than I anticipated! The little creep hasn't given up, and he is gaining more knowledge of the Father." The beast continued to pace, his massive tail bashing into the cavern walls.

"The brat is becoming equipped for war. War! I will give Samuel and his annoying friends a war." The creature abruptly stopped and thought a moment. "I will reach the people of Zion before he does," he snarled. "Yes, that's what I will do. While Samuel's know-it-all Father wastes time showing the child how special He is, I will destroy the Father's favourite city. Zion will become my hideout! Ha ha!" The evil laughter echoed through all the cavern chambers. "Yes! How exciting this will be. While Samuel and his Father are bonding, I will overtake Zion. Yes, yes, yes! This is perfect. Since I can't depend on you useless Spittles to steal the fruit from two measly children, I will destroy the people they are taking the fruit to! Muwhahaha! There will be no people left alive to receive the precious, life-giving fruit from the Father! Ha ha ha—I'm so brilliantly wonderful!"

As the evil laughter arose, more smelly gases were released into the cavern. "Yes, I will capture the people before the fruit arrives to strengthen them!" The beast rubbed his spindly fingers together as he thought.

"Zion will be my property! I will suck the goodness out of the people. They will be caught off guard as I slither my way in with my brilliant charm. Oh, who can resist my alluring trinkets of power, wealth, and success? What mortal can defend themselves against my twisted, deceitful lies? Yes! This will be so diabolical. Not only will I have stopped the fruit from coming to the people and empowering them, I will own more territory!" The monster laughed, releasing even more noxious gas into the cavern. The hideous beast smacked his lips and started to drool at the thought of destroying the people of Zion. "Ha ha ha—mortals always love to take my wealth and power. Oh, how I savour bringing them into my den of iniquity! Once they have succumbed to my ways, I will suck the life out of them! Mwahahaha!

"Deceiving the people gives me such pleasure."[9] Beelzebub grabbed a Spittle and began squeezing the vapour as he brought it near his face and stroked it with his long, sharp fingernail. "The people are always so naïve when they haven't been feeding on the Father's fruits." The creature was speaking in an unnerving high-pitched voice, as if he was talking to a small child. "Deception is so much fun. It is one of my favorite gifts to dangle in front of the unsuspecting mortals. It's like giving poison candy to a baby! Eh, eh, eh!" His childish voice changed and was now deep and methodical. "I will make them think evil is good.[10] Oh yes, and I will entice them with the candy of sin." The beast began to froth green slime from one corner of his grimacing scowl. "Oh yes, wonderful sin! Deliciously tasty, tantalizing, tempting sin." The frothy green slime dangled from Beelzebub's mouth. The creature turned his large head and looked down the dark hall of the cavern. The little Spittles all remained perfectly still as the ghastly creature remained deep in thought.

"Hmmm, not just sin—I will send my principalities[11] to oppress the people," Beelzebub said slowly. "Yes! Since I cannot get near Samuel or the treasured fruit guarded by Shear-Jashub and their Forever Friends, my principalities will attack the people of Zion. Then I will be able to devour all those that the pesky brats care about, and the brats too! First Zion, then the children.

Oh how I enjoy having a full meal! Bwahahaha! I will consume all those that the Father 'loves.' Argh, I hate that word!" Beelzebub released the Spittle and spat on the cavern floor, disgusted by the taste of the word "love" in his mouth. The green slime from his mouth dropped on the damp floor and sizzled.

THE THIRD DAY

Then the beast took a deep breath in and belched loudly. A toxic green gas cloud was formed. Out of the gases, evil faces emerged and began to scream as they were released into the atmosphere. The unusual spooky figures moved violently about and then disappeared through the damp walls of the cavern. They were going into the deep underworld to awaken the cruel principalities. Beelzebub delighted in the grotesque wickedness he had belched up. His pride was visible upon his hideous face. "Mwahahaha!" The beast released his menacing laughter and then a high pitched, ear-piercing scream, the official seal of his desire to release the villainous principalities from deep within his evil world.

The Spittles moved away from their master. The unnerving noise made the evil vapours shake. A booming slow thud could be heard repeatedly from deep within the center core of the earth. The loud boom was slowly making its way towards the cavern which housed the vapour puffs. The unleashed principalities moved slowly out from the depths of the earth.

The principalities from the deep emerged with a loud ghastly cry, stalking their way towards Beelzebub. An eerie silence hung in the cavern as the creatures glared at Beelzebub. The evil Spittles remained planted next to the cold, slimy cavern walls.

Beelzebub grinned, and glared back at the principalities. The despicable master was proud of all the dark evil around him. He loved to be in the atmosphere of doom and terror. Slowly the beast sneered and then laughed. "Zion shall be mine! Do not disappoint me!" Beelzebub hissed at the vile creatures. "Take as many of the little Spittle demons as you need. Hmmm... Discouragement, Discouragement!" the beast roared. "Discouragement, get over here!" The vapour quickly moved towards Beelzebub, keeping himself an arm's distance from his master. "Go with them and this time do your job properly! I want to claim this territory as mine. Mine! Do you understand me?" Beelzebub placed his spindly hand in front of one of the principalities. "Let me know when I can arrive to enjoy my meal. Now get out of my sight." Haunting laughter exploded out of Beelzebub and echoed throughout the underworld.

Questions to Contemplate

1. Why do you think this chapter is called "The Third Day"? What other important third days can you find in the Bible?

2. Why does Samuel need to use caution with his curiosity?

3. Why do you think God uses fire to purify us? Do you know of other people in the Bible who survived going through fire? What do you think the fire might represent?

4. *Yahweh Shammah*, "The Lord Is There," is described in Ezekiel 48:35: *"The distance around the entire city will be 6 miles. And from that day the name of the city will be 'The Lord Is There.'"* Do you feel like God is there with you? Psalm 46:1 says, *"God is our refuge and strength, a very present help in trouble"* (ESV).

5. What do you think Zion represents in the story?

6. What do you think is inside the fruit that makes it so powerful?

THE THIRD DAY

[1] Acts 1:8: "But you will receive power when the Holy Spirit comes upon you."

[2] Psalm 89:13: "Your arm is endowed with power; your hand is strong, your right hand exalted" (NIV).

[3] Psalm 18:34: "He trains my hands for war, so that my arms can bend a bow of bronze" (ESV).

[4] Zechariah 13:9: "I will bring that group through the fire and make them pure. I will refine them like silver and purify them like gold. They will call on my name, and I will answer them. I will say, 'These are my people,' and they will say, 'The Lord is our God.'"

[5] 1 Peter 4:10: "God has given each of you a gift from his great variety of spiritual gifts. Use them well to serve one another."

[6] Psalm 50:2: "From Mount Zion, the perfection of beauty, God shines in glorious radiance."

[7] Luke 18:16b–17: "For the Kingdom of God belongs to those who are like these children. I tell you the truth, anyone who doesn't receive the Kingdom of God like a child will never enter it."

[8] Psalm 68:4: "Sing praises to God and to his name! Sing loud praises to him who rides the clouds. His name is the Lord—rejoice in his presence!"

[9] Revelation 12:9: "…the great dragon was thrown down, that ancient serpent, who is called *the devil and Satan, the deceiver of the whole world*—he was thrown down to the earth, and his angels were thrown down with him" (ESV, emphasis added).

[10] Isaiah 5:20: "What sorrow for those who say that evil is good and good is evil, that dark is light and light is dark, that bitter is sweet and sweet is bitter."

[11] Ephesians 6:12: "For we wrestle not against flesh and blood but against principalities, against powers, against the rulers of the darkness of this world, against spiritual wickedness in high places" (KJV).

Chapter Thirteen

Deceit

It wasn't long into their journey before the trio became aware of disaster ahead. It started when Samuel pointed to a burnt tree he noticed. As they travelled towards Zion, more and more of the lush landscape had been scorched. They all knew the devastation they were encountering would likely mean havoc for Zion.

Near the end of the day, their speculations were confirmed. Where the city of Mount Zion should have been was a dense, black mound of darkness.[1] The darkness had settled over all of Zion as a thick blanket of evil.

Dunamis and Ruach, descended to the ground some distance from the darkness. All three were silent as they stared at what should have been a large city of splendour and glory. For a time, no one spoke. They just peered out over the complete desolation.

Little yellow and red eyes peeked out from under the blanket of darkness. Sixty-six of the evil Spittles had noticed Samuel in the distance. With their little tails uncurled, they now propelled themselves towards the young warrior. The Spittles wasted no time in whispering lies into Samuel's head. "You have lost. Go home. Your Father has let you down. He has failed you. He doesn't care about you. This was a set-up to make you look foolish." The Spittles bombarded the atmosphere with their unending lies.

DECEIT

Samuel couldn't contain his disappointment any longer. "Dunamis, why would my Father send us into battle if the battle has already been lost? Why didn't the Father help us to arrive before Beelzebub? I can't believe this has happened."

A loud whinny was heard. Dunamis shook his royal head and mane, releasing golden sparkles into the air. The horse pounded his front hooves on the ground. "Samuel, we are *not* too late. Your Father is never late with anything. His timing is just different from ours. He will bring justice to Beelzebub." Dunamis shook his mane and gold dust drifted everywhere. "Look into the darkness. What do you see, Samuel?"

"I see a lost battle! We didn't even get to fight. What good is this splendid armour if I can't use it? It's just decoration!" Samuel swiped at his cape in disgust.

"Look again, Samuel. What do you see? What do you hear? Father, give him eyes to see and ears to hear; may he look beyond what is in the natural world, and focus on the unseen realm.[2] May understanding and wisdom come to him, Father."[3]

Dunamis rose up on his powerful hindquarters. Samuel clung tightly to the silken mane and gripped the horse's stomach firmly with his legs. The pair landed with a loud thud as gold dust billowed up around them. "Look again, my friend. Look again!" Dunamis was attempting to shake off the discouragement he knew his rider was experiencing.

The evil Spittles backed away from Samuel and hovered in the distance, waiting for their next opportunity to strike. They knew Dunamis was aware of their presence. Discouragement grinned at the mighty horse, his beady yellow eyes watching and waiting for another chance to sabotage Samuel's destiny. The vapour of evil was not about to give up.

Samuel looked down at Dunamis. What did this incredible horse see that Samuel could not? What did Dunamis know that Samuel had yet to figure out? "Father, I need insight and understanding!"[4]

More Spittles arrived from the darkness. When they felt it was safe, they slowly approached Samuel and continued their unending lies. Doubt hovered over the warrior, pressing down on his thoughts. Frustration came up close to Samuel and breathed his foul breath of destruction into Samuel's nose. The Spittles looked at each other. Their squinchy red eyes or beady yellow eyes were peering at Samuel, waiting for his response.

Samuel let out a deep groan of frustration. The vapours grinned at one another, proud of their success. Whenever the young warrior was beginning to feel like he understood some of this new world, he came up against another challenge. *Oh Father,* Samuel said in his head, in his heart, *I want to be able to grasp onto the reality of Your world. I want to be able to know You and Your ways. I want to understand Your Kingdom. My heart is teachable, but my mind can't comprehend.* Samuel continued looking out at the suffocating blanket that had encased the once magnificent city of Zion. He tried to reason out what had taken place.

Samuel looked down again at his extraordinary new friend. Dunamis began to prance, lifting his powerful legs upwards, only to pound his hooves upon the ground beneath them. The mighty horse shook his massive neck wildly, releasing sparkles of gold from his flowing mane.

As Samuel's legs gripped the horse tightly, he reflected on his short but incredible journey. Since he had chosen to enter into the Father's Tabernacle, the presence of his Father seemed to be with him. Even when he didn't see his Father, Samuel knew he was now working in union with Him. "Father," Samuel said quietly as he sat upon the mighty beast Dunamis, "I do believe in you. I do trust you." The confusion and lack of understanding in Samuel's mind were replaced with a sense of peace, calm, and reassurance.

DECEIT

The Spittles looked at one another. They were losing their hold on Samuel's thinking. Slowly they backed away and regretfully returned to the darkness over Zion.

* * *

Beelzebub sniffed the air. He had been enjoying his meal. The principalities had quickly claimed hold of Zion. The people had eagerly bitten into the bait of greed, power, sin, and instant wealth, allowing the principalities to gain complete control over the region.

Beelzebub sniffed the air again and slammed his fist upon the table. He turned abruptly and flew out of his den of iniquity. With a blast of scorching flame, he erupted into the edge of the blackness which held the people of Zion captive.

"What are you doing back?" His beady red eyes were almost popping out of his head in rage. "I told you to discourage the brat! He is still out there." The creature grabbed a Spittle by its neck and shook the vapour violently. "Must I do everything? I can't be in two places at one time! Grrrrrr," the beast growled. "Ohhh, how I wish I was able to move like the Father![5] *Aaaaagh!* I am limited! I can only be at one place at a time. Grrrrr, so frustrating! That is why I have you idiots!" Beelzebub said through clenched teeth. "You Spittles are to be my hands and feet. Except you're incompetent!" The vapour wobbled back and forth in the clutches of the beast as it was being violently shaken. "How can I suck the life out of these people and defeat the boy, as pathetic as he is, at the same time?"

Beelzebub stopped and cocked his head slightly. His red eyes darted back and forth through the darkness. The beast hissed. "Something is happening—I can feel it! I am losing my hold. Everyone to your positions! I will not lose this battle!" the beast fumed.

* * *

FOREVER FRIEND

Samuel now realized the Father had always been with him and was for him.[6] Although the journey had been confusing at times, he was growing in his understanding of the Father and the Father's Kingdom. He was developing trust and a dependency upon his Father. He was no longer relying on his own understanding and strength, no longer relying on his own reasoning, but on that which the Father was pouring into him.[7]

The warrior looked out onto the horizon. He strained his eyes to see—to see anything. All he saw was darkness over Zion. Evil had fallen on the great city.

As Samuel was studying the darkness, he turned his head slightly. *What is that sound?* he thought. The sound of a trumpet could be heard far in the distance. Then a beautiful melody, as if there was singing in the wind. Carried on the wind, Samuel heard a still small voice. The voice of his Father was calling to him.[8] "My child, listen to Me and treasure My instructions. Tune your ears to wisdom and concentrate on understanding. Continually cry out for these gifts. Understanding will keep you safe. Wisdom will save you from evil." [9]

Samuel smiled, absorbing what he had just heard. He felt strengthened by the words. "Did you hear what the Father said, Dunamis?" Samuel beamed, knowing he was able to hear from the unseen realm.

"What did the Father tell you, Samuel?"

Samuel was about to share what he had just heard, when a flash of light near the darkened city caught his eye. He strained his eyes and moved himself higher on Dunamis's back, hoping to see further into the horizon.

"What is it, Samuel—what do you see?" Dunamis questioned, knowing the young warrior's senses were becoming heightened.

"I don't know. There was a flash of light beside the darkness. Look, there—do you see it? The light is coming this way! Can you see it? It's small,

DECEIT

but it came from the darkness! Should we be ready to fight?" Samuel placed his hand upon his sword.

"Samuel, the light is with us. Light is always with us.[10] Wait for the light to arrive." Dunamis looked out over the darkness. "You felt you were too late to do battle, but the battle has yet to begin. Beelzebub would love for you to believe the fight has been lost without a war." The royal hose whinnied loudly. "He is such a coward! Deception—he has hidden behind deception again. Hoping you will retreat, believing his lie. Always remember—he comes to kill, steal, and destroy.[11] Deceit and lies, that's what he carries for weapons. Don't believe his lies or his deception. Once the light is here, it will reveal the truth to us. The truth will set us free— free to do the work we were destined to accomplish."[12]

Samuel sat on Dunamis, watching ever so intently as the light came closer to the three of them. The closer the light came to them, the dimmer it became. The ready warrior looked down at his Forever Friend. Ruach seemed to have a smile on his face. His blue eyes looked lovingly out at the fading light. Samuel furrowed his eyebrows as he wondered what was coming towards them. Whatever it was, Ruach seemed excited about it.

Soon Samuel could see a form within the light. It slowly became more visible as the intensity of the light disappeared. Samuel realized a person was coming towards them. As he rubbed his eyes, he realized the person was a young girl. She was running steadily towards them. Her long, black hair was flowing behind her as she ran. Samuel could see the terror in her face as she drew near. When she was a short distance away, she fell to the ground, whimpering loudly.

Dunamis slowly went towards the girl. He bent down and placed his head by hers. Dunamis gently breathed onto the girl and whinnied. She looked up at the magnificent face of the horse and began to pat the soft, golden nose. Then she lowered her face and continued her soft sobs.

Samuel looked down at her and saw the tears that had flowed from her eyes as she patted the nose of Dunamis. He jumped off the muscular stallion and cautiously moved towards the girl, who continued to make a soft whimpering sound. As Samuel listened to the soft sound of her cry, he realized he had heard that sound before.

Samuel knelt by the girl and spoke softly. "Please, tell us what's happening. We are here to fight for the people of Zion. Have they all perished?" As Samuel looked down upon the girl and listened to her cries, he recalled his dream. The sound was the same whimpering he had heard in his dream.

The girl looked up at Samuel and stared into the warrior's eyes. She was obviously still in shock. Samuel stood up and put his hand out towards her.

Dunamis whinnied softly and said, "Talitha Koum." The royal horse touched the girl gently with his nose as golden sparkles descended upon her. He spoke again. "Little girl, little one, get up!" Then the mighty horse breathed onto her again. Her long dark hair moved slightly with Dunamis's breath.

The girl reached for Samuel's arm, and he gently pulled her up onto her two still shaking legs. The girl looked towards the darkness. "Our people are in great danger. My Father said He would send us mighty warriors to defend us. We waited, but no one came."

The girl brushed her long-tangled hair away from her eyes. "Beelzebub's evil principalities came over us quickly. They wasted no time in releasing their subtle lies and tricks. At first, the people thought the principalities were charming as they dangled their vile trinkets in front of the people. They were crafty and sly. They were disguised. I recognized their tricks and warned the people, but they wouldn't listen. Beelzebub had this well-planned. He'd been watching us." The girl looked about her. "He

DECEIT

is always watching us, and invariably ready to pounce in and attack. Once the principalities were in control, they released the little Spittle demons to entice the people of Zion with overnight access to riches, wealth, and fame. The people thought they had gained power, but it was false power."

The child wiped the tears from her tiny cheek before she continued speaking. "When the people realized what had happened, it was too late. Beelzebub's presence had been allowed into Zion through agreement. Once the people accepted and tolerated evil, they had literally opened a gate that led them down a wide path of destruction.[13] The creatures had already poisoned most of our people.

The child placed her hand to her forehead and let out a small whimper. The girl looked up at Samuel. "The people then began fighting against one another for Beelzebub's treasures. The community abruptly became corrupt. They started to believe evil was good.[14] Soon Beelzebub and his Spittles were choking everyone with hatred and chaos. Beelzebub's creatures had suddenly taken over Zion. The principalities had gained a stronghold over this land."

The young girl shook her head in disgust. "Zion has fallen. It has become a hideout for evil creatures..." she paused and shut her eyes for a moment, "...a den for dreadful beasts. The people lost sight of what was promised to them from the Father." The child released a loud sob. "There was no fruit!" She sobbed again. "No leaves, nothing for the people to nourish themselves on." The young girl shook her head; her long black hair flowed back and forth with the movement. She let out a loud sigh and gazed out towards the darkness. She whimpered softly. "Overnight, a city of splendour and glory, loyal to the Father..." She paused as she looked up at Samuel. "...came crashing down!"

The young girl's eyes filled with tears as she looked down at her soiled clothes and bare feet. Again she whimpered, this time loudly. She couldn't contain her sorrow for the people she loved. She turned and looked back at her beloved city. Her tears continued to flow slowly over her soot-covered cheeks, leaving a clear streak upon her delicate face. Samuel could feel her pain in his heart.

***!

Fire erupted under the darkness which clamped down on Zion. Beelzebub was having a tantrum. He took anything he could grab hold of and violently threw it in the air. "She has escaped! The child is partnering with the boy. They are building up an allegiance to the Father." The creature thought for a moment. Steam was rising from his ears.

"Division, come to me." There was a long, unnerving pause from the explosive creature. Beelzebub's voice changed pitch. "Yes, you—my powerful weapon of war." The vapour cautiously moved towards the beast. "This is your moment," the beast stated smoothly. "You can change the course of history." The beast's short, spindly hands waved through the air; his claws outstretched as he calmly nodded his head at Division. Beelzebub grinned and slowly continued, giving thought to his unfamiliar words of encouragement. "All you need to do is separate the little children from becoming friends. That's not too hard, is it? You have accomplished this feat thousands of times."

The vapour slowly nodded his head in agreement. Witnessing Beelzebub in a state of calm and composure was unnerving to the demon. The Spittle remained just outside his reach.

Beelzebub continued to think as the steam hissed out of his ears and now his nose. He slowly lifted his scrawny hand and lunged forward, capturing the small Spittle. Venomous laughter erupted. Beelzebub drew the vapour close to his gigantic mouth, exposing his rows of yellow and brown teeth.

Beelzebub continued his evil laugh, then looked the Spittle in the eye. "Do not fail me on this mission," the beast demanded in his usual deep, threatening, growling voice. "Separate those children! Bring Irritation, Confusion, and...." The beast thought a moment as more noxious gases and steam arose from his body. A sly grin formed on Beelzebub's face. "Hopelessness. Yes, call upon Hopelessness." He released Division and then quickly snatched him by the tail. The little vapour spun around quickly. "Do not return defeated! Do you understand?" Beelzebub spoke slowly as he made his demand.

The beast opened his mouth widely and licked the green saliva which was dripping from his lips. "Bring all the vapours you need. Just don't come back here without a victory." The ruling creature threw the vapour through the air towards the edge of the suffocating blanket of evil. Now outside the grip of Beelzebub, Division nodded his head slowly, acknowledging his assignment—and his destiny, should he return without a win.

* * *

The young girl took a deep breath of the fresh air. She was grateful she had escaped the clutches of Beelzebub. The girl glanced towards the dark blanket of evil and sighed. She looked up at the majestic horse and gently stroked its soft golden nose. She studied the unusual white feather wings, which seem to be illuminated like crystal with sun moving through cut glass. Then the young girl continued to explain her predicament to Samuel. "I had stayed, hidden in paga. I wanted to believe my Father's words, that He would send us great and mighty warriors. As the end came and I pagaed, a door opened slightly in the darkness. There was only light beyond the door. I knew the light was from my Father. I squeezed my way through the narrow opening and arose, outside of the darkness. I was miraculously outside the city of Zion. I was now away from Beelzebub's presence. I could make out your shapes as forms moving. I ran towards you, believing you to be the warriors sent by my Father." She turned, staring at the darkness for a moment, and then looked into the eyes of Samuel. "The people are all alive, but they are suffering great persecution. Beelzebub is tormenting everyone. He is slowly, mercilessly sucking the life out of them."

Samuel was trying to digest all the girl had told him when he was distracted by a piercing cry in the air. The warrior instantly drew his sword from his side and turned towards the sound, stretching his opposite arm out in front of the young girl to protect her. Glaring towards the setting sun, Samuel squinted, straining his eyes to decipher what was soaring through the air above them.

Questions to Contemplate

1. Have you ever questioned or wondered about God's timing?

2. Dunamis speaks about a natural world and the unseen realm. What do you think might be the difference between the two worlds? Where in the Bible does it talk about the unseen realm? Have you ever seen into this world? Can you explain or draw a picture of what you saw?

3. The author writes, "Even when he didn't see his Father, Samuel knew he was now working in union with his Father." Have you ever experienced this? Can you describe what you felt?

4. The Father told Samuel, "Tune your ears to wisdom and concentrate on understanding. Continually cry out for these gifts. Understanding will keep you safe. Wisdom will save you." How can understanding keep you safe and wisdom save you? Have you ever experienced these gifts helping you?

5. Beelzebub says "Must I do everything? I can't be in two places at one time!" Did you know that God is omnipresent? God is not limited by space or time. God is present, everywhere, all at the same time. Read Psalm 139:7–12. Verse 7 says, *"I can never escape*

DECEIT

from your Spirit! I can never get away from your presence!" Does knowing God is always with you make you feel more secure? He is Yahweh Shammah.

6. This chapter is called "Deceit." What deceit was happening in this chapter?

---

[1] Isaiah 60:2: "*See, darkness covers the earth and thick darkness is over the peoples*, but the Lord rises upon you and his glory appears over you" (NIV, emphasis added).

[2] 2 Kings 6:17: "Then Elisha prayed, 'O Lord, open his eyes and let him see!' The Lord opened the young man's eyes, and when he looked up, he saw that the hillside around Elisha was filled with horses and chariots of fire"; Matthew 11:15: "Anyone with ears to hear should listen and understand!" (NLT).

[3] Proverbs 2:6: "For the Lord grants wisdom! From his mouth come knowledge and understanding."

[4] Proverbs 2:3–4: "Cry out for insight, and ask for understanding. Search for them as you would for silver; seek them like hidden treasures."

[5] Matthew 28:20b: "And be sure of this: I am with you always, even to the end of the age."

[6] Isaiah 8:10b: "For God is with us!"

[7] Proverbs 3:5: "Trust in the Lord with all your heart; do not depend on your own understanding."

[8] 1 Kings 19:12b: "And after the fire came a still, small voice" (BSB).

[9] Proverbs 2:1–3: "My child, listen to what I say, and treasure my commands. Tune your ears to wisdom, and concentrate on understanding. Cry out for insight, and ask for understanding"; Proverbs 2:11–12: "Wise choices will watch over you. Understanding will keep you safe. Wisdom will save you from evil people, from those whose words are twisted."

[10] John 8:12: "I am the light of the world. If you follow me, you won't have to walk in darkness, because you will have the light that leads to life."

[11] John 10:10: "The thief's purpose is to steal and kill and destroy. My purpose is to give them a rich and satisfying life."

[12] John 8:32: "And you will know the truth, and the truth will set you free."

[13] Matthew 7:13–14: "Enter by the narrow gate; for wide is the gate and broad is the way that leads to destruction, and there are many who go in by it. Because narrow is the gate and difficult is the way which leads to life, and there are few who find it" (NKJV).

[14] Isaiah 5:20: "What sorrow for those who say that evil is good and good is evil…"

Chapter Fourteen

The Choice

As Samuel glanced towards the setting sun, he was relieved to see the silhouettes of Gimel and Shamar. Samuel let out a loud cry of joy.

The winged friends landed a short distance away from Samuel. Shear-Jashub quickly jumped off the back of Shamar and ran towards Samuel. The two hugged one another tightly, lifting each other off the ground in jubilation as they laughed.

"Shear-Jashub, wow, look at you! You're all armoured up and ready for battle!" It was true. Shear-Jashub had transformed into a fighting warrior. His armour was heavier than Samuel's, and golden in colour. On his head he wore a magnificent helmet which held one large, exquisite turquoise feather.[1] Across the forehead of his helmet was written the word "salvation." His chest was encased in a gold breastplate, boldly engraved with the word "righteousness." He wore a sturdy gold belt declaring "truth" which wrapped firmly around his waist. Upon his feet were leather moccasins. Across the top of the moccasin was the word "peace," spelled out with tiny ruby red gems delicately sewn into the leather. He held onto a dented old shield, which had the word "faith" written in large letters.[2] The shield must have endured many battles, for there were numerous dents upon it. He also carried a long gleaming sword. Though the edge of the sword appeared razor sharp, the handle was notably well-worn.

Shear-Jashub's sack had also been changed. It was larger now, and seemed to be moving as if something inside it was alive. The golden fabric of the sack was now smooth and shiny, shimmering with sparkles so bright it was hard to look upon.

"What's in your sack?" Samuel asked his friend, as the sack bounced about on Shear-Jashub's hip.

"Wait till you see what the Father gave me! All the fruit I've been carrying from the garden has changed. Look!" Shear-Jashub reached into his sack and pulled out an amazing ball of fire. It was jiggling in Shear-Jashub's hand.

"Astounding! What is it?" Samuel inquired, stepping back a bit from the flames which were erupting on Shear-Jashub's bare hand.

"It's a fireball. Ezekiel told me about these when I was training with him at the Tabernacle. They are a rare, powerful gift from the Father."

"Why is it moving?"

"The fireball hates evil. If it detects any sin, corruption, or any trace of evil, it will attack and purify or completely destroy the evil. It constantly jiggles, waiting anxiously to move into action."

"How can you hold onto fire?" asked Samuel, completely enthralled with what Shear-Jashub was showing him. He moved a little closer to his friend as he studied the flaming object jiggling in the warrior's outstretched hand.

"It just tingles a bit; the fire doesn't hurt me. The Father prepared me for this as I went through an amazing, thick wall of fire." Shear-Jashub tucked the fireball delicately back into his sack, with the other fireballs which were visibly bouncing around inside.

"You have changed too my young friend. In fact, you are no longer young!" Shear-Jashub said as he placed his hands-on Samuel's shoulders, admiring the younger warrior. The warrior looked over Samuel's shoulder and noticed the winged horse. "Hey! Not only are you now armoured up for battle, you have been introduced to Dunamis!" The mighty horse cantered over to Shear-Jashub and whinnied in acknowledgement. "How's it going, my magnificent, powerful friend?" Shear-Jashub ran his hand across the side of the enormous horse as golden flecks swirled about. The warrior gazed upon Dunamis's wings. "I could stand here all day and just stare at your mesmerizing, glassy wings. You are not only powerful but beautiful as well," the warrior stated. "It has been awhile since we travelled together." The majestic horse whinnied and nodded his head in agreement. Shear-Jashub looked back at Samuel. "Tell me more about your journey."

"Dunamis, Ruach, and I went through a gigantic firewall too!" Samuel exclaimed excitedly. "As I rode through the fire on Dunamis, the flames actually danced around us! It was unbelievable! We weren't harmed! We were transformed by the scorching flames," Samuel proclaimed.

Shear-Jashub smiled at Samuel and nodded his head in agreement. His large turquoise feather moved majestically. "The Father purifies us in the fire.[3] We are either strengthened and made pure, or we remove ourselves from the pressure of the intense heat and return to what we were. I am grateful we have all endured the pressure and the flames." Shear-Jashub grinned as he studied his friend's new armour. "Samuel, we should never be surprised at any fiery trouble which we go through. It is a test. A test to try us and make us better. We should actually be rejoicing in the midst of the test!" He laughed. "Yes, my friend, we both have been tested and strengthened by the hands of our Father."[4]

Shear-Jashub reached into his belt of truth and pulled out his sword. The warrior admired the weapon for a moment. "As I was in the blazing inferno, a magnificent angel came to me and said, 'Take the sword of the Spirit, which is the word of the Father; it is a gift to you from *Jehovah-Makkeh*, the Father who molds us.'" Shear-Jashub gazed upon the sparkling sword as he moved it thought the air, catching the sun's rays. "Yes! The

THE CHOICE

Father was really molding me in that fire! Wowee!" The warrior let out a happy war cry and lovingly hit Samuel lightly on his back as he continued to study his new sword, which was raised into the air with his opposite hand. Obviously, Shear-Jashub was still enthralled with the experience and all he had been given. "The incredible angelic being was dancing in the flames as I was handed my treasure." Shear-Jashub relinquished his sword to Samuel, who waved it through the air.

Shear-Jashub looked over at the city of Zion, covered in the shroud of darkness. Samuel returned the sword to his friend, and standing shoulder to shoulder, the two looked upon the devastation.

"He can't take it without a fight!" declared Shear-Jashub. "It is not over yet. I am onto his tricks, his deceit. Beelzebub doesn't get it without a fight!" the experienced warrior repeated. The two warriors continued to look upon the destruction of Zion a while longer. Then Shear-Jashub shook his head, as his beautiful turquoise feather moved in rhythm with him. "Shamar, what are we to do next?" As Shear-Jashub turned to talk to the great lion he gasped, startled at seeing a young girl. "Who is this?" Shear-Jashub asked.

"She emerged out of the darkness covering Zion. Her Father told her he would send warriors to fight Beelzebub. I don't know her name. She arrived just before you." The young girl was standing, staring out towards the darkness over her fallen city.

"What is your name?" Shear-Jashub asked as he walked slowly over to the young girl, who was a distance away.

The girl turned and looked at Shear-Jashub. "Shear-Jashub, it is I!"

Shear-Jashub looked at the girl in disbelief. "Wow!" he yelled, running towards the child. Gently, he put his arms around the small girl and looked down upon her. Shaking his head in disbelief, he said, "Thank goodness you're alright."

The girl smiled and gently touched the fabric the warrior was wearing. She stepped back and grinned at him. After pausing for a moment she reached up and touched the soft turquoise feather moving above his head and giggled. "How many times have you bravely brought me the treasured fruit or leaves from the Father's garden? Always risking your life for the people of Zion." The girl sighed as she turned her head. Then her eyes widened, and she smiled excitedly as she glanced over and saw Shamar, who was positioned behind the warrior.

The child gracefully walked over to Samuel. "I need to introduce myself to you. I am Ruhamah. My Father called me this to remind the people of His great love for them. My name means 'the ones I love.'"[5] The girl then quickly walked over to Shamar, and knelt before the great beast. "I am so glad you are here with me, my friend! I have missed you!" The girl looked up at the face of the massive creature. She put her tiny arms up towards the lion's face, and the two embraced. "Though we were not together, I felt your presence, I heard your words, I followed your instruction." She sobbed for a moment and then regained her composure. "How is my Father? Did He give you a message for me?"

"What, your Father?" Samuel exclaimed. "Shamar lives with my Father in the Tabernacle. Wait a minute. Does your Father live there also?"

Shamar put his massive head on the girl's back. Two of his six wings wrapped around her as they continued to embrace. After a short while, Shamar looked over at Samuel. "We have much to explain to our friend Samuel," his deep voice boomed. "He does not yet fully understand or really know the Father. His life and teaching in the Tabernacle were interrupted by Beelzebub."

THE CHOICE

"I do know the Father!" Samuel stated defiantly. "I saw Him in the dry valley. He came to me. It was amazing—like nothing I've ever experienced or seen before. He was dressed in a robe of light, clothed in dazzling splendour.[6] His brilliance overtook me. His voice was riding on the wind.[7] The Father spoke to me—He spoke to *me*!" Samuel tapped his hand on his chest. "I was transformed in His presence! Not only that, I was cleansed when the water fell upon me. The Father gave me this sword and shield." The younger warrior waved his sword through the air and lifted his shiny shield skyward.

The others remained still; their eyes fixed upon Samuel. Samuel ran over to Dunamis and stroked the powerful golden horse. "Dunamis can testify this is true. He was given to me, as a new friend. The Father wanted me to go forward, so Dunamis was supplied to me. I understand now—the Father supplies all our needs!"[8] Samuel looked at the others, who were now all smiling at him. "I do know my Father!" Samuel's voice rose in frustration.

The little Spittles had arrived in time to hear Samuel defending himself. They grinned at each other, pleased with the frustration that was rising in his voice. Division proudly started to declare lies into Samuel's ears. The vapour's small tail curled round and round as he arrogantly delighted in the evil he was releasing. "They don't believe you. They think you're lying. They are insulting you. They think they know more then you. They think they're better than you. Don't listen to them! Walk away from this group. Do it right now. They don't understand you. You don't belong with them. Go out on your own. You will be better alone." The vapour hovered closely beside Samuel's ear, not wanting Ruach to know he was there.

"Samuel, we believe you. We all believe you!" chuckled Shear-Jashub. "There is something you need to understand. I've been meaning to

FOREVER FRIEND

tell you this. We are all children of the Father." He smirked at Samuel. "Not just you," he chuckled again. "We are the King's kids too!"

"What?! All of us?! We're all His children?![9] We're related? How is this possible?" Samuel asked. The thought of being related to everyone did not appeal to him.

The large lion let out a heavy sigh. He gently rubbed his soft mane against the young girl. Her arms were still wrapped around part of the massive neck of the mighty creature. Shamar spoke gently and slowly so Samuel could absorb all he was hearing. "We are all citizens of the Kingdom of the Father. People are His own special possession.[10] The Father, *Jehovah-Mekoddishkem*, has sanctified all who call on His name. He has set us apart." The lion roared. "We are all one family, in one Kingdom."[11]

Samuel looked out over the darkness and the shroud of evil that had clapped down upon the great city. Dunamis placed his soft nose on Samuel's neck, nudging the warrior slightly.

The Spittle moved away quickly.

The gallant horse and Samuel both stared out towards the darkness for a time. Samuel was once more trying to understand this strange new world he had abruptly been thrust into. "Samuel, there is still more for you to learn about your Father," said Dunamis softly. "And about yourself. We are here to help you gain the knowledge you need to work with your Father."

"*Our* Father," Shear-Jashub interrupted emphatically. The warrior grinned and then emphasized the word "our" once again.

Dunamis nudged Samuel gently on his neck again, regaining the warrior's attention. "I want to tell you about the Father's amazing power. I know you experienced some of it in your encounter." The gallant horse moved his wings slowly, excited to share more about the magnificent

Father. "There is still more, much more for you to learn about the Father and His kingdom. It is by His power the earth was created."[12]

"The whole earth!" Samuel stated. He abruptly turned from looking at the darkness over Zion and faced the gallant horse. "The *whole* earth!" repeated Samuel.

Dunamis raised his mighty head up and down in agreement as sparkles released into the atmosphere. "I know it is hard to comprehend. Yet it is truth. The Father merely spoke, and the world began! It appeared at His command. His wisdom gave shape to the world. The Father breathed and the world and all the stars were born.[13] He thunders, and rain pours down. He launches the wind.[14] The Father created this kingdom." Dunamis rose up on his back legs and whinnied loudly. He cantered around Samuel, the gold dust from his body being thrown into the air. "This you need to understand and believe. Beelzebub has no defense against the power of the Father. Your Father, our Father. The beast must bow down in His magnificent presence."

Samuel watched the royal horse as he continued to canter around the young warrior. Gold dust slowly settled on the ground at Samuel's feet. He listened intently, still trying to understand what was being spoken. The recently commissioned warrior trusted his new companion and believed all he was being told, but it was a matter of understanding and digesting all this new information.

"Beelzebub is nothing but stale smoke," Dunamis stated with a loud whinny. "That evil, monstrous beast will be destroyed. His days on earth are numbered!"[15] But the Father will last forever."[16] Upon saying the word forever, the majestic horse jumped up into the air and flew over Samuel, only to land on the opposite side of the warrior. "Forever!" he shouted loudly.

Ruhamah, Shear-Jashub, and Shamar all repeated the word "forever" at the same time, agreeing with Dunamis's statement.

The horse continued. "The Father has always been and always will be![17] The Father is the creator of everything that exists, including people."

Samuel thought about this information for a while and then asked, "If the Father is greater and Beelzebub must bow down to the Father, then why is Beelzebub allowed to roam the earth? Why doesn't the Father destroy him?" Samuel raised his hands into the air in frustration and looked out at the darkness covering Zion. The others all remained silent as they continued to stare out towards the destroyed city of Zion. They knew they needed to give Samuel time to comprehend this new information.

After awhile, Samuel turned and looked at the others. "Why is Beelzebub allowed to kill, steal, and destroy, like Dunamis told me earlier? How did Beelzebub even come into existence? Where did such evil come from?" Samuel looked back at the darkness covering Zion, shaking his head in disbelief. "And why doesn't the Father destroy him?!"

Division and his gang of vapours continued to infiltrate Samuel's thinking with their lies and attacks. "They are lying to you. Nothing they say is true. It's all lies to confuse you."

Dunamis gave a loud nicker, flaring his nostrils and rapidly moving his head, the colourful mane wildly dancing as he released a bounty of dazzling sparkles. "The Father created Beelzebub, just as he created all of us."

"The Father!? The Father created that beast?" Samuel shouted in disbelief. "Why would He do that?"

Dunamis whinnied. Shear-Jashub giggled loudly, patted the large, muscular horse, and walked over to his Forever Friend, Gimel. Dunamis looked at Samuel. He knew this information was hard to absorb, let alone believe. "Yes Samuel, the Father created all things. All means all, my friend. Things on earth and things in the heavens."

The noble horse walked next to Samuel and touched him gently with his nose. Dunamis knew he had to keep Samuel's full attention. This was important information the warrior would need to understand if he was going to be successful at defeating Beelzebub. "The Father created the visible and invisible. He is the creator of rulers, powers, and authorities. All things have been created through him—and more importantly, for him."[18]

Samuel looked at Dunamis with furrowed eyebrows. "Really?!" the warrior exclaimed. "You're telling me the Father actually created that beast, that monster?!"

"Yes, Samuel. The Father created Beelzebub. But he created him to glorify the Father. Beelzebub was the greatest worshipper that ever existed. His whole body was created in song for the Father. With every movement he made, his body worshipped the Almighty Father. He was once the most magnificent of all the heavenly beings,"[19] Dunamis explained. "Yes, Samuel—it's true. Beelzebub—that evil, vile beast—was once more glorious than all of the creatures and beings the Father had ever created."

The vapours were circling around the Father's chosen assembly. They were unable to penetrate though the atmosphere of faith and truth which was building. They listened to the words being spoken about Beelzebub, remembering their master's glory days. They remembered when they too had been celestial beings, worshipping the Father. The vapours all cringed at the fate they had chosen.

The words being spoken about the Father's goodness and power were cutting into the demons, causing them to slowly deflate. The words of truth were more than irritating to the Spittles—they were causing some of them to convulse. A Spittle would randomly begin to shake violently and then deflate completely, spewing out all of its evil.

Division looked back towards the defeated Zion. He knew his fate should he return without accomplishing his mission. His small, squinty red eyes glared at the remaining vapours.

Slowly he moved his head back and forth, motioning the others. The demons slowly backed away from the words being said about the Almighty Father. They lurked in the shadows, knowing they had to wait for their opportunity to strike. They continued to float outside the tranquil atmosphere. They were used to waiting—there was no cause to rush. Humans always gave them time to invade and defile.

Shamar spoke up now, his deep voice booming. "Then one horrible day, Beelzebub thought he was too beautiful and great to worship the Father. He fell in love with himself. He fell into pride and arrogance."[20] Shamar let out a loud roar of disgust. "The Father knows all our thoughts before we think them,[21] so the Father knew what the despicable creature was up to. Nothing can ever be hidden from the Father. The Father cast Beelzebub out of heaven with a third of all the heavenly beings, who were in agreement with Beelzebub.[22] In a single moment, Beelzebub fell from the heavens and was sent to earth."[23] Shamar was pacing as he spoke to Samuel, clearly agitated as he recalled this event.

Samuel looked at the great lion. "I still don't understand. Why is Beelzebub allowed to harm us? You said the Father is greater than Beelzebub, and the Father loves us. So why hasn't He destroyed the creature?" Samuel shook his head in disbelief. "If the Father truly loves us, why does he permit this to happen? Why? How is it that this beast is walking on the earth and tormenting us? He's just allowed to kill, steal, and destroy, even though the Father is greater?! This clearly doesn't make sense!"

Samuel spoke loudly, his heart and mind in turmoil. He shook his head, questioning all the information. "I don't understand," the warrior admitted, feeling hopelessly defeated.

THE CHOICE

Hopelessness snickered quietly. He didn't want to be discovered by the Father's creatures, but he was so proud of his diabolical plan of breaking slowly through the atmosphere of faith. He remained close to Samuel and continued to whisper his unending lies.

"Because we allow him to." The soft, gentle voice of Ruhamah broke the mounting tension.

"What?!" Samuel exclaimed. He turned his back on the girl and looked towards the fallen city of Zion, shaking his head.

"Yes—sadly, we allow Beelzebub to steal from us, to kill with detestable diseases, and to destroy us. We live in a fallen, sinful world. A world where Beelzebub is roaming about, spreading his lies and his evil. But the Father is at work too!" Ruhamah said excitedly. "He is advancing His kingdom through us." The girl walked over to Samuel and pulled on his cape, getting his full attention. "You see, the Father has given us free will. We freely choose who we want to serve, which kingdom we want to be a part of." The girl looked out at Zion and then back at Samuel. "We can choose the Father and work with the Father's agenda, enabling us to receive the Father's protection, guidance, and training, so we can conquer Beelzebub.[24] Or," she sighed, "we can choose Beelzebub, allowing him access to kill, steal, and destroy." Again she sighed and waited for a moment to regain her thoughts. Ruhamah tugged on Samuel's cape once more, but he continued to stare out at Zion, refusing to look at the girl. "Samuel, when we partner with the Father, we have the ability to rise above the beast and his dreadful world of sin."

Samuel turned and looked down upon the child. He wondered how she had acquired so much knowledge of the Father and His Kingdom at such a young age.

Ruhamah smiled at Samuel. "The Father loves us so much, but He wants our love for Him to be pure. The Father will never force us into anything—not even loving Him." Ruhamah walked over to Dunamis and stroked his soft fur. Golden flecks moved across her small hand. "Samuel, our Father wants a relationship with us that is built on love and trust—never forced, never demanded or manipulated. We have a choice. We always have a choice."

Samuel looked over at Shear-Jashub, who was now resting beside Gimel. The seasoned warrior raised his eyebrows and nodded his head in approval of what the young girl was saying.

"Our Father waits patiently for us to choose to engage in this battle with Him. He doesn't need us to work with Him, but He desires for us to become involved with Him. If we choose to engage with the Father, He will give us the armour and weapons to fight Beelzebub. If we turn from our Father, then we have placed ourselves in the hands of Beelzebub. It's that simple. There are only two sides to be on, and we must all choose our side. There is no neutral ground, because neutral is actually siding with the enemy, Beelzebub. And Beelzebub gets to claim the undecided vote."

The young girl smiled as she looked at the two mighty warriors. "Just think, Samuel," the young girl said excitedly, "the creator of this world chooses us. All of us, each and every person. Whether we are weak or strong does not matter." The girl began to laugh. "Actually, I think He prefers the weak!"[25] She continued to giggle. "Yes, amazingly our Father waits patiently for us to join Him in this fight."[26]

Samuel rubbed his neck. A cold chill was settling upon him. "So how did Beelzebub capture an entire city like Zion?" Samuel asked, still trying to understand all he had been told.

Confusion wrapped his tail around Hopelessness. He had pushed his way into the atmosphere of truth. The two smiled at each other, their beady eyes darting back and forth to make sure the heavenly creatures didn't notice them.

THE CHOICE

Shear-Jashub looked over at his sack of fireballs. They were moving about wildly inside the sack. *Hmmmmm,* he wondered. He placed the sack closer to Gimel and repositioned himself comfortably by the feet of his Forever Friend. This was taking longer than he had hoped, but the seasoned warrior knew Samuel needed to understand this information.

Dunamis spoke with authority. "Remember when Ruhamah explained that she had begun to paga as Beelzebub engulfed the city of Zion?"

"Yes," Samuel said, wanting to learn more.

Shamar spoke now as he paced back and forth. His noble mane bounced as he took large strides in front of the small girl. "If you stay in paga," his deep voice of authority boomed, "focusing on the Father, you cannot be touched by Beelzebub. Pray, paga at all times and on every occasion, in the power of your special, secret language. Stay alert and be persistent in your prayers for all people.[27] This is crucial. Ruhamah knows how to do this—she has been trained well. She is a mighty intercessor for the Father, interceding in paga. Ruhamah stands in the gap for those who aren't quite ready or trained up in paga, in prayer."

Samuel looked at the small girl and then out towards the darkness hovering over Zion. "How can paga or praying help? Praying or *paga*," Samuel said, emphasizing the strange word, "obviously didn't help the people of Zion!"

The young girl put her hand over her mouth, gasped, and shook her head as she stared at Samuel.

"There's your proof!" Samuel stated as he extended his arm towards Zion and shook his head in disbelief.

Ruhamah took another large gasp of air, her hand still placed over her open mouth. Her eyes opened wide in shock at Samuel's words. The girl glanced over at Shear-Jashub, who was now on his feet and pacing back and forth in front of Shamar, shaking his head. The beautiful turquoise feather emphasized his disapproval with its movement.

Ruhamah raised her hands beside her head in total frustration, gesturing for Shear-Jashub to intervene.

Division smiled. He addressed the young intercessor. "Samuel is a fool! He has no faith. Why would you want to be with him? He doesn't understand. He doesn't care about the people of Zion like you do. Why don't you leave this group? They don't know what they are doing. They're not the soldiers the King sent for. They're impostors."

The young girl looked out towards the darkness. She stood in disbelief, looking out at her beloved city. Shear-Jashub continued to pace as Samuel sat down on the ground for a moment. Ruach came over to the warrior and snuggled up close to him. Everyone was silent. No one was talking.

Ruhamah let out a grunt of frustration. *No one is defending the power of paga!* she thought. *What am I doing here?*

"Walk away. You can do this yourself. You don't need any of them." The vapour grinned. Division nodded his head for the other vapours to continue their evil rant of lies.

The atmosphere of faith had been fully invaded. Irritation was now engaged. He continued to poke his lies at the girl. Other Spittles came and crowded around Ruhamah. They continued to spit lies at her. Their master would finally be somewhat satisfied with their work— though they knew, only too well, that nothing truly made Beelzebub happy or fully content.

The girl rubbed the back of her neck and looked down at her bare feet. *Could Samuel really be one of the Father's mighty warriors?* she wondered. She sighed as she looked back out over her beloved city of Zion.

THE CHOICE

Division continued to bombard the child with thoughts of giving up and running away. The little vapour was going to hold onto the ground he had gained in the thoughts of the girl. The Spittles all watched her every gesture for more clues to their victory. Irritation lingered close to Ruhamah's mouth, intently listening for any words she might release which would give the vapours more ammunition to fight with. The girl was clearly irritated. The vapour grinned at his effectiveness.

Hopelessness and Confusion stayed close to Samuel, edging him on. Confusion looked over at the group of Spittles hovering around Ruhamah. He grinned and nodded his head in approval of their evil gang attack.

Division smirked and nodded back at Confusion, as he intently watched the young girl. *Yes, humans always give themselves away with their words and gestures,* he thought. *I will not be going back to Beelzebub without my victory!* The evil vapour snickered ghoulishly to himself.

The lion let out a huge roar, which caught everyone's attention—including that of the Spittles. He brushed his soft mane up against Ruhamah's face and shoulder. Division and the other vapours quickly departed into the shadows away from the mighty Forever Friends. The vapours knew the powerful creatures were aware of their presence.

"Ruhamah knows her identity in the Kingdom." The mighty beast once more rubbed up against the girl, shaking off any discouraging thoughts along with the irritation that was mounting inside her. "She is a princess." The lion released another mighty roar. It was long and loud. The little Spittles moved further back into the darkness. "Ruhamah knows her identity," Shamar repeated. "She is a princess. Not any princess, but the King's princess. She is the King's daughter!"

Ruhamah is a princess? Samuel thought to himself. He hadn't realized he was speaking to royalty, though Shear-Jashub had stated earlier that they were all the King's children. Samuel looked over at the young girl.

She certainly didn't look like a princess. She was wearing a torn brown gown and had no sandals on her feet. *Well, she has just come out of a battle—but shouldn't there be something distinguishing about her?* he thought. *A small piece of jewelry... something to show her royalty?*

Ruhamah reluctantly looked at her amazing Forever Friend. She grinned as the beast continued to rub gently against her small frame. Ruhamah smiled as she felt the love from the majestic creature flow into her heart. Shamar knew her so well. The irritation lifted. The girl giggled. Yes, Shamar knew all her needs and her thoughts. He was her great Forever Friend!

The lion continued. "As Ruhamah was in paga, the Father heard her words, her *paga*." Shamar emphasized the word as he looked at Samuel. "The Father did hear her prayers, and He did answer them, Samuel. He bends down and listens to us.[28] The Father felt her anguish for the people, and He provided Ruhamah's escape. She is a remnant of those who believe."

Shamar continued to rub his massive head gently against Ruhamah as she caressed his tawny fur. Shamar clearly cared for the small girl. "Paga works!" he declared loudly. "How the Father orchestrates everything out is not always understood by mankind. It is also not for mankind to question the Father's ways. The Father sees the beginning from the end, and He knows what He is doing.[29] This is where your faith and trust in the Father come into play. These are two great qualities that please the Father very much when He finds them inside of you.[30] Ruhamah's prayers were effective, even if it looks like Beelzebub has captured Zion. This war has not ended yet." The lion roared again as if he was releasing laughter. "It hasn't even begun, my young warrior." The lion lay down comfortably near Ruhamah.

"You must take all this information in, young Samuel. Into your mind and into your soul. It is actually quite simple how Beelzebub was able

THE CHOICE

to capture the city of Zion. All of Zion's people believed the lies he whispered," the impressive lion roared once more. The breath from his massive mouth moved the young girl's hair wildly as she continued to stroke his thick mane.

The strong wind of truth from the mouth of the Father's trusting guard pushed Division further back into the barren land, along with the other Spittles.

Shamar continued. "Unendingly, Beelzebub and his demons tell lies and shift the truth. Beelzebub transformed evil to look like good,[31] and the people willingly took the bait. Only Ruhamah believed the Father and held fast to the truth." The mighty lion roared. "Ruhamah chose righteousness. The princess chose the right direction, the right path."

Dunamis spoke now. "Samuel, our war with Beelzebub isn't finished. Just like Shamar said, it hasn't yet begun. The evil creature wants us to think he has overtaken and won. How despicable he is! Deceitful coward!" The horse whinnied loudly. "The Father wants to fight this war with us side by side. He already has the victory planned out for us! We must choose to step into this victory."

The gallant horse cantered around Samuel, who was still sitting on the ground beside Ruach. Dunamis placed his nose on Samuel's neck, his breath warming the young warrior. The Spittles Hopelessness and Confusion flew quickly into the comfort of the shadows.

Ruach looked up at the air and nodded his head in approval. The ram knew what Dunamis was doing. He knew the Spittles were trying to change Samuel's mind and heart. The Forever Friends always knew when the Spittles were near. They were constantly aware of all that was happening in both realms. The Forever Friends were never threated by the presence of evil, and they never gave any attention or focus to the vile creatures. Ruach remained close to Samuel and continued to warm the warrior with his presence, with his love.

The Spittles all waited and listened for their next chance to disrupt Samuel's thinking. Sly as they were, the little vapours didn't realize the Forever Friends were always aware of their presence—their every move and every word.

"When you saw the Father, Samuel, what did He look like?" Ruhamah asked. She had now fully forgiven Samuel for his comments.

The warrior looked over at the young girl. His mind was still trying to absorb the fact that Ruhamah was a princess. He looked at Shear-Jashub, knowing now they were all related in the Father's Kingdom. They looked different from one another, yet they were from one family, one Kingdom. His mysterious Father belonged to all of them.

"What... what did you say?" Samuel asked, regaining his thoughts, and not knowing how he should address a princess.

Ruhamah smiled at the warrior. "Tell me again what the Father looked like when you saw Him. I have yet to meet my Father face-to-face, though Shamar comes to me often, carrying words from the Father's heart. These are the words I share with my people." She paused. "When they will listen to me."

Samuel smiled and made a loud sigh. "He was indescribable—mostly a dazzling white, gold, and silver light[32] radiating from within. So warm, so brilliant; it made me feel at peace. All my senses were aware of the Father's presence. I could barely stand under the weight of His... His...?" Samuel couldn't fully express how he'd felt in the presence of his Father. Ruach rubbed up against Samuel's leg. The warrior looked down at his beloved Forever Friend and smiled. Ruach's head was resting on Samuel's lap, his brilliant blue eyes gazing into Samuel's eyes.

"His love for you, Samuel," said Shamar. "It is His love you felt. It is unlike any known to man. Greater than any earthly love.[33] It is pure. It comes from the source of love itself, for that is what and who the Father is: love."[34]

"Ah," said the young princess as she tried to envision what Samuel had described. "I experienced a light also, but in a different form. The light I ran through was the Father bringing me into a new dimension. In the Father's light, you can experience many things. We *all* have much to learn, Samuel." Ruhamah placed emphasis on the word "all." Samuel grinned at her. The young girl's heart was now filled with compassion for the new warrior. She wondered how much training he had received before Beelzebub had tried to destroy him.

Shear-Jashub's laugher broke the solemn mood. He stroked the silky feathers of Gimel, who was standing beside the warrior. "Sometimes the best learning comes through experiencing life for yourself." He looked up at his stately Forever Friend and continued to stroke its chest.

"Isn't that right, Gimel?" The miraculous eagle stretched open its large wings to affirm what had been stated. "Sometimes we must cry out to the Father—not knowing, but believing. In the Father's kingdom, Samuel, you can't always reason things out. You must trust your inner knowing. Trust your Forever Friend's nudging. You will somehow know you're going in the right direction, no matter what your surroundings look like." The mature warrior tapped Gimel's chest. "We have done that many times—right, my friend?" The eagle let out a confirming squawk. Shear-Jashub laughed. "We have gone through some very strange stuff together!" The warrior continued to stroke Gimel's large, stately chest.

The princess smiled. "Yes! That's exactly what I experienced when I went through my light from the Father! I had absolutely no idea where I was going. I had to trust that the Father was showing me a way out. And look, it has brought me to all of you. My prayers were answered, Samuel. Just not in the way I thought they would be answered."

The lion let out a loud yawn and shook his mane. "It is your choice. It is always a choice. Choose wisely, my friend—life with the Father, or death with Beelzebub."

Samuel looked at all of them. He knew the choice he had to make. The warrior smiled as he looked down upon Ruach, nestled close to him. He gently rubbed his companion. "I choose... the Father," Samuel stated softly as he gazed down upon his Forever Friend. He looked up at the others and smiled. Confidently, he repeated his statement. "I choose the Father!" he stated a little louder. Ruach pushed his large silver and gold horns into Samuel's chest and batted his large blue eyes at the warrior. Samuel stood up. "I choose the Father!" Samuel announced proudly. The Father's united group all gave a big cheer as Ruach nodded his head with its impressive gold and silver horns, emphasizing his approval.

Questions to Contemplate

1. Would you like to hold a fireball in your hands?
2. What would you throw a fireball at, and why?
3. How is our earthly family different from our heavenly family? How is it the same?
4. What choice did Samuel make in this chapter?
5. *Jehovah-Mekoddishkem* means "the Lord who sets you apart."[35] What are people are set apart from?
6. The author writes, "The Father will never force us into anything, not even loving Him." Did you know it is our choice to love God? Do you love God?

THE CHOICE

[1] According to Ira Milligan in *Understanding the Dreams You Dream* (Destiny Image Publishers, 2010), a turquoise feather means spiritual authority, covering, and protection.

[2] Ephesians 6:13–18: "…put on every piece of God's armor so you will be able to resist the enemy in the time of evil. Then after the battle you will still be standing firm. Stand your ground, putting on the belt of truth and the body armor of God's righteousness. For shoes, put on the peace that comes from the Good News so that you will be fully prepared. In addition to all of these, hold up the shield of faith to stop the fiery arrows of the devil. Put on salvation as your helmet, and take the sword of the Spirit, which is the word of God. Pray in the Spirit at all times and on every occasion. Stay alert and be persistent in your prayers for all believers everywhere."

[3] Isaiah 48:10: "Indeed, I have refined you, but not as silver; I have tested *and* chosen you in the furnace of affliction" (AMP).

[4] 1 Peter 4:12: "Beloved, do not be surprised at the fiery ordeal which is taking place to test you [that is, to test the quality of your faith], as though something strange or unusual were happening to you" (AMP).

[5] Hosea 2:1: "In that day you will call your brothers Ammi—'My people.' And you will call your sisters Ruhamah—'The ones I love.'"

[6] Job 37:22: "So also, golden splendor comes from the mountain of God. He is clothed in dazzling splendor."

[7] Psalm 104:2–3: "[You are the One] who covers Yourself with light as with a garment, Who stretches out the heavens like a tent curtain, Who lays the beams of His upper chambers in the waters [above the firmament], Who makes the clouds His chariot, *Who walks on the wings of the wind…*" (AMP, emphasis added)

[8] Philippians 4:19: "And this same God who takes care of me will supply all your needs from his glorious riches, which have been given to us in Christ Jesus."

[9] 1 John 3:1: "See how very much our Father loves us, for he calls us his children, and that is what we are!"

[10] Deuteronomy 7:6: "For you are a people holy to the Lord your God. The Lord your God has chosen you out of all the peoples on the face of the earth to be his people, his treasured possession" (NIV).

[11] John 1:12: "But to all who believed him and accepted him, he gave the right to become children of God."

[12] Revelation 4:11: "…You created all things, and because of Your will they exist, and were created and brought into being" (AMP).

[13] Psalm 33:6, 9: "The Lord merely spoke, and the heavens were created. He breathed the word, and all the stars were born… For when he spoke, the world began! It appeared at his command."

FOREVER FRIEND

[14] Jeremiah 10:13: "But it is God whose power made the earth, whose wisdom gave shape to the world, who crafted the cosmos. He thunders, and rain pours down. He sends the clouds soaring. He embellishes the storm with lightnings, launches wind from his warehouse" (MSG).

[15] Therefore rejoice, O heavens and you who dwell in them [in the presence of God]. Woe to the earth and the sea, because the devil has come down to you in great wrath, knowing that *he has only a short time [remaining]!"* AMP emphasis added

[16] Psalm 102:12 *"But You, O LORD, shall endure forever,* And the remembrance of Your name to all generations." NKJV emphasis added

[17] Revelation 1:8b: "I am the one who is, who always was, and who is still to come—the Almighty One."

[18] Colossians 1:16: "…for through him God created everything in the heavenly realms and on earth. He made the things we can see and the things we can't see—such as thrones, kingdoms, rulers, and authorities in the unseen world. Everything was created through him and for him."

[19] Ezekiel 28:12b: "You were the seal of perfection, full of wisdom and perfect in beauty" (BSB).

[20] Ezekiel 28:15, 17: "You were blameless in all you did from the day you were created until the day evil was found in you… Your heart was filled with pride because of all your beauty… So I threw you to the ground and exposed you…."

[21] Psalm 139:2b: "You know my thoughts before I think them" (ICB).

[22] Revelation 12:4: "His tail swept away one-third of the stars in the sky, and he threw them to the earth."

[23] Luke 10:18b: "I saw Satan fall from heaven like lightning!"

[24] Psalm 91:9–11: "If you make the Lord your refuge, if you make the Most High your shelter, no evil will conquer you; no plague will come near your home. For he will order his angels to protect you wherever you go."

[25] 2 Corinthians 12:9: "My grace is sufficient for you, for My strength is made perfect in weakness" (NKJV).

[26] John 15:16: "You didn't choose me. I chose you."

[27] Ephesians 6:18: "Pray in the Spirit at all times and on every occasion. Stay alert and be persistent in your prayers for all believers everywhere.

[28] Psalm 116:1–2: "I love the Lord because he hears my voice and my prayer for mercy. Because he bends down to listen, I will pray as long as I have breath!"

[29] I make known the end from the beginning, from ancient times, what is still to come. I say, 'My purpose will stand, and I will do all that I please.' Isaiah 46:10 NIV

[30] Hebrews 11:6: "But without faith it is impossible to [walk with God and] please Him, for whoever comes [near] to God must [necessarily] believe that God exists and that He rewards those who [earnestly and diligently] seek Him" (AMP).

[31] Isaiah 5:20: "Woe to those who call evil good and good evil…" (NIV).

THE CHOICE

[32] Psalm 104:1b–2: "You are robed with honor and majesty. You are dressed in a robe of light."

[33] 1 John 4:7b: "…for love comes from God."

[34] 1 John 4:8: "But anyone who does not love does not know God, for God is love."

[35] Chris Poblete, "The Names of God: Jehovah Mekoddishkem," *The Blue Letter Bible Blog* (https://blogs.blueletterbible.org/blb/2012/08/14/3926/).

Chapter Fifteen
The Unveiling

Ruhamah rested at the feet of Shamar. They all took some time to regain their thoughts as they stared at the dark shroud covering Zion. It had been another day full of adventure for all of them. Everyone was becoming weary. The sun was quickly fading, and a gentle night breeze was beginning to blow.

Samuel was the first to break the silence. "I have another question."

A loud groan was heard from the group. Shear-Jashub pushed his head into the chest of the large eagle, his turquoise feather bent backwards. The seasoned warrior then lifted his head, looked at Ruhamah, and grinned. The young girl smiled back at him knowingly, then looked back at Samuel waiting patiently for his question.

"Why didn't my mother tell me any of this?"

Shamar let out a loud roar and began to pace between Ruhamah and Shear-Jashub. Shear-Jashub released a giggle as he continued to stroke the feathers of his powerful Forever Friend. He shook his head, knowing this could be a long night.

Shamar began, "Your mother is a very loving and wise woman. A woman of paga, a woman of prayer. She is a prayer warrior for the Father. Your mother knew the experiences you were about to have would change you and mold you into a mighty warrior for the King, your Father. Your mother has been in prayer for you since she left you at the Tabernacle door.

She knew you needed to experience this journey on your own." Shamar was still pacing as he spoke.

"Your mother hasn't stopped praying for you. She has asked the Father to give you complete knowledge of His will and to give you spiritual wisdom and understanding."[1] Shamar lay down beside Ruhamah.

"We all have a destiny," the resting lion continued. "It is up to us to choose the destiny the Father has placed before us. Your mother knew you would have decisions to make— decisions that would change your life and history. Your mother knew you had to figure this out for yourself, being guided by Ruach." The ram's big blue eyes looked lovingly up at Samuel, as he batted his long black lashes. "Your experience with the Father is your testimony. Beelzebub and his demons can't lie about what you have experienced with the Father. Sharing your testimony with others is power in action—power Beelzebub does not want you to possess." The great creature rested his massive head on his paws.

Confusion inched his way over to Samuel's ear and began his unrelenting lies. "How could Shamar know your mother? He is lying! This is a trick, and you're falling for it. You're a fool. Shamar has never met your mother."

"Wait a minute, Shamar—you know my mother?" Samuel blurted out. "How?" The confused warrior scratched his head and furrowed his eyebrows. "When... when did you meet her?"

Shamar raised his head and looked at Samuel. There was still a young boy's mind inside the young man. Shamar could see the resemblance of Samuel's earthly father in Samuel's face and frame.

The noble beast let out another loud roar and once more shook his head. He rose and settled on the ground near Samuel. "Your mother and your earthly father were very close to me. Your father and I had many great battles together. Many great battles!" the lion repeated. He grinned as he thought of the exploits they had done together and the territory they had gained for the Father. "Beelzebub also knew your father. His hatred for your father grew in vehemence. It was Beelzebub who eventually took your father from us." The noble beast paused a moment. "Your father was one of our greatest warriors—this is why Beelzebub despised him. You were just a mere babe when all this happened."

Confusion quickly retreated back to the other Spittles. Division needed a stronger plan. He had to prevent the Father's creatures from sharing any more information with Samuel. The warrior was gaining to much knowledge of the Kingdom. And worse, the group was becoming united.

The lion bellowed an angry, fierce roar. "Beelzebub also knows who you are. That is why he is trying to destroy you. He knows you carry the mantle of your earthly father—you are also a great warrior. Beelzebub wants to destroy you before you have a chance to accomplish the destiny that your heavenly Father has arranged for you."[2]

"I carry a mantle? What's that?" Samuel looked above himself—there was no door he could see.

The lion laughed. "The mantle you carry is the authority and responsibility that the Father has wrapped around you. You are a chosen spokesman for Him. There is also an anointing which the Father has given you. You, Samuel, carry your earthly father's anointing plus your own anointing. You have received a double portion.[3] You can't see your anointing or mantle, Samuel—but it's real; it exists. It is like..." Shamar thought a moment, "...an invisible cape you are always wearing. It has been wrapped around you by the Father. As you open the cape up, you can grab the tools which rest inside you—like your own personal testimony of meeting the Father. Your experiences are like tools you can use to help build up and fix others. The anointing and the mantle you receive aren't jewels or capes merely to be worn on display, but qualities to be used in extending the Kingdom for the Father, and for fighting against Beelzebub and his dark world."

Ruach now nuzzled up to Samuel's side. The warrior touched the soft, silky wool as he considered the new information.

"The Father has equipped all his children with power and tools to accomplish His will," Dunamis added, catching their attention with a whinny and pounding his hooves on the ground, creating an explosion of gold sparkles. "The Father has given you all spiritual gifts.[4] These are great tools to advance the Father's Kingdom on earth as it is in heaven."[5]

Samuel looked at Shamar. The great beast lay peacefully on the ground. Ruhamah had snuggled close to her heavenly Forever Friend. She seemed like a small lamb next to the noble lion. Samuel remembered how his precious Forever Friend had been brutally thrown against the mountain wall. Samuel continued to stroke the back of Ruach. "Oh Ruach, I'm so glad you survived being thrown against the cavern rock wall. Beelzebub is really awful. He is pure evil."

Division now tried to change Samuel's thoughts. "They're making this stuff up. This can't be true. This has all been a delusion." The Spittle thought of more lies. He knew it was his last attempt to thwart the plans of the Father. "The beast didn't throw Ruach. The ram tripped. This is a bunch of lies. Would anyone in your tribe believe any of this? No! No one would believe any of it!"

The younger warrior shook his head and continued to stroke his Forever Friend. Samuel quietly looked out over the horizon for a time. He turned and looked at Shamar with a puzzled face. "So, the Father in the Tabernacle isn't my father? My father was a great warrior who died fighting Beelzebub? Umm, who's in the tabernacle? And why do we call Him Father? What's going on?!"

FOREVER FRIEND

Samuel thought back to his mother leaving him on the top steps of the Tabernacle. Her parting words had been, "Your Father waits for you on the other side of the door."

Samuel scratched his head a moment and thought. "Who is my Father?" he said loudly in frustration. The Spittles all grinned at each other, their little tails twirling. Division nodded his head slowly, claiming an early victory over Samuel's thoughts.

"Samuel, all people have an earthly father and a heavenly Father," said Dunamis. "Creatures like myself have only our heavenly Father. Our Creator. We were created to assist and serve the people, to help them learn about the Father and move into a greater love for Him."[6]

Shear-Jashub now spoke up. "Samuel, we also have our Forever Friend. The Father has given us our Forever Friend to be our helper[7] and comforter.[8] Our Forever Friend will guide, teach, reveal the truth, and correct us."

Shear-Jashub looked up at his loyal eagle and gently stroked the feathers on Gimel's breast. "Our Forever Friend brings us great power[9] from the Father, and the Father's priceless love.[10] Our Forever Friend also helps us in all our weakness, especially in our paga[11] to the Father. There are other gifts we receive as we learn to partner with and listen to our Forever Friend. Our Forever Friend is one of the greatest gifts from our Father." The older warrior tenderly rubbed the chest of the mighty eagle. "Our Forever Friends will always direct us towards our glorious Father. Always! We just need to listen and obey."[12]

Samuel sat down on the ground. Everything was overwhelming. Ruach knew Samuel was trying to absorb all that he had heard. The ram once more lay down beside Samuel and put his head in the young man's lap. Samuel ran his hands through the ram's beautiful silken wool, amazed at all his Forever Friend could do for him, and had been doing for him.

THE UNVEILING

Samuel journeyed back in his mind to his first encounter with the ram. How thrilled Samuel was to have a friend—a Forever Friend.

Samuel thought about all the changes that had occurred since his mother had left him at the Tabernacle door.[13] Not only had he changed in appearance—his heart, mind, and soul had also changed. His mind was opened and being transformed with each new concept.[14] He had obediently entered the Tabernacle believing he would discover his earthly father, only to now discover he had a heavenly Father! Not a distant god he would pray the same prayer to night after night, like the people in his tribe. No, he had been introduced to his heavenly Father, who had chosen him and wanted a relationship with him. Even more amazingly, it would be a relationship built on trust and love. *Wow*, he thought. *A relationship with the creator of the universe!* He grinned as he looked over as Shear-Jashub and Ruhamah. He now belonged to a new family, a Kingdom family. Samuel smiled down at his gentle yet powerful friend, Ruach, who was still resting his head on Samuel's lap. Ruach's big blue eyes gazed into Samuel's soul. Samuel grinned at his loyal companion.

"We need to help free the people!" Samuel said, as if the thought and words had come from a different source than his own. Or rather, they'd come from a deeper place inside of him— a place he was just now discovering. His soul was coming into agreement with his heavenly Father, and his Father's Kingdom mandate.

The Spittles all looked at each other as they remained in the shadows. They had failed, and they knew it. They would have to return to Beelzebub and receive the fate that awaited them. Slowly they retreated. The fragrant aroma of hope was building, causing the vapours to gag. Already they had spent too much time listening to positive words and being in the presence of goodness. Evil was where they belonged.

Samuel looked at the unimaginable group. He was now aligned with a body of warriors who understood so much more about his Father's Kingdom. He was glad he had chosen to move forward in his journey. He felt like he was properly positioned for his destiny. He was slowly beginning to understand his Father's Kingdom. Their Father's Kingdom. This was Samuel's appointed time for victory.[15]

"We need to free the people!" Samuel shouted the words this time as he abruptly stood up.

"Awwww!" Shear-Jashub let out a sudden, loud cry. He was glad the teaching session was over. He was a man of action, eager to take part in escapades for the King. He began to dance wildly, his feet moving in jerky fashion. He raised his shield and shouted, "This is a kairos moment! I can feel it in the atmosphere. We are about to receive the battle plan," the warrior prophesied. "Let's paga together as we wait for the Father to give us his instructions to defeat Beelzebub. Praise is the first weapon—the first tool we are given to whirl at Beelzebub."

Shear-Jashub raised his sword towards the sky. He moved aggressively, as if he was already engaged in battle with an invisible enemy, his majestic turquoise feather dancing above his powerful movements.

"There is a sound of war!" Shear-Jashub's feet banged louder beneath him. "A sound of engagement! This sound will defeat our enemy. Listen for that sound. Wait for that sound. Let it erupt within us. Then we move forward!"[16] The young warrior let out a piercing cry similar to the shriek of his Forever Friend, Gimel. The sound sliced through Samuel and Ruhamah's bodies, creating a passion to engage with him.

"There is power in our unity,[17] power in our praise." Shear-Jashub circled around Gimel as he continued in his war dance.

THE UNVEILING

Gimel opened up his wings and took flight, penetrating the atmosphere with a loud screech. The wind from the eagle's large wings blew upon all the warriors. Gimel soared swiftly above the group.

Dunamis looked over at a log lying by itself on the ground. The horse gazed intensely at the log, his fiery red eyes glowing, until the log began to burn brightly with fire.

Dunamis began his war dance around the fire, lifting his long, strong legs high into the air. His head moved up and down, allowing his beautiful mane to flow and dance too. His tail swished around and around, creating a current of gold sparkles. Dunamis's crystalline glass feathers created an iridescent glimmer around him as he slowly moved his wings up and down.

Ruhamah wasted no time. She quickly ran behind Dunamis, catching the dancing sparkles in her arms and throwing them back up into the air. The sparkles danced over her. None of them descended to the ground; they just bounced all around the young girl. Her torn brown gown flowed about her as if in its own current of wind. She laughed as she happily twirled and clapped her hands above her head and moved her bare feet to a rhythm that seemed like pure joy. She sang so sweetly, consumed in her love song to her Father, the King.

Ruach bounded into the dance. He shook his silky wool as if he was wet again. As he did, diamonds and other glistening stones flew into the air, creating a rainbow of jewels around the ram.

Samuel laughed and laughed. He could barely contain himself with laughter and joy. Samuel fell to the ground as he continued to laugh. He remembered how he had laughed when he'd first entered the Tabernacle and the lights were tickling him. Samuel felt this same sensation now. His laughter was uncontrollable. Samuel felt so alive.

Shamar took one giant leap into the air and landed in front of Dunamis, making a loud thud. The lion began to strut, revealing his mighty form. His mane was thrown about wildly as he moved his magnificent head. The long tawny tail circled around and around, keeping beat with the movement of the others. In the midst of the dancing, the lion let out a huge roar that caught everyone's attention. They all began to laugh louder and sing praises to their King, the Father.

Shear-Jashub released another war cry, his feet dancing wildly. Sparkling crystal water mysteriously poured out from the ground he was dancing on. The young man moved in his jerky warrior dance as he sang in his secret, special language. He'd possessed this gift from the Father for some time, and he used it often. As he danced and sang, the water splashed about his feet.

Then Gimel, who had been soaring over the group, suddenly opened his immense wings and flew directly upwards into the sky. The eagle let out a penetrating cry and dove down towards the warriors, only to rise again a second before impacting the fire. The wind from the beautiful raptor created a whirlwind above the fire, which rose up towards the sky. Gimel kept repeating this action, causing the whirlwind to grow outward and upward. The diamonds, jewels, and gold sparkles all became captured in the whirlwind and rose with the current. The occasional spark from the fire would also be captured in the whirlwind of jewels, and the atmosphere would suddenly explode in brilliance.

His laughter having subsided, Samuel sat on the ground looking out towards his friends. What a splendid assembly they were. What marvellous qualities they all possessed. They were all so very different, yet together they created a body of splendour. He stood and watched the dance a few moments more. Then, with a burning inside his heart, he too joined the dance of a lifetime.

THE UNVEILING

Samuel held his shield up towards the sky. "Father, now I paga for You—for Your presence to come to us in greater glory. We wait on Your words of wisdom. For the battle is Yours, Father,[18] and the victory will be ours." The burning in Samuel's chest intensified. For the Father was working in Samuel, giving the warrior the desire and the power to do what pleased Him.[19]

Samuel took his sword out of its sleeve and began to move it around, as if fighting an enemy of darkness. Instantly his shield began to burst forth with colours and flashes, all beaming up towards the heavens. Samuel's shield had come to life. Samuel moved the shield into different positions, memorizing all the qualities of the colours in his shield. The power from the light flashes would burn the remaining nearby trees. Samuel had a flaming fighting shield.

"Hey Samuel, be careful where you point that thing!" yelled Shear-Jashub. He had to duck as a bolt of lightning shot by him, just missing the top of his turquoise feather.

Samuel looked at his friend and laughed. Then he noticed his ram's horn lying nearby. He picked it up and blew. Samuel continued to march around the circle of fire, blowing his ram's horn. The sound was so majestic and powerful. He loved the music and rhythm his horn produced.

The warriors danced together late into the night. They were waiting patiently for the battle plan to be revealed to them. They all knew that without the Father they would perish, even with the amazing armour they all carried. With the Father, the victory was won. Singing together in harmony and joy, they willingly awaited the voice of the Father.

The Father looked down from heaven's throne and smiled upon his children. He was well pleased!

***

From the cover of darkness, Beelzebub glared out towards the small fire. He saw the glow of glory coming from the united group. Quickly the beast turned around in rage and breathed a fiery breath of putrid fumes. Noxious gases were released into the atmosphere.

"I hate that grotesque noise!" the vile beast growled through clenched teeth. "Who gave that kid that confounded horn? That noise is deafening! Awwww, my ears!" Beelzebub placed his scrawny hands over his ears as the horde of flies moved around the top of his head.

The enemy of the Father wouldn't give up easily. Beelzebub moved over to the edge of the shroud of evil and abruptly sat down on the dark blanket. His long, spindly fingers grasped tightly to the blanket of evil he had covered the people of Zion with. "Arghhhhhh," the creature groaned unrelentingly throughout the night as the worship continued unceasingly.

Questions to Contemplate

1. The author called this chapter "The Unveiling." What do you think was unveiled?

2. The anointing and mantle you receive aren't jewels or a cape merely to be worn on display, but qualities to be used in fighting against Beelzebub and his dark world. Do you have an anointing or mantle from God? What is your gift, and how do you use it?

3. Praise is the first weapon—the first tool we are given to whirl at Beelzebub. Do you think of praise to God as a weapon?

4. Do you know what the Father's Kingdom mandate is? The prayer Jesus taught His disciples might help you understand and answer this question. Luke 11:2 says, *"So He said to them,*

    a. *'When you pray, say: Our Father in heaven, Hallowed be Your name. Your kingdom come. Your will be done on earth as it is in heaven" (NKJV).*

5. The chapter ends with the Father looking down from the throne room. The Father is well pleased with the children. Why?

6. Do you think God can be well pleased with you?

---

[1] Colossians 1:9–10: "So we have not stopped praying for you since we first heard about you. We ask God to give you complete knowledge of his will and to give you spiritual wisdom and understanding. Then the way you live will always honor and please the Lord, and your lives will produce every kind of good fruit. All the while, you will grow as you learn to know God better and better."

[2] Psalm 37:23: "The Lord directs the steps of the godly. He delights in every detail of their lives."

[3] 2 Kings 2:9: "And Elisha said, 'Please let a double portion of your spirit be upon me'" (NASB).

[4] 1 Peter 4:10: "Each of you has been blessed with one of God's many wonderful gifts to be used in the service of others. So use your gift well" (CEV).

[5] Matthew 6:10: "May your Kingdom come soon. May your will be done on earth, as it is in heaven."

[6] Hebrews 1:14: "Therefore, angels are only servants—spirits sent to care for people who will inherit salvation."

[7] John 14:26: "But the *Helper*, the Holy Spirit, whom the Father will send in my mane, he will teach you all things and bring to your remembrance all that I have said to you" (ESV, emphasis added).

[8] John 14:16: "And I will pray the Father, and he shall give you another *Comforter*, that he may abide with you for ever…" (KJV, emphasis added).

[9] Acts 1:8: "…you will receive power when the Holy Spirit comes upon you."

[10] Romans 5:5b: "…God's love has been poured out into our hearts through the Holy Spirit, who has been given to us" (NIV).

[11] Romans 8:26–27: "…the Holy Spirit helps us in our weakness. For example, we don't know what God wants us to pray for. But the Holy Spirit prays for us with groanings that cannot be expressed in words."

[12] James 1:22: "…don't just listen to God's word. You must do what it says."

[13] 2 Corinthians 3:18b: "And the Lord—who is the Spirit—makes us more and more like him as we are changed into his glorious image."

[14] 2 Corinthians 5:17: "Therefore, if anyone is in Christ, the new creation has come; The old has gone, the new is here!" (NIV).

[15] Esther 4:14b: "And who knows but that you have come to your royal position for such a time as this?" (NIV).

[16] Barbara J. Yoder writes in *Taking on Goliath: How to Stand Against the Spiritual Enemies in Your Life and Win*, "There is a sound of war, of engagement in battle, that will defeat the enemy. Listen for that sound and move forward: take the next step when the sound ignites your spirit with faith" (Charisma House, 2012, p. 83).

[17] Genesis 11:6: "The people are united, and they all speak the same language. After this, nothing they set out to do will be impossible for them!"

[18] He said, "Listen, all you people of Judah and Jerusalem! Listen, King Jehoshaphat! This is what the LORD says: Do not be afraid! Don't be discouraged by this mighty army, *for the battle is not yours, but God's.* 2 Chronicles 20:15 NLT emphasis added

[19] Philippians 2:13: "For God is working in you, giving you the desire and the power to do what pleases him."

Chapter Sixteen
The Battle Plan

Nightfall had now covered the Father's unified army. After an exhilarating time of praising the Father and dancing together, Samuel, Shear-Jashub, and Ruhamah had settled in next to their Forever Friends and had quickly fallen asleep.

Ruhamah now stirred and opened her eyes, gazing upon the moon and the brilliant display of stars shining towards the earth and lighting the ground around her. Shamar's massive head was resting beside hers. Ruhamah moved her head slightly to marvel at all the sparkling crystals and golden flakes lying on the ground around the fire. Parts of the ground had pools of crystal liquid where Shear-Jashub had been dancing.

The princess yawned and slowly arose, not wanting to wake the others yet. The dawn would be breaking through the night sky shortly. The young girl knelt down beside a small pool of the shining liquid. The moon and stars were illuminating the pools, creating a shimmering effect upon the crystal water.

Ruhamah scooped some of the crystal water into her hands and took a drink. The water was cool and refreshing. She crawled over to another spot and scooped up more water. Ruhamah looked into the sparkling water and saw her illuminated reflection shining back at her in the crystal liquid. She could see the dirt and dust streaks upon her pale skin. The princess splashed water onto her face again. The water felt so wonderful and refreshing. She kept speaking softly in her own special language to her Father.

Ruhamah was so grateful that she now had friends who would stand with her—friends who believed as she did. She had been a remnant of hope for so long by herself. The people in Zion had so quickly lost hope. Suddenly, they just didn't seem to believe the warriors would come, or that they even existed. The princess had held fast to the promise from the Father. She had remained loyal to His words. Only Ruhamah was left standing in belief.

Ruhamah found more crystal-clear water and splashed it onto her face, removing the tears that were quickly falling. She had found her tribe—others who would fight with her. Ruhamah looked over at the mighty warriors. They were each so powerful and noble. She looked down at her torn brown dress. It was soiled with dirt and smoke. She thought of the sins the people had committed and tried to erase them from her mind, though they lingered, making her feel soiled in their sins too. A strain of hair fell across her face. She noticed her long black hair was now scraggy and unkempt.

Ruhamah didn't care how she looked; instead, she wondered what gifts were inside of her. What had the Father given her to fight Beelzebub? She felt simple and plain. What could she possibly do to help these great warriors fight this battle? She wanted to join in with them; waging war against an enemy she despised—an enemy that had stolen her people, her family.

A gentle wind blew. It blew only around Ruhamah. She felt a stirring in her heart. She stood up and examined herself. Her hair was still tangled, her clothes still soiled, but in her heart she felt a well pumping forth new blood, new strength. Something inside her was building, bubbling up.

FOREVER FRIEND

The young girl looked towards the darkened, star-filled sky. The stars were more numerous than during any night she had ever remembered. Then the stars began to part in the black sky. She rubbed her eyes and looked again. *Could this be happening?* she wondered.

In awe, she watched as an opening in the night sky appeared. A glorious light like none other shone forth. Out of the light came beautiful beings.[1] Some were riding on horses of fire, and some were being carried on chariots with wheels of blazing fire.[2] As the glorious beings moved through the night sky, a burning fire trail streaked behind the chariots. Other beings were dressed in an armour unlike any on earth—far more magnificent than Shear-Jashub or Samuel's. All the beings were gigantic in stature.

The young girl continued to stare, as she observed glorious angelic hosts coming forth bearing a long, flowing cloth of silk. The cloth seemed to be endless as it came down from the night sky. The cloth carried living sparks of life. Gold and silver were bouncing off the cloth, with crystals moving on it. Ruhamah could see through the cloth, yet its beauty appeared strong. The cloth was mostly transparent, with gold and silver threads woven throughout its fabric.

The army of the Father came forth and began to dance around her sleeping warrior friends. Ruhamah could barely believe her eyes. Shear-Jashub and Samuel both began to stir. Shear-Jashub raised his arms above his head and released a loud yawn. As he stretched, he took his foot and tapped Samuel on the back. Samuel was still nestled up closely to Ruach. The older warrior nudged him again, only harder. Samuel turned over and threw some gold-dust and sparkles at his friend. "Okay," he murmured. The two sleepy warriors sat on the ground, gazing out into the darkness, totally unaware of the majestic army which had joined them.

Ruhamah looked beside her, and there stood the most glorious angel of all. His dazzling apparel gleamed like lightning.[3]

THE BATTLE PLAN

"I am the commander of the Father's army."[4] The angel's words echoed, as if it spoke into a valley. "You wondered what gift you have been given from the Father." The large angel pointed towards the Father's army. "Your gift is that of a seer. Not all will see into the realm of the Father. He has given you the gift to see what others overlook.[5] Your gift is also that of faith.[6] For in faith, you have held fast to truth."

The large angel smiled down at the young girl. "The Father has chosen you, Ruhamah, to speak His battle plan. You have a very important place in His army. Since you held onto the Father's words believing, you will now speak the words given to you by the Father. You will bring forth for the Father the battle plans which will defeat the enemy of your people—for the Father love's, Zion."

Ruhamah looked at her still-soiled clothes. She looked at the most magnificent angelic being she had ever seen. Her humanity was now humbler and more fragile then ever before.[7] Ruhamah fell to the ground. "Please, make me worthy of all the Father desires of me!"

"You are worthy, my child. Do not look at yourself with your earthly eyes—look at yourself as the Father sees you. He sees you in all His glory and strength!"

Ruhamah wiped the tears from her eyes. She stood on shaky legs and glanced down at her dirty bare feet. "See myself as the Father sees me?! Father, how do You see me?"

Instantly she was transformed into true royalty—a human jewel. Her dress was now the same splendid cloth that had been brought down from the heavenly skies. She was a princess, dressed in a gown woven with gold.[8] Her hair was silken, and glowed with gold, purple, and amber, which intermingled with her dark hair. The Father had gently woven into her hair rows of delicate pearls, cascading down her back and around her head. The princess gently touched the pearls when she realized a golden crown had been positioned upon her head. On her feet she wore feathered white slippers that seemed to allow her to float in a heavenly cloud. The slippers had sparkles of silver, which left a powdery presence. When she moved her hands, she noticed each finger held a ring. The Father had adorned her with exquisite rubies and pearls, delicately placed upon her fine small fingers. Her tiny wrists were decorated with jewelled bracelets.

She glanced down and noticed the large pearl necklace she was now wearing. As her delicate fingers touched the smooth, iridescent pearls, she realized a cape was draped across her shoulders. Large purple gems were positioned on top of the cape above each small shoulder, causing the cape to ruffle around her arms. The princess's eyes were captivated by the sparkling large gemstones which glistened as she moved. Ruhamah touched the fabric of the cape and marvelled at the silken texture and shiny metallic shimmer of the cloth. It appeared as though all the colours of the rainbow were dancing within the weave of the garment. The Father had turned her into a true work of art.[9]

"The Father sees me like this!?" She was totally amazed by her splendour.

"The Father began working in you long ago, and He will continue His work until it is finally finished."[10] When you begin to see yourself as the Father sees you, then you will be able to use all He has placed inside you for His glory." The angel smiled at the transformation that had taken place. The glorious being had waited a long time to show Ruhamah the clothing she had long possessed. Now the child was armoured up and ready to partner fully with the Father. "Your Father is *El Roi*, the Father who sees you!" declared the angel of the Father. "He has clothed you with the garment of salvation. He has covered you with the robe of righteousness. He adorns you with jewels."[11]

Ruhamah moved her feet, totally thrilled by the cloud slippers the Father had adorned her with. As the princess wiggled her feet, she began to float up into the air on a pillow of clouds. The angelic hosts began to sing over her. Then she heard the voice of her Father, speaking to her with compassion and love. "For you returned to me and waited for me. You will be saved. For in quietness and confidence is your strength."[12]

"Wow!" yelled Shear-Jashub. "Look at Ruhamah!" He stared at the young girl, who was now floating high above them on her cloud. The princess's hair flowed freely around her, and the purple gems on the shoulders of her cape were radiating beautiful light beams. Ruhamah's gown was waving in the gentle breeze, which had stayed with her.

"Do you see the army of our Father?" Ruhamah asked the two young men as she looked down upon them.

"We are the army!" Samuel shouted, as he quickly stood up and glanced around.

Ruhamah floated over to Samuel and landed beside him. The cloud now disappearing.

"No," she stated, softly yet firmly. "We are but a crystal speck in the army of our Father. We are only a piece in this fight—but an important piece. The crystal which must be in place for the Father's army to come and join us. We are a piece of His battle. The Father, *Jehovah-Sabaoth*, the Lord of armies, has sent his heavenly beings to fight with us. He is the Father of the angelic armies."

Ruhamah took a moment to absorb all the splendour around her. "The Father's love for Mount Zion is passionate and strong."[13]

"Where—where are his men?" Samuel was looking all over for warriors. His eyes strained. He saw nothing except darkness. "And how did you float in the air?" he asked, totally perplexed. "Where did your royal clothes come from?"

Ruhamah placed her small hands, now adorned with rings, on Samuel's eyes. "Oh Father, impart to Samuel eyes to see into Your realm. He already has ears that hear Your voice and a heart that hungers for You. For it is not by might, nor by strength, but by the Father's power."[14]

Ruhamah removed her hands from Samuel's eyes, and he gasped at what he saw. There before him stood millions of warriors, mightier than anything he could have imagined. Suddenly Samuel felt the depth of his own pride and fell to his knees. "Father, forgive me! My strength is in You. My strength is in Your supply, Your power. Father, thank You for Your mighty army. May I be worthy to hold a shield into battle for one of Your magnificent soldiers."

Samuel felt himself being raised to his feet by an invisible force. The beautiful music he had heard before nightfall filled the atmosphere again. Riding on the wind of the music, Samuel once more heard the gentle whisper of His Father. "My child, My grace is all you need. My power works best in your weakness.[15] My son, you have been made perfect, in My image.[16] You will fight with My hosts. You, Samuel, will lead the way. For you, My son, are Judah. You are jubilee; you will go forth first, in a sound of song and praise. You will declare My victory before the battle has even begun. You are my precious star jewel, for you are my treasured possession."

Shear-Jashub had been listening to the conversations, but he had heard only the words of his friends. He didn't see or hear the heavenly hosts, or the whispered words from the Father on the wind. Ruhamah came over to him, bent down, and placed her delicate hands on his eyes and then his ears. She gently blew into his face. Shear-Jashub felt the gentle breeze, and then he saw the golden sparkles carried on her breath. He looked about in total amazement as he saw the angel armies of the Father. For the first time, the seasoned warrior was speechless. Ruhamah stepped backwards and smiled down at her warrior friend, who no longer had a sleepy look on his face. Shear-Jashub's eyes and mouth were both wide open in awe.

Shear-Jashub steadied himself against his great beastly friend, Shamar, as he rose from the ground. He was wide awake now, to both the natural world and the supernatural world around him. Shamar had been aware of the presence of the heavenly beings and angelic hosts. This was the world all the Forever Friends had come from—and the glorious world Shamar knew would be created here on the earth. The powerful lion placed his huge head against Shear-Jashub, then let out a resounding roar.

Shear-Jashub breathed in all that was around him. "The angels of the Father! You mighty ones who carry out His commands. You armies of angels who serve the Father and do His will!"[17] Shear-Jashub stared upwards at the large army, which seemed to grow in number unceasingly. "We are honoured to partner with you, oh mighty ones."

Shamar released a thundering roar. "It is time, my friends, to do battle. You three are the remnant that remains to fight for the Father." Once more the powerful lion roared, violently shaking his mane. "Shear-Jashub, your name was given to you by the Father. Your name was meant to remind the elders of what was to come. It means 'a remnant will return!'[18] The Father has woven His remnant together."

Shamar began to pace before the remnant as he spoke. "Never was this battle intended to be fought alone. The Father has always planned for you to battle with the help of the heavenly hosts.[19] The Father has sent His great Tsebaah, a humongous army of angels, to partner with the remnant.[20] The Father had to wait for the pure in heart, for those who were without spot or wrinkle.[21] He has chosen you and set you apart from the very beginning of time."[22]

"The time has now come for the battle of all battles."

The large glorious being smiled down at Ruhamah and handed her a large scroll. The young girl placed the scroll near her heart and praised the Father, proud to declare the battle plan. Ruhamah then carefully opened the ancient scroll and spoke with gentle authority. "We will attack at morning light. We will be in place before the first ray of light is birthed. Samuel will go forth first, for he is Judah. He will sound his ram's horn repeatedly. Samuel will march around the city of Zion, announcing the presence of the Father, *Jehovah-Sabaoth*, and his angel army." With the speaking of the Father's name, *Jehovah-Sabaoth*, the angelic host began to cry out "Holy, Holy, Holy!" Ruhamah looked upwards towards the massive army of the Father.

When the worship softened, she continued declaring the battle plan.

"Ruach will go with Samuel. His crystal pellets will fly and protect Samuel from any fire or smoke from Beelzebub. The pellets will cover Samuel in an impenetrable seal of diamond strength. Samuel and Ruach will give praise and thanksgiving to our Father."

Ruhamah looked up at the angelic being who had first spoken to her and had given her the battle scroll. She continued to gaze upon the glorious angel. "The armies of our Father know their place and positions. They receive their orders from the Father, and will take their stand above us, fighting in the spiritual realm." The beautiful young princess smiled as she paused, acknowledging the angelic hosts.

"Shear-Jashub, you will march further back from Samuel. Gimel will protect you with a current of wind from his mighty wings. The wind will keep all evil from touching even a hair on your head. You will dance, and sparks of fire will be ignited by your feet. The fire will begin to break down the hold Beelzebub has on our people. The fire from your feet, from your steps, is pure love—love from the Father, which Beelzebub cannot tolerate." The princess smiled as she read the next part of the scroll. She looked up at the warriors. "Beelzebub cannot hold out against love. Once love touches the grip he has over Zion, he will have to leave. His evil claws will retreat!"[23]

"Behind Shear-Jashub, a distance away, I will walk, declaring my faith in the Father. Declaring His goodness and our victory. The heavenly cloth is that of righteousness. Righteousness will flow over all of us as the cloth surrounds all of Zion. We will all march, dance, sing praises, and release shouts of joy and victory to our Father as we encircle the city. Love will be unleashed!" Again Ruhamah paused. "The heavenly host will accomplish the will of the Father. Dunamis will gallop around us. He knows his position, and has battled Beelzebub many times before. Shamar will be working closely with the Father and declaring His orders to the heavenly hosts." Ruhamah returned the scroll to the radiant being.

"We will prepare now in song, praise, and paga," continued Ruhamah. "The battle plan has been given. We are the remnant which has endured. We are the ones born for such a time as this," said Ruhamah as she reached out and stroked the thick mane of her enormous friend Shamar.

The group stood in silence as they listened to the music of the heavenly choir from above. The sound was like none they had ever heard. The angels were repeating the word *Elohim* over and over again. Then other names of the Father could be heard coming from the hosts of heaven. "Holy, Holy, Holy," was mixed within the names of the Father.

Shear-Jashub could stay still no more. He beat his hands against his legs and chest in rhythm with the heavenly hosts. His feet began to dance wildly.

Samuel let out a war cry. His tongue suddenly seemed to move once more in unusual ways. The warrior continued making utterances and phrases he didn't understand.[24]

FOREVER FRIEND

Samuel smiled as strength arose inside him.[25] The warrior remembered the sounds that came out of him in the valley of dryness, when His Father had touched him. He realized he too was able to speak in his own secret, special language to the Father.[26]

Ruach rubbed up against Samuel's leg. Samuel glanced down at his Forever Friend. Ruach smiled and nodded in approval. The words continued to flow out of Samuel's mouth. He didn't have the capacity to stop them, nor did he want to. Louder and louder he exclaimed the new syllables and sounds. The warrior knew powerful sentences were being spoken.

A fragrant perfume enwrapped them all, as if a meadow of flowers was releasing its scent. Ruhamah smiled at her surroundings. She breathed in deeply, wanting the aroma to fill every part of her being.

The wait was over. The endurance had been worth everything it had taken from her. The victory was already sweeter than any she had hoped for, pagaed for. As she breathed in the sweetness of the air, she began to dance in a soft wave of grace. The end was near for evil. A new world was about to be birthed on earth.

***

"Hold onto that cover! Do not let go!" The little Spittles were shaking violently as they held onto the black shroud of evil over Zion. "Do not release your grip!" demanded Beelzebub. Some of the Spittles were shaking so violently they actually evaporated in a puff of dust. The worship from the remnant was affecting the atmosphere inside of Zion. The music was invading the darkness. Beelzebub had his scrawny little hands over his ears, trying to muffle the noise.

"I hate that detestable noise! Everyone, keep gripping the evil blanket of darkness. Awwwww!" yelled the beast, as he moved deeper into the center of Zion to avoid the sound of praises to the Father.

THE BATTLE PLAN

Questions to Contemplate

1. Ruhamah felt simple and plain at the beginning of this chapter. Have you ever felt like this? Ephesians 2:10 says *"we are God's masterpiece."* Can you draw a picture of how God sees you?

2. Ruhamah was told her gift was that of a seer. Can you explain this gift?

3. Why are the three main characters referred to as a remnant?

4. Where else in the Bible did people march around a city?

5. The angel told Ruhamah quietness and confidence would be her strength. How can these qualities give you strength?

6. The warriors were each given a specific gift to defeat the enemy. Do you think Samuel's gift of praise, Shear-Jashub's gift of love, and Ruhamah's gift of faith are powerful weapons?

---

[1] Hebrews 1:7: "Regarding the angels, he says, 'He sends his angels like the winds, his servants like flames of fire.'"

[2] 2 Kings 6:17b: "The Lord opened the young man's eyes, and when he looked up, he saw that the hillside around Elisha was filled with horses and chariots of fire."

[3] Luke 24:4: "As they stood there puzzled, two men suddenly appeared to them, clothed in dazzling robes."

[4] Joshua 5:14: "I am the commander of the Lord's army."

[5] 1 Samuel 9:11: "As they were climbing the hill to the town, they met some young women coming out to draw water. So Saul and his servant asked, *'Is the seer here today?'"* (emphasis added).

[6] 1 Corinthians 12:8–9: "To one there is given through the Spirit a message of wisdom, to another a message of knowledge by means of the same Spirit, *to another faith by the same Spirit..."* (NIV, emphasis added).

[7] Isaiah 6:5: "Oh no! I will be destroyed. I am not pure and I live among people who are not pure. But I have seen the King, the Lord of heaven's armies" (ICB).

[8] Psalm 45:13: "The bride, a princess, looks glorious in her golden gown."

[9] Ephesians 2:10: "For we are God's masterpiece. He has created us anew in Christ Jesus, so we can do the good things he planned for us long ago."

[10] Philippians 1:6: "And I am certain that God, who began the good work within you, will continue his work until it is finally finished on the day when Christ Jesus returns."

[11] Isaiah 61:10b: "…He has clothed me with the garments of salvation, He has covered me with the robe of righteousness. As a bridegroom decks *himself* with ornaments, And as a bride adorns *herself* with her jewels" (NKJV).

[12] Isaiah 30:15: "This is what the Sovereign Lord, the Holy One of Israel, says: 'Only in returning to me and resting in me will you be saved. In quietness and confidence is your strength.'"

[13] Zechariah 8:2: "This is what the Lord of Heaven's Armies says: My love for Mount Zion is passionate and strong; I am consumed with passion for Jerusalem!"

[14] Zechariah 4:6: "It is not by might nor by power but by my Spirit, says the Lord Almighty" (NIV).

[15] 2 Corinthians 12:9: "Each time he said, 'My grace is all you need. My power works best in weakness.' So now I am glad to boast about my weaknesses, so that the power of Christ can work through me."

[16] Genesis 1:27: "So God created human beings in his own image. In the image of God he created them; male and female he created them."

[17] Psalm 103:20–21: "Praise the Lord, you angels, you mighty ones who carry out his plans, listening for each of his commands. Yes, praise the Lord, you armies of angels who serve him and do his will!"

[18] Isaiah 7:3 & footnote: "Then the Lord said to Isaiah, 'Take your son Shear-jashub and go out to meet King Ahaz.'" [Shear-jashub means, "A remnant will return"]; Isaiah 10:21: "A remnant will return; yes, the remnant of Jacob will return to the Mighty God."

[19] Psalm 91:11: "For He will command His angels concerning you to guard you in all your ways" (NIV).

[20] "Tsebaah, a mass of angelic beings organized for military service, equipped for war." Tim Sheets, *Angel Armies: Releasing the Warriors of Heaven* (Destiny House, 2016), p. 41.

[21] Ephesians 5:27: "…and to present her to himself as a radiant church, without stain or wrinkle or any other blemish, but holy and blameless" (NIV).

[22] John 15:16: "You did not choose me, but I chose you…" (NIV); Ephesians 1:4: "For he chose us in him before the creation of the world to be holy and blameless in his sight" (NIV).

[23] Song of Solomon 8:6: "Set me as a seal upon your heart, as a seal upon your arm, for love is strong as death, jealousy is fierce as the grave. Its flashes are flashes of fire, the very flame of the Lord" (ESV).

[24] Acts 2:4 All of them were filled with the Holy Spirit and began to speak in other tongues as the Spirit enabled them" (NIV).

[25] 1 Corinthians 14:4: "A person who speaks in tongues is strengthened personally…."

[26] 1 Corinthians 14:2: "For anyone who speaks in tongue does not speak to people but to God. Indeed, no one understands them; they utter mysteries by the Spirit" (NIV).

Chapter Seventeen
The Agreement

The drumbeat was slow, steady, and intense. The atmosphere was changing, becoming more and more charged. Samuel could feel the currents of energy in the air. He was Judah, and he would go forth first! What an hour, what a privilege, what an honour! Samuel began his steady march, fearlessly, towards the darkness that was over Zion.

Samuel looked down at Ruach, who was by his side. The now full-grown ram bounced beside Samuel, springing up and down as he walked alongside his Forever Friend. The mighty warrior looked down at his faithful companion[1] and grinned. The ram looked up at Samuel and smiled, his blue eyes glistening. The ram's silken wool flowed up and down. Diamonds were gently rising from the ram and floating up into the air.

Samuel wondered if Ruach knew the intensity of the battle that was to come. He wondered if the ram knew life or death for both of them could come without warning. This was not a game. This was a real, history-changing war.

The ram continued to smile at Samuel. It seemed like his blue eyes were telling a story. A thought suddenly entered Samuel's mind: *As long as I am with you, my friend, and you are with the Father, we are strong together.* Samuel knew this new thought was not his own. *We are a three-stranded cord, Samuel. The Father, you, and I. Nothing can stop us or harm us as long as we are woven together.*[2]

THE AGREEMENT

Samuel scratched his head and looked down at the ram. Ruach nodded his head, his long, thick eyelashes batting up and down as his brilliant blue eyes stared up at Samuel.

"I can understand your thoughts, Ruach?"[3] Samuel asked. The ram looked up at the magnificent young warrior and smiled. This time the ram smiled broadly, showing his pearly white teeth. Ruach's face beamed as Samuel finally understood the bond of their friendship, and the growth that had occurred in the hands of their great Father. The ram continued nodding his head in agreement.

"Yes! We are a three-stranded cord. That's amazing. Nothing will break us from the Father, my Forever Friend. We are both unbreakable and unstoppable with Him."

The drumbeat intensified, this time with the addition of trumpeters. After a short while, harmonizing voices were heard. The angelic host continued to declare "Holy, Holy, Holy" as they proclaimed the names of God.

Ruhamah was now floating in the air. She had become so absorbed in the music she didn't realize she was rising up to the host of angels. Her white, feathered cloud slippers were moving wildly in dance to the sound being birthed.

Shear-Jashub reached through the cloud and grabbed the train of her elegant robe. "Hey, I thought you were walking into battle with us. You've overtaken my position." Shear-Jashub laughed. He loved the enthusiasm of the small girl.

Ruhamah looked about and realized she was floating. She laughed too and lowered herself beside Shear-Jashub. "I can barely believe all that has happened. I thought I had a great imagination, but this is far greater than anything I could have dreamed up!"

"I know. The Father's thoughts are so much higher and greater than ours."[4]

The two walked together for a time. Samuel was a few meters ahead of them, talking to Ruach. The young girl thought about her friend Shear-Jashub, and how long they had known one another. "Shear-Jashub, it seems like you have been with the Father longer than Samuel and I. Have you always been a warrior for the Father?"

Shear-Jashub looked down at Ruhamah and smiled. He reflected a moment on his life, then released a long sigh and took a deep breath. "I have been with the Father awhile," he hesitated, "but not always." Shear-Jashub took another deep breath, looked down at the dainty princess and smiled. He felt compelled to tell Ruhamah the truth. The truth was a magnificent testimony of the Father's love for him—and the Father's search for all his lost children.

"I fell into agreement with Beelzebub." Shear-Jashub looked at Ruhamah again, whose eyes were wide in astonishment. "Yeah, I know—a little shocking isn't it?—but sadly…"—the warrior paused a moment—"…true. My mom died when I was young. It was a really hard time for me. I became confused. I was sad. I was hurt, and then eventually I became angry. Really angry. Angry and upset with everyone. I questioned why my mom had died. I wanted answers, and no one had the answers for me."

The warrior looked up at the star-filled sky. Even now it was difficult to remember, yet he felt he needed to share his testimony. "I had just turned ten when my mom passed away. I was so young. It was hard for me to understand what was happening at the time. I began to hate everyone, and I especially hated my father, who was away at war fighting Beelzebub when my mom died. Another one of Beelzebub's evils came and took my mother from me. It was sickness. The evil disease caught us all off guard. I thought my father should have been there to protect us! To paga for us. Instead, he was fighting for strangers." Shear-Jashub shook his head in disgust. His elegant turquoise feather magnified his movements. "I felt abandoned by both my mom and dad." The warrior kicked the sand under his feet and looked down upon the graceful girl.

Ruhamah tenderly smiled up at her friend. She knew he was recalling painful memories, and wanted to give him all the time he needed. The two walked in silence for awhile.

"After my mom was gone, I wouldn't allow anyone to speak to me or love me. I didn't want anyone to come near. I put up a high wall. I thought if I didn't love anyone, I would never get hurt again. But really, I just couldn't bear the pain of losing anyone else." Shear-Jashub looked up at the multitude of stars.

"There was a deep ache in my heart, and my life became empty. The ache was slowly filled with despair. The emptiness was filled with loneliness and self-pity. Evil and hatred crept into my life, burning and growing within me, within the walls I'd built. I lived in darkness. It was dark because I would not accept the light or love others tried to show me. Hatred breeds hatred. Beelzebub came into my dark world, because that's where he resides. He lives in our darkness, when we shut out others who care. When we shut out love."

Shear-Jashub choked up for a moment. He swallowed hard, not wanting to show his deep emotions. He looked over in the distance at Samuel and Ruach marching together. He was glad he had been able to convince Samuel to fight with him. He was grateful to have the younger warrior in his life. *Wow!* he thought, *how much I've changed from those dreadful days.*

The warrior took another deep breath and began again. "When we shut out others who care about us, evil, resentment, anger, and fear exist to torment us. Isolation and darkness can feel like great friends. But they shouldn't be." The warrior looked down at his feet, remembering how alone and isolated he'd once felt. "Beelzebub then slowly creeps into our pit of despair and keeps us locked in self-pity and hopelessness."

Shear-Jashub kicked some sand as he walked. "Beelzebub slowly told me many lies, because he is the father of lies.[5] It is his identity. I believed them all." Shear-Jashub shook his head. He looked down at the young girl. In her eyes he saw compassion. Shear-Jashub smiled at her and looked away, staring at the darkness over Zion. "It's strange, but I felt empowered by my hatred."

"Ohhh!" Ruhamah gasped as she put her hand over her mouth.

Shear-Jashub looked down at her and smirked. "I know, hard to believe—but sadly, that's the truth. I felt empowered by my hatred, but it was a false sense of power. My hatred continued to grow and boiled over onto all who dared to come near me."

Shear-Jashub continued sharing as he scanned the horizon. "Beelzebub had taken me in. I thought I was safe. I was greatly mistaken! The truth is, no one is ever safe with that monster. He will use and abuse everyone who willingly joins him. His only agenda is for himself. Beelzebub sent me forth to spread and share my evil and my hatred. I told many lies to others. It was actually fun at first, watching others being drawn into deceit. Those who were in the light, but questioning and double-minded,[6] they could be easily led astray." The warrior shook his head, the tall feather on his helmet swaying with the motion.

Shear-Jashub once more kicked the sand and dirt beneath him as they continued on their journey towards the fallen city of Zion. "Anyone— and I mean anyone—near the darkness or approaching the darkness was an easy target for me to persuade away from the light of the Father's presence. They would fall quickly into corruption and become part of Beelzebub's team. Soon many others believed my lies. This may seem strange, but we felt like a family together. We all shared hatred. We all shared our hurts and loneliness. Our pain actually drew us together and formed our bonds. Yet we were, each one, very much alone and still in pain. We didn't receive relief from our sorrow while we remained with Beelzebub, only more pain." Shear-Jashub looked down at the young princess. She was listening intently.

"Then one day, Beelzebub persuaded me to do an unspeakable act. Just before I was to perform it, I felt an unusual presence. I saw a light, and in that light was a beautiful being. The being was very large with glowing white wings. Beams of light radiated all around it. Its face was glowing, so I was unable to recognize any detail. I just knew it was an angelic being of some kind.

"Then within the brilliant light beams I could see the angelic being was holding a box. He stretched out one hand to me as he held it. Then the angel opened the box and a colourful liquid light came out and moved all around me. I felt peace, joy, and love like never before." Shear-Jashub smiled.

"I remember I fell to my knees. Then the angel began speaking to me, saying, 'This is a taste of the atmosphere of heaven. In the presence of the Father, love resides. Choose wisely. Know that what lies ahead for you can be peace, joy, and love—but you must choose them.' The angelic being's voice seemed to boom as it said, 'Love is the greatest.'[7] I was overcome by the experience. These words can't begin to describe the true atmosphere and astonishing phenomenon I was witnessing. Then, as suddenly as the angelic being had appeared to me, the wall of hatred I had built began to crumble. I could feel my heart becoming unravelled from all the toxic feelings of hate, bitterness, anger, and betrayal." The warrior gazed up at the stars again.

Ruhamah took a deep breath in as she looked up at the young man.

"Immediately I realized that what I was about to step into was wrong. It was sin. Sin is waiting to attack and destroy us. We must fight it!"[8] Shear-Jashub shook his head and looked down at his feet. He was remembering all he'd felt on that great day.

He looked over at Ruhamah, knowing she would not judge him. He continued speaking, his emotions stirring. He wanted to share everything with her. He wanted her to know the whole truth of who he was, and how he'd been set free of his sin. "Instantly I fell to my knees and asked the Father for forgiveness. I was ashamed of who I had become.[9] Then I felt the hand of the Father upon me. He immediately picked me up from that dark hole I had crawled into and carried me tenderly to the Tabernacle. The Father gently placed me at the top steps of the Tabernacle. I was filled with joy, thanking Him.

"When I looked up, Ezekiel was standing before me. He was waiting for me in front of the door to the Tabernacle."

"Ezekiel—who is Ezekiel?" asked Ruhamah.

Shear-Jashub chuckled, remembering the first time he'd seen Ezekiel. "He is a trusted friend of the Father. He is magnificent, full of laughter and joy. Ezekiel's first words to me are stamped into my memory. He said, 'How blessed is the one whom the Father chooses to bring near to Him, to dwell in His Tabernacle.'[10] Ezekiel said if I wanted to enter the Tabernacle, I could. The choice was mine. I would be allowed into the home of the Father, or I could return to Beelzebub. Ezekiel said my life would be forever changed the moment I made my decision. I could share the inheritance that belongs to the people who live in the light, or receive the fate that awaits all who do not embrace the Father."[11]

Again the warrior looked up towards the night sky. "The Father wanted to rescued me—me!" Shear-Jashub beat his chest with his hand. "The Father would rescue a confused, angry kid, from the kingdom of darkness—and He would transfer me into His Kingdom[12] if I chose to enter. Think about that! Think about the trade we get to make!"

Shear-Jashub laughed heartily. "I chose the Father's house, the Father's heart, the Father's presence, and I have never looked back. I know there was some rejoicing going on that day."[13] The warrior continued to laugh, his turquoise feather bobbing up and down majestically.

"Evil still tries to tempt me and trick me." The warrior laughed loudly. He looked down at his young friend walking beside him. The girl's eyes were open wide in wonder. Shear-Jashub winked at her as he continued to smile. "But now I know the smell of evil! I know its stench. I know the source of evil. I know its name. I detest, despise, and hate evil with every cell in my body."

"Amazing! Absolutely amazing!" Ruhamah thought a moment and then asked, "What was it like for you when you entered the Tabernacle?"

"First I had to get through the Tabernacle door. Ezekiel disappeared in a white cloud after I made my decision to enter in. I was alone, yet I felt an invisible force working against me as I tried to open the large heavy door. I cried out to the Father. I told Him I desired Him more than anything else. I wanted more of the invisible love I had experienced. It was like a burning or a hunger inside of me for more of the Father. I began to cry..." Shear-Jashub looked at Ruhamah, raised his eyebrows and tilted his head. "Actually, I sobbed like a baby. I fell to my knees and realized how sinful I had become." Shear-Jashub looked up again into the beautiful night sky. The stars were more brilliant than any night he could remember.

Ruhamah gently touched him on the arm. "Can you share what happened next?" she softly asked.

Shear-Jashub let out a deep sigh. He was still gazing up at the multitude of stars. "It is hard to explain to anyone what happened next. As

I knelt in a heap before the Tabernacle door, a presence came before me—a breathtaking, amazing man. He had the most loving, caring blue eyes, which seemed to look into my heart and soul. The man wore a simple, long, plain white robe and had long, curly brown hair. The most extraordinary golden sash was around His chest.[14] He did not speak, but He heard my thoughts and I could hear His. He told me, 'The thief, Beelzebub, comes only to steal, kill, and destroy. I have come that they all may have life and have it to the fullest.'[15] Then He said that He was the one and only Son of the Father.[16] He had purchased our freedom and had forgiven our sins.[17] He had gone before me and made a way for me to enter into the Father's home. He said He had died on a cross for all of mankind's sins. He actually bore all these sins on Himself. My many sins were included!"

Shear-Jashub shook his head as he looked down at his feet. "He said to me, 'I hold the keys of death and the grave.'[18] That all the sin I had was now washed off of me, because of his death on the cross."[19]

"He said the Father had now forgotten my sins because I had confessed them and asked for forgiveness. I had repented, turned from my sinful ways. He said my sin was as far from me as the east is from the west."[20]

"How... how could anyone do this? How is this possible?" asked Ruhamah.

"The Son of the Father said I had to believe He did this out of His great love for mankind and His love for the Father. Beelzebub had been defeated at that very moment in time.[21] Then the Son went to heaven, to the Father's throne room in heaven where He's sitting right now with His Father. That is where He had come from. He said He prays, pagas for us day and night, so that all of us will come into a relationship with the Father.[22] So we will be able to believe in the Father, to love the Father. The Son is praying for us right now!"[23]

THE AGREEMENT

Ruhamah gasped. "I didn't know about the Son!"

Shear-Jashub grinned as he looked down at the young princess. Her face was full of wonder. "You're not alone. A lot of people don't know about the son & what he did for all mankind. The marvellous Son told me the Father is passionate for us. The Father pursues us with His love. It is the Father's greatest desire that we know Him and love Him. The Father actually longs for us to love Him! Can you believe that? Even more astonishing, the Father is continually thinking about us.[24] Then the man with the loving blue eyes, the Son, said to me, 'Because of My blood, which was shed for all of mankind on the cross, the door to the Tabernacle is now open to anyone who knocks.' I immediately stood up and knocked. The door opened slightly. I squeezed my way through, and there I saw the throne room of the Father."

"Oh, I have so much more to learn about my Father and now His Son." Ruhamah twirled around, her arms outstretched as she gazed into the heavens. "Describe to me what you saw when you were in the Tabernacle!"

"Oh, wow! Where do I begin? There is nothing like it anywhere else in this world. Everything is more vibrant and brighter; more real and alive. There are no words to explain what awaits you inside the Father's house. It's too amazing to describe. You have to see it and feel it for yourself! But I will tell you about the garden."

"What, there's a garden?" The girl's voice rose in wonder.

"Yes! And inside this magnificent garden there is an amazing stream that flows with—get this—crystals bouncing off the top of the water!" The warrior shook his head as he fondly remembered the splendid garden. His turquoise feather moved in sync with his motions. "Every detail of the garden is different from the world we walk in now. Even the stones on the beach are covered in golden specks, and if you skip them across the water, they hop over and over again almost unendingly on the surface." Shear-Jashub laughed, remembering the small firework display which would light up when the rock finally began to sink. How much fun he'd had by the water's edge.

"What?" Ruhamah interjected.

"That's nothing. The trees...." He thought a moment. How would he ever be able to describe the trees? "The trees are not only unique—well, you know that the fruits and leaves I bring to your people are priceless. Their healing qualities are a treasure given to us by our good and perfect Father"[25]

Ruhamah tried to imagine what Shear-Jashub was describing to her. She observed her friend, who had a faraway look in his eyes. Peace was visibly present on his face. Something inside her told her this was pure, without exaggeration—the truth. She too had a burning, a hunger for more of the peace, joy, and love which seemed to ooze out of both Shear-Jashub and Samuel when they spoke about the Father or the Tabernacle.

"Someday I too will enter the Tabernacle!" said Ruhamah with boldness and confidence. "Oh Father, I do want to enter into Your home. I want to meet Your Son! I, too, want to gaze into His beautiful blue eyes!"

Shear-Jashub looked down at her and smiled. "You will have to care for the garden. That is the first responsibility you will be given."[26]

"I will nurture the garden with passion!" Ruhamah said; then she jumped into the air and flew up into the cloth of righteousness. She wrapped herself in the majestic cloth and was comforted by its silken texture and dazzling jewels.

Shear-Jashub smiled at the adorable princess. She too was a great and powerful warrior for the Father—for she had believed what was spoken to her. She tucked the spoken words into her heart and her mind. Great was her faith.

The eyes of the Father were watching His chosen children, who were committed to Him. The Father smiled upon them as He continued to strengthen them. [27]

* * *

Beneath the thick, black blanket of evil, the enemy of the Father was plotting his defence as the little Spittle demons clamped down on the edges of the suffocating blanket. "The mere mortals will try to stop us by crying out to their Daddy. Argh, why didn't you silence them when you had the opportunity at the Tabernacle door?" Beelzebub was again in a rage, grabbing at any of the Spittles who were within his reach. The morbid beast would shake the small beings and then slam them against the closest object. "Over and over again you have failed! Never stop the lies. Never cease confusing the pathetic mortals. Why do I tolerate you failures near my great and magnificent presence?" The beast blew fire from his mouth.

"Where are the creatures from below?" Beelzebub began to laugh. Not just any laugh, but his evil, sinister, menacing laugh. The Spittles knew their master was devising a new scheme. "Where have they sulked off to? I need all my army on high alert! I will not lose this war!" The evil beast now yelled obscenities as he paced back and forth under the cover of darkness. The massive scaly tail with the many spikes banged into anything around the monster. This created an eruption of fear and destruction. No one was safe from the ghastly Beelzebub.

"Creatures of the night, arise—arise from below!" bellowed the nasty beast. "I have a scheme. Mwahahahaha!" Beelzebub began to snicker and then slowly, more evil laughter erupted from the beast. Beelzebub's loud shrieks and ear piercing, hideous laugh began to stir the underworld. The eerie sound awoke the horrifying beings who had been resting in the lower darkness, awaiting their moment to enter the planet's atmosphere. A bloodcurdling roar was heard as the massive creatures from the night moved upwards towards the surface of the earth. They bashed their way through the decay of Zion, splitting the earth beneath the evil shroud of darkness.

The Spittles stood back in suspense. They had yet to witness the effect of this gruesome entangled thing upon the earth. A loud boom was heard. Then another. The resounding sounds shattered the stillness. An unnerving sound of ghastly laughter erupted from the creatures of the night and the gruesome Beelzebub. "Vengeance is mine!" declared the enemy of the Father. The chilling laughter continued on throughout the night as the evil creatures and Beelzebub plotted their destruction against the Father's Kingdom. They were certain of the warriors' impending doom. Having the city of Zion was only the first course in the beast's meal. Dessert would be even tastier for Beelzebub!

Questions to Contemplate

1. The author begins this chapter with, "The atmosphere was changing, becoming more and more charged." What do you think the atmosphere was being charged with?

2. The author named this chapter "The Agreement." Two very different agreements were described in this chapter. Which agreement do you think was the easiest to make? Why? Which agreement is the best?

3. Who do you think the Son is?

4. Shear-Jashub states, "Anyone—and I mean anyone—near the darkness or approaching the darkness was an easy target for me to persuade away from the light of the Father's presence." How do you feel about this comment?

THE AGREEMENT

5. Why do you think the Father's first responsibility for those who enter the Tabernacle is to care for the garden? Who else in the Bible was asked to care for a garden? What happened to them and to the garden?

6. Hebrews 7:25 says, *"Therefore he is able, once and forever, to save those who come to God through him. He lives forever to intercede with God on their behalf."* Interceding is praying on someone's behalf. Jesus is interceding—praying for you right now! How do you feel about this truth?

---

[1] John 14:16: "And I will ask the Father and he will give you another Savior, the Holy Spirit of Truth, who will be to you a friend just like me—and he will never leave you" (TPT).

[2] Ecclesiastes 4:12: "A person standing alone can be attacked and defeated, but two can stand back-to-back and conquer. Three are even better, for a triple-braided cord is not easily broken."

[3] 1 Corinthians 2:10–12: "But it was to us that God revealed these things by his Spirit. For his Spirit searches out everything and shows us God's deep secrets. No one can know a person's thoughts except that person's own spirit, and no one can know God's thoughts except God's own Spirit. And we have received God's Spirit (not the world's spirit), so we can know the wonderful things God has freely given us."

[4] Isaiah 55:8–9: "'My thoughts are nothing like your thoughts,' says the Lord. 'And my ways are far beyond anything you could imagine. For just as the heavens are higher than the earth, so my ways are higher than your ways and my thoughts higher than your thoughts.'"

[5] John 8:44b: "When he [Satan] lies, it is consistent with his character; for he is a liar and the father of lies."

[6] James 1:7–8: "That person should not expect to receive anything from the Lord. Such a person is double-minded and unstable in all they do" (NIV).

[7] 1 Corinthians 13:13: "Three things will last forever—faith, hope, and love—and the greatest of these is love."

[8] Genesis 4:7b: "Sin is crouching at the door, eager to control you. But you must subdue it and be its master."

[9] 2 Corinthians 7:10: "For the kind of sorrow God wants us to experience leads us away from sin and results in salvation. There's no regret for that kind of sorrow. But worldly sorrow, which lacks repentance, results in spiritual death."

FOREVER FRIEND

[10] Psalm 65:4: "What joy for those you choose to bring near, those who live in your holy courts."

[11] Deuteronomy 30:19: "Today I have given you the choice between life and death, between blessings and curses. Now I call on heaven and earth to witness the choice you make. Oh, that you would choose life, so that you and your descendants might live!"

[12] Colossians 1:12–14: "He has enabled you to share in the inheritance that belongs to his people, who live in the light. For he has rescued us from the kingdom of darkness and transferred us into the Kingdom of his dear Son, who purchased our freedom and forgave our sins."

[13] Luke 15:10: "In the same way, there is joy in the presence of God's angels when even one sinner repents."

[14] Revelation 1:13b: "He was wearing a long robe with a gold sash across his chest."

[15] John 10:10: "The thief comes only in order to steal, kill, and destroy. I have come in order that you might have life—life in all its fullness" (GNT).

[16] John 3:16: "For God so loved the world that he gave his one and only Son, that whoever believes in him shall not perish but have eternal life" (NIV).

[17] Colossians 1:14: "…who purchased our freedom and forgave our sins."

[18] Revelation 1:18: "I am the living one. I died, but look—I am alive forever and ever! *And I hold the keys of death and the grave*" (emphasis added).

[19] Colossians 2:14: "He canceled the record of the charges against us and took it away by nailing it to the cross."

[20] Psalm 103:12: "He has removed our sins as far from us as the east is from the west."

[21] Colossians 2:15: "In this way, he disarmed the spiritual rulers and authorities. He shamed them publicly by his victory over them on the cross."

[22] Romans 8:34: "…he is sitting in the place of honor at God's right hand, pleading for us."

[23] Hebrews 7:25: "Therefore he is able, once and forever, to save those who come to God through him. He lives forever to intercede with God on their behalf."

[24] Psalms 139:17–18: "How precious are your thoughts about me, O God. They cannot be numbered! I can't even count them; they outnumber the grains of sand! And when I wake up, you are still with me!"

[25] Ezekiel 47:12: "Fruit trees of all kinds will grow along both sides of the river. The leaves of these trees will never turn brown and fall, and there will always be fruit on their branches. There will be a new crop every month, for they are watered by the river flowing from the Temple. The fruit will be for food and the leaves for healing."

[26] Genesis 2:15: "The Lord God placed the man in the Garden of Eden to tend and watch over it."

[27] 2 Chronicles 16:9: "The eyes of the Lord search the whole earth in order to strengthen those whose hearts are fully committed to him."

Chapter Eighteen

Fearless

They stood shoulder to shoulder. No one spoke a word. Samuel reached for Ruhamah's hand. As Ruhamah felt his touch, she smiled and felt strength enter into her. The strength of unity and oneness. She reached for Shear-Jashub's hand. He was caught off guard by her touch, and jumped into a defensive position. Ruhamah again reached for his hand as she continued to stare at the devastation. Shear-Jashub locked his grip into hers.

Their Father had skilfully pieced them together. They were His remnant. The remnant now had a name: righteousness. For it was the warriors' faith in the Father that put them in right-standing with the Father, *Jehovah-Tsidkenu*.

"You are the remnant," exclaimed Shamar, who moved before the three young warriors. "You were chosen for such a time as this." He looked at each one of them. To anyone else they would have just been three young people—ordinary, insignificant. Yet to the Father, they were His chosen children.[1] They had a purpose. They had a vision.[2] They were fearless.

Shamar let out another loud roar of authority, shaking his noble mane wildly, and then spoke again to the remnant. "The Father has commissioned us to bless you and anoint you." As Shamar was speaking, the heavenly host moved a massive vessel resembling a horn above the remnant. The large horn being carried by the angelic hosts was clear, so the three could see the gold oil that was held within it. The container was poured slowly over the three, dripping down from the sky like thick honey.

The warriors felt the warmth of the oil on their skin. The liquid then penetrated deep into their pores, into their hearts, minds, and souls. Every cell became immersed in the oil from heaven, and a new fragrance began to fill the air. The threesome looked at one another in awe. They could feel their bodies being refreshed and revived. New strength and energy was flowing into them. They were now awakened with an exhilaration of might.[3]

Dunamis spoke now as he cantered in front of the warriors, who were saturated in the heavenly oil. "You are now strengthened with all the Father's glorious power and His might, enabling you with the endurance you will need.[4] May you be filled also with the oil of joy.[5] For the joy of the Father is your strength."[6]

The odour from Beelzebub could no longer be smelled. Instead, a wondrous aroma engulfed them. Scents of cinnamon, lilies of the field, and frankincense were mixed together, saturating the air around them.

Shamar continued to parade in front of the remnant as he spoke. "You have been supernaturally charged!" The magnificent lion released a loud roar and breathed in the aroma of heaven that had fallen upon the mighty warriors. His large wings moved slowly up and down as if his entire body was being rejuvenated with the fragrance from heaven.

The three warriors looked up to the heavenly hosts, who then parted, releasing a beam of radiant crystal light. A loud crack of thunder was heard as lightning simultaneously shot from the heavens. A voice came out of the light and spoke. "You are My fearless children! You are fearfully and wonderfully made.[7] I love you with an everlasting love."[8]

Again, a bolt of lightning was released from the thundercloud above the warriors. "Go forth, knowing I will go with you. Because I love Zion, I will not keep still.[9] I have prepared a way for you in the darkness. I am the bright morning star."[10] The voice thundered from above, reverberating all around. Flashes of lightning and loud bursts of thunder could be heard and seen far off in the distance. The members of the remnant were centred within a mighty storm of glory about to be discharged throughout the land.

Dunamis pounded his mighty hooves on the ground. "The first ray of light will be birthed shortly. Move into your positions. Remain fearless at all times. Fear is the enemy which will destroy you.[11] Do not allow fear into your hearts or minds. Know this: as you resist Beelzebub, he will flee from your presence."[12] The royal horse rose up on his back legs and came down upon the ground with a hard thud. Gold dust burst from his body and danced around him.

"Believe in who you are, heirs to the throne of the King. Identify as heirs, ruling ones![13] You are the warriors of the new day, the new dawn. Go!"

Dunamis shouted, then leaped into the air. His eyes blazed a way for him in the last moments of the darkness, creating a red hue over the remnant. From the distance, the remnant could hear Dumamis exclaim, "Every place that the sole of your feet shall tread upon will be given to you by the Father!"[14] The royal horse's voice boomed throughout the land.

Samuel looked down at Ruach. "It has begun, my Forever Friend. This is the day the Father has made; I will rejoice and be glad![15] Judah goes forth first, in praise and celebration." The warrior began to laugh. The excitement inside his chest, his heart, was uncontrollable. "Your anointing, Father, has made me strong and mighty. You've empowered my life for triumph by pouring fresh oil over me!"[16]

Samuel proudly took a deep breath and blew into his ram's horn. Instantly, the first ray of light began to climb from behind the horizon. The morning light and the morning star were with them. Samuel began his march around the city of Zion as he continued to blow his horn. Joy and excitement energized his steps as he celebrated a victory yet to be created. The blast from the ram's horn grew stronger and louder. By his side was his Forever Friend, Ruach.

***

"Why does he blow that blasted horn?" Beelzebub had his scrawny hands firmly planted over his ears. "I can't stand that noise! Awwww... and the praises, the shouts of joy, aaaaiiiieeee! Keep that blanket as close to the ground as you can," demanded the beast. "I want to drown out as much of the worship and praise as I can. Creatures of the night, get ready. It will not be long now till you will be able to devour those brats! I will tell you when you can attack. Agh... aaah, I can't stand this!" bellowed the monster.

***

The fearless warriors marched tirelessly around the destroyed city of Zion. Theirs was a march of victory and strength. Samuel continued to blow his horn in perfect harmony with the angelic hosts above them. Ruach would shake his silken wool, which formed a crystal barrier of diamond strength. Shear-Jashub danced wildly as Gimel swooped over the flames produced by the warrior's feet, fanning them towards the darkness. Ruhamah danced to her own song of worship to the King as she continued to declare by faith their victory. She was moving between two worlds, both of which held her heart.

The noon-day sun had shone brightly. Now it was mid-day. The warriors were still singing and praising as strongly as when they had begun. Truly, the spirit of might was upon them.

Then, without warning, the ground beneath the young warriors began to violently shake. The dry land moved and shifted with a laborious groan. The sound of the enemy army was rising. Evil was beginning to reveal its ugly head. The noise of growls, piercing screams, and hideous cries arose from the underworld. The earth broke open in large, wide cracks. The jagged openings were spewing out embers of hot black coals. Smoke and a foul odour arose from the depths of the earth.

Dunamis flew towards the warriors. "Do not be frightened. Do not hold onto fear!" The muscular horse flew over all of them, releasing a wind of strength from his miraculous, glassy, white-feathered wings.

The shaking continued as the warriors tried to steady themselves. The ground beneath them moved forcefully. The movement was unrelenting, but the remnant kept hold of the words from Dunamis and did not fear. They remained steady as they marched on the shaking ground.[17]

Ruhamah looked up into the sky. She noticed the angels of the Father were battling with large ghastly black monsters and evil beasts. The black beings were chanting the word, "doomed, doomed, doomed," over and over again, with their hollow voices echoing into the void around them. The unnerving wails, screeches, and hisses were reverberating with the repeated word. All the repulsive beasts were moving quickly to and fro, yet they could not get away from the larger, invincible angelic force.

The angels all held swords of brilliant light and were moving them in rhythm and splendour. As the beasts were screaming, the angels in the chariots of fire spoke commanding words from the Father's book. Ruhamah's eyes were drawn to the Father's book, which the radiant angels were holding open. Flashes of lightning were released from the pages of the glorious document. Out of the lightning, words from the Father's book could be seen visibly entering into the gruesome beasts. The evil creatures would scream in agony as the words touched them. Then they would disappear in a puff of black smoke as simultaneously the ground beneath them shook.[18]

The warriors continued to march and dance for the Father. The trembling of the earth made the movements of the warriors more difficult, but they continued on, undeterred. Samuel looked over at the city of Zion and noticed whenever he blew his ram's horn in a particular rhythm, the black blanket of evil would release a portion of its death grip on the city. There was now a small space between the ground and the suffocating blanket of darkness. Each time Samuel played his horn with the particular rhythm, the crevasse grew slightly larger. Samuel continued to blow his horn, not knowing exactly what impact the rhythm was making on the enemy. He just knew whatever was happening was for the glory of the Father. *If the Father is for us,* Samuel thought, *then who could possibly be against us?*[19]

A loud groan and then an ear-rending scream was heard. The earth suddenly shook with extreme intensity. The warriors stopped and stood wobbling, staring at the black blanket of evil. As the ground continued to vibrate, five immense devil heads rose out of the blackness. The heads had burst out of the blanket of darkness. Each head was screaming and raging war against the young warriors of the Father. The entangled creatures of the night had been released!

The heads and necks of the entangled creatures moved separately from one another; attached to one large scaly black body. The blanket of darkness was encased around the torso of the massive, bulging body. The thick necks of each of the beastly heads would suddenly become long and lunge towards the remnant. The monstrous heads bellowed out snarls and roars while spewing slimy drool from their open mouths. The creatures repeatedly charged, screaming loudly and thrashing their heads violently as they spat slime at the warriors. Their evil mouths were wide open, revealing rows and rows of brownish, yellow teeth, anxious to devour all who stood with the Father. Upon the grotesque heads appeared horns which released thick, toxic smoke and steam.

Shear-Jashub wasted no time to engage in battle. The seasoned warrior placed his fingers in his mouth and whistled loudly for Gimel, who flew instantly to his side. Shear-Jashub jumped on the back of his large Forever Friend. Gimel immediately leaped into flight. The giant eagle dove brazenly at one of the devil heads. He used his razor-sharp talons to slash at the beast, tearing shreds of scaly black skin from the evil creature.

Shear-Jashub quickly grabbed a fireball from his sack. Holding onto the blazing ball, the warrior took precise aim at the beast. With a powerful and steady arm, he threw the fireball at the head of the monster. The insidious creature looked up, wailing in rage, as the fireball began to eat away at its armoured scales. The smell of burnt flesh filled the air. The demon, undeterred and looking upward, steadily moved toward Shear-Jashub and Gimel. Fearlessly, the duo rose high into the air and plummeted with supernatural speed towards the demon.

The eagle's talons opened and then clamped down, gouging the eyes of the evil creature. The monster let out a terrifying roar. Yellow-green pus gushed out of the morbid beast's eyeballs. Shear-Jashub and Gimel again soared upward, preparing to take aim at another beastly head.

Samuel had watched as Shear-Jashub gallantly jumped onto the back of his majestic eagle. Samuel looked down at Ruach. The ram smiled lovingly up at Samuel and blinked his large blue eyes innocently. "Hmmm," Samuel said as he rubbed his chin and thought. "Do you think you can carry me into battle?"

The ram nodded his head yes. Ruach opened up his impressive fluorescent dragonfly wings with amber burning through them. The amber glowed brighter now, almost blinding Samuel's eyes. The ram looked back at his wings, beamed, and then smiled at Samuel. Gentleness, love, joy, and loyalty[20] were just some of the many qualities Ruach possessed.

Samuel grinned as he looked at his faithful Forever Friend, then jumped onto his back. The valiant warrior's legs were bent, and his feet still touched the ground. *Will I be too large and heavy for my Forever Friend?* With that thought, the ram leaped swiftly and effortlessly into the air, quickly joining the war.

Laughter rang out loudly. Samuel raised his sword above his head, musing inwardly as he found himself laughing in the face of his enemy. The two rose up into the battle zone. Samuel did not need to worry about his Forever Friend—he knew Ruach would fight with him till the end. Samuel realized the ram was so much stronger and braver than he appeared. The warrior also recognized the purest qualities of strength were found within oneself, not dependent on one's outer appearance.

Samuel placed his shield in front of himself. His sword was in his right hand. The ram's horn was now tucked securely into the sheath which usually held his sword. Samuel was prepared and eager to do battle. He didn't have to think about his actions or his motive. Now that his heart was right, he was ready to fight without question. His burning love for the Father propelled Samuel into action. He was a warrior for the King, for his Father!

The two quickly gained height over the evil heads. Samuel held tightly to his shield and aimed it at the beasts. The colours seemed to know what to do, as if they were reading the movements of evil on their own. Fire and lightning burst forth from Samuel's shield.

Samuel glanced over at Ruhamah, who was standing on the ground. One of the beast's heads was coming extremely close to the young girl. Ruhamah was standing perfectly still. It appeared she was speaking to someone and not engaged in the battle.

Samuel was concerned for the princess. Would she be caught off guard? Had she stumbled into distraction? The second form was hard for Samuel to see—he couldn't quite make out who Ruhamah was talking to.

The warrior aimed his shield towards the devil heads, releasing more lightning strikes.

Samuel quickly glanced down again. The form he had seen with Ruhamah appeared to be a man.

As Ruach continued to soar over the battle zone, his diamond pellets were being released and forming an impenetrable shield against the toxic vapour rising out of the horns of the beasts. Samuel quickly glanced towards Ruhamah once more, his concern for her safety mounting. He was fearful the beast would destroy the princess.

Just as his concerns about Ruhamah became intense, the warrior was instantly sucked into the mouth of one of the giant heads. The warrior looked around and realized where he was. The rows and rows of brownish yellow teeth were chewing only a few feet away—he was close to being eaten alive. The repulsive smell made Samuel want to gag. He saw dewy saliva dripping inside the mouth of the beast with black bugs moving throughout the slime. The warrior could hear the sound of sucking as the black bug-like creatures moved about inside the slime.

Then Samuel heard a different sound—voices. As the warrior looked around, he saw small creatures that resembled puffs of vapour. The black vapours were yelling out at Samuel from inside the large creature's throat. "Stupid, worthless, fool, defeated, loser, doom, doom, doomed," they all began to bellow together. The little vapours' menacing laughter erupted as they continued to chant. "Now you are ours! Defeated! Doomed, doomed, doomed! Ours! Ours! Ours!"

Flying above the creature, Shear-Jashub noticed Samuel's predicament and impulsively flung a fireball down the open throat of the beast. The beast immediately coughed Samuel and Ruach out. Samuel looked down at the still-open mouth and noticed drool dripping from it. The morbid creature licked its jagged yellow teeth, looked up at Samuel, and hissed. A red tongue extended from its mouth, jerking back and forth.

Dunamis flew over to Samuel. "Do not allow fear to enter your body, mind, or soul. It is the tool of our enemy. Remember who you are! Keep your thoughts fixed on the Father."[21] Dunamis flew around Samuel once and then went back to the battle which raged above them.

Samuel again looked down at Ruhamah. The ram was now hovering in the air a safe distance from the beastly heads. Samuel watched as the evil creature lunged at the young girl, coming frighteningly close. But when the beastly head was inches away from Ruhamah, she opened her mouth and spoke. Samuel noticed she was not speaking in anger, fear, or hostility—he could tell Ruhamah was calmly speaking the same word over and over again. The ghastly beast could not fight her. The word from her mouth was paralyzing it. The beast released a blood-curdling scream, became a puff of black smoke, and vanished from sight. Samuel was totally astonished.

"Samuel, I could use a little help over here." Shear-Jashub and Gimel were caught between the four remaining giant heads. The beasts were lunging at them and drooling. Slime fell from their horrible faces and dripped onto the black blanket of evil which was directly beneath them.

The image was nauseating. "Ewww," Samuel exclaimed, trying not to throw up. The warrior swallowed hard and concentrated on the battle and his identity in the Father.

The four heads surrounding Shear-Jashub roared loudly, snarled, and displayed their razor-sharp teeth. The heroic warrior was being tossed about in gusts of grey air from their putrid breath. The creatures were gloating as they taunted the warrior, throwing Shear-Jashub and Gimel back and forth in currents of toxic airwaves. Gimel was having difficulty controlling his flight, as the moisture from the putrid breath of the beasts was saturating his feathers. Moving his wings became strenuous. The impenetrable wind of protection was slowly diminishing.

Samuel remembered the words Dunamis had spoken. "I am a warrior for the Father! Immanuel!" he proclaimed loudly. The word came out of Samuel's mouth without hesitation, declaring the presence of the Father. He and Ruach ascended high into the sky and came soaring down, plunging into the gray air currents of evil. Now the two warriors were back-to-back. "Two will stand strong together,"[22] Samuel stated to Shear-Jashub.

Shear-Jashub was barely able to hold onto Gimel as they were propelled violently through the repulsive currents of bad breath. The warrior's helmet and turquoise feather sat crookedly on his head. Shear-Jashub looked over at Samuel, baffled. He crinkled up his face at his friend's response. "Thanks for the words of encouragement, but how about some fire action to back up your words?!" The older warrior straightened himself on Gimel and continued to fling his fireballs at the hideous monsters.

Samuel grinned. He skillfully used his shield to hurl lightning bolts and fire bursts at the beasts. Not one of his bolts of lightning or bursts of fire missed. *Wow!* thought Samuel. *It's like I have favour for perfect aim. Nothing wasted and nothing misses!*

Samuel then remembered his ram's horn. He took it out of the sleeve and drew in a huge breath. The warrior of Judah let out a loud trumpet blast. The beasts all shrank back to the black blanket of evil, groaning in agony. The sound from the ram's horn was both deafening and painful to the evil creatures. "Yeah! Everything is possible with the Father!"[23]

Samuel watched as Ruhamah ran fearlessly toward the blanket of evil. She seemed to be holding the hand of another person as she ran. Samuel heard the voice of a man yelling, "Come!"[24] to Ruhamah. The person was hard to see clearly, but Samuel thought it was a man wearing a plain, long white robe with a gold sash across his chest.[25]

Quickly, Ruhamah and the man ran up to the monstrous heads now lying on the blanket of evil. The beasts were clearly still in pain as they rocked their massive heads back and forth, groaning. The princess spoke her powerful word again. Samuel was amazed as each of the heads became paralyzed. The creatures each let out one last terrifying roar and then vanished in an immense puff of black smoke. The smoke rose high into the air and completely covered the warriors and their Forever Friends. Very, very slowly the filth descended towards the ground, landing on the blanket of evil.

The two warriors looked down at the young Ruhamah, amazed at what had just transpired. Samuel quickly looked around and realized the mysterious figure was now nowhere to be seen. Ruhamah smiled innocently up at them. "I think we won that fight," announced the princess softly as she straightened her crown and adjusted her large pearl necklace.

The two warriors looked at each other and then back down at the girl. The young men were covered in black smoke and soot, but the princess was immaculately clean. The warriors' faces had been smeared with ashes. They looked at each other and began to laugh and laugh. The soot was puffing off them as they continued their belly laugh.

"You both look like mighty, fierce warriors to me," Ruhamah stated proudly.

"You are one precious jewel," proclaimed Samuel.

"A lifesaving jewel," said Shear-Jashub as he continued to laugh.

The two warriors descended to the ground and dismounted their flying friends. The soot-covered warriors brushed the filthy residue from their noble armour. Gimel and Ruach shook the black ashes off their bodies.

The trio stood now looking at each other, then, at the same moment in time, they all said out loud, *"No fear!"* The three laughed and hugged each other.

Ruhamah fell to the ground and praised the Father. "Our lives are in His hands, and He keeps our feet from stumbling!"[26]

Samuel looked all about himself. The devil heads were gone, but the black blanket of evil still held the people of Zion hostage. Samuel began to praise his Father for the first victory. "Father, thank you for protecting us with your shield of love."[27]

Shear-Jashub was dancing wildly to his own music in his head. He was shouting glorious words of praise in his own special language.

As the remnant was praising the Father, the angelic army symphonized into the exaltation, declaring the names of the Father. "Holy, holy, holy" resounded from the heavens.

The word "mighty, mighty, mighty" entered in harmony.

The warriors looked up and saw the cloth of righteousness. The angelic armies had hooked their enemies and pulled them into the cloth of righteousness.[28] The creatures of evil were all captured and entangled within the heavenly cloth. The beady eyes of the multitude of vapour puffs were bulging open in horror. The sound from the angelic army was intensifying. "Holy, holy, holy, is the Lord of heaven's armies! The whole earth is filled with his glory!"[29] was proclaimed as the drumbeat grew steadily more intense and powerful.

Shamar flew directly above the remnant. "Dunamis and I will take the enemy back to the lake of eternal fire.[30] The battle continues on in the city. All that is evil must be returned to the lake of eternal fire. Nothing can remain that is evil. Leave nothing unturned. All iniquity must be destroyed. Only the pure in heart and righteous can remain.[31] There are no exceptions."

The heavenly cloth of righteousness continued to hold all the screaming, evil creatures. The angelic army was positioned around the creatures. The words proclaiming the Father's goodness were being declared loudly, tormenting the hideous beasts. Suddenly a rumbling sound was heard, accompanied by a deep groaning from inside the earth. The three placed their hands over their ears, for the noise was so great.

"Look!" cried Ruhamah. She pointed to the earth that had opened up. A large dark chasm appeared in the ground. The area was as large as all of Samuel's tribe's community. The warriors stood astonished as they watched the armies of the Father, who had captured all the demons in the cloth of righteousness, now descend into the large black hole. The screams from the demonic realm could be heard as the evil creatures were brought back into the darkness from where they had emerged.

"I want to see into the pit!" yelled Shear-Jashub. He began to run towards the opening in the ground. Ruhamah and Samuel followed close behind. Screeches, howling, wailing, and gnashing of teeth could be heard from within the ground.[32]

The remnant stopped, inches away from the depths of the abyss. Thick smoke was rising from inside the earth, carrying the disgusting stench of death and evil.[33] The warriors looked carefully into the chasm which seemed to go on forever. The screams coming from inside the pit were frightening. They could hear the wailing of a far greater number then those who had just been cast into the lake of eternal fire. An eerie chill came over the warriors.

"Ruhamah, what do you see?" asked Samuel.

"I see a large black hole," she responded slowly, studying the depths.

"Well, I see that—what do you see beyond that, in the supernatural realm?" he asked anxiously.

"Only a large black hole with foul smoke rising. I do not believe we are to see what is inside the pit. I believe it is too evil for our eyes, even our spiritual eyes."

"She is right!" declared a gentle voice.

The three turned in amazement and saw Ezekiel standing before them in all his splendour. His cape now vibrated with the colours it held. His dark skin seemed to have more gold sparkles then the warriors remembered, alive and dancing on the Father's friend. Laughter erupted from the belly of the eccentric, stately man.

Ruhamah stared at Ezekiel as he stood laughing heartily and towering over the remnant. She was thrilled to meet the man both Samuel and Shear-Jashub had spoken of so highly.

The large, tall frame of Ezekiel bent down and embraced the three friends. They all hugged one another and gave cheers and shouts of joy. Then the remnant shared their adventure of conquering the five-headed beast. The young warriors gave all the glory to the Father and rejoiced over the victory.

"The Father and I watched from heaven. He is so pleased with all of you. You have each used the gifts given to you with skill and fearlessness.[34] You have worked together as one, calling out in agreement, creating a unity of power, unsurpassable by the evil world of darkness."[35] Ezekiel looked down at the remnant with delight. He tenderly put his hand on Ruhamah's head and touched one of the many pearls woven into her long, dark hair. The peculiar man observed each of the mighty warriors, nodding his head in approval. The friend of the Father grinned and released a booming laugh. "Well done, warriors—well done!"[36]

The tall man looked out at the darkness that encased the city of Zion. "Your work is not finished yet," said Ezekiel. Again his laughter echoed. "You must still destroy all evil within Zion. There still lies a blanket of evil darkness over the great city." The extravagant man gazed out across the large pit. He shook his head in disgust as he squished his nose up. Sniffing the foul air, Ezekiel announced, "Ackkkkkkk, leave the dead to bury their own[37] in the pit; we have work to do. We must leave this place."

The four walked towards the city of Zion. Gimel flew over the blanket of darkness with Ruach. There was no movement within the covering of evil. The air was still—not a breath of wind. Samuel was thinking about how they would release the people from the darkness. Then he remembered that as they were fighting, there had been a space between the earth and the blanket of darkness. It had occured when he'd blown his ram's horn in a certain rhythm. Curiously, he asked Ezekiel, "What do you suggest we do to remove the blanket of evil?"

Ezekiel glanced down at Samuel, his colourful cape moving more wildly than before. A loud giggle erupted from within the imperial statesman for the Father. Ezekiel put his hand on Samuel's shoulder. "You know what to do, mighty warrior of Judah. Where is this powerful ram's horn of yours? The rhythm must be that of before, when you saw the crack appear beneath the darkness."

Samuel smiled. He had suspected this would be the next weapon of war. A rhythm and sound from heaven, purer than any known to man or beast, was soon to be released into the atmosphere.

"Shear-Jashub, I want you to go to the north side of the city. Ruhamah, you must stand on the south side. I will be to the west and Samuel will be to the east. When we are in our positions, Gimel and Ruach will land by their Forever Friends. Shamar will come and be with you, little princess." Ezekiel smiled at the delicate child. "Samuel will know when it is time to sound the ram's horn. Let's get into our positions."

The three young warriors looked at one another. "No fear!" shouted Shear-Jashub. He placed his hand high into the air.

"No fear!" declared Samuel as he placed his hand on top of Shear-Jashub's. Ruhamah looked warmly at her new friends. She smiled and placed her delicate hand, decorated in the Father's jewels, on top of their strong hands. "No fear and strength in our Father. We are united in unity and purity. Clean hands, pure hearts.[38] We go forth with love in our hearts. Love for our people, love for our great Father, and—" her delicate face became serious as she lowered her voice and exclaimed forcefully, "—death to all evil!"

They looked at one another. The remnant gazed into each other's eyes—souls. They had all transformed into young people of integrity, yet there was more work to be done. Evil had not yet been eliminated from the land. They knew their strength was in the Father. They were learning how to pull from His strength and wisdom. They were learning much about themselves and the character of the Father. They were becoming the ripened fruit of the garden.

As the three walked to their positions, the Father's smile radiated on them from heaven.

FEARLESS

Questions to Contemplate

1. The author refers to the Father as *Jehovah-Tsidkenu*. This name of God means "righteousness." What does righteousness mean to you?

2. Do you think joy can be a strength? How?

3. Dunamis said, "Fear is the enemy which will destroy you." Do you believe this to be true?

4. *Immanuel* means "God with us." Why did Samuel shout this name out?

5. Samuel was told to keep his thoughts fixed on the Father while he was in battle. How would this help him?

6. The angelic hosts were reading from the Father's book. What book do you think the author is referring to? What words do you think were going into the beasts?

7. When Samuel sat on his Forever Friend, about to enter battle, he was obviously too large for Ruach. How do you think Samuel felt? Did feeling this way hinder him from moving into battle? Have you ever felt like this? What did you do?

8. Samuel discovered that the strength of a person is not determined by their outward appearance, but what is inside them. How do you feel about this? What quality of strength do you have inside of yourself?

9. The heavenly hosts took the evil beasts to the lake of eternal fire. Do you think this lake really exists? What do you think its purpose is?

10. The remnant was "becoming the ripened fruit of the garden." What do you think the author means by this statement?

FOREVER FRIEND

[1] Deuteronomy 7:6: "For you are a holy people, who belong to the Lord your God. Of all the people on earth, the Lord your God has chosen you to be his own special treasure."

[2] Proverbs 29:18: "Where there is no vision, the people perish: but he that keepeth the law, happy is he" (KJV).

[3] Isaiah 11:2: "The Spirit of the Lord shall rest upon Him, The Spirit of wisdom and understanding, The Spirit of counsel and might, The Spirit of knowledge and of the fear of the Lord" (NKJV).

[4] Ephesians 6:10: "Finally, my brethren, be strong in the Lord and in the power of His might" (NKJV).

[5] Isaiah 61:3: "…the oil of joy instead of mourning…" (NIV).

[6] Nehemiah 8:10: "…for the joy of the Lord is your strength!"

[7] Psalm 139:14: "I will praise You, for I am fearfully *and* wonderfully made; Marvelous are Your works…" (NKJV).

[8] Jeremiah 31:3: "The Lord appeared to us in the past, saying; 'I have loved you with an everlasting love; I have drawn you with unfailing kindness'" (NIV).

[9] Isaiah 62:1: "Because I love Zion, I will not keep still."

[10] Revelation 22:16b: "I am the bright morning star."

[11] Psalm 27:1: "The Lord is my light and my salvation—so why should I be afraid?"

[12] James 4:7b: "Resist the devil, and he will flee from you."

[13] Romans 8:17: "*And since we are his children, we are his heirs.* In fact, together with Christ we are heirs of God's glory. But if we are to share in his glory, we must also share in his suffering" (emphasis added).

[14] Joshua 1:3: "I will give you every place where you set your foot, as I promised Moses" (NIV).

[15] Psalm 118:24: "This is the day the Lord has made. We will rejoice and be glad in it."

[16] Psalm 92:10: "Your anointing has made me strong and mighty. *You've empowered my life for triumph* by pouring fresh oil over me" (TPT, emphasis in original).

[17] Hebrews 12:26b–27: "'Once again I will shake not only the earth but the heavens also.' This means that all of creation will be shaken and removed, so that only unshakable things will remain."

[18] Isaiah 11:4b: "The earth will shake at the force of his word, and one breath from his mouth will destroy the wicked."

[19] Romans 8:31b: "If God is for us, who can be against us?" (NIV).

[20] Galatians 5:22–23: "But the Holy Spirit produces this kind of fruit in our lives: love, joy, peace, patience, kindness, goodness, faithfulness, gentleness, and self-control."

[21] Isaiah 26:3: "You will keep in perfect peace all who trust in you, all whose thoughts are fixed on you!"

[22] Ecclesiastes 4:12: "A person standing alone can be attacked and defeated, but two can stand back-to-back and conquer."

[23] Mark 10:27: "Humanly speaking, it is impossible. But not with God. Everything is possible with God."

[24] Revelation 22:17: "The Spirit and the bride say, 'Come!' And let the one who hears say, 'Come!'" (NIV).

[25] Revelation 1:13b: "He was wearing a long robe with a gold sash across his chest."

[26] Psalm 66:8–9: "Let the whole world bless our God and loudly sing his praises. *Our lives are in his hands, and he keeps our feet from stumbling*" (emphasis added).

[27] Psalm 5:12: "For you bless the godly, O Lord; you surround them with your shield of love."

[28] Ezekiel 38:4: "I will turn you around and put hooks in your jaws to lead you out with your whole army—your horses and charioteers in full armor and a great horde armed with shields and swords."

[29] Isaiah 6:3: "They were calling out to each other, 'Holy, holy, holy is the Lord of Heaven's Armies! The whole earth is filled with his glory!'"

[30] Matthew 25:41: "Then he will say to those on his left, 'Depart from me, you who are cursed, into the eternal fire prepared for the devil and his angels'" (NIV).

[31] Matthew 5:8: "Blessed are the pure in heart, for they will see God" (NIV).

[32] Matthew 13:42: "And the angels will throw them into the fiery furnace, where there will be weeping and gnashing of teeth."

[33] Revelation 14:11: "The smoke of their torment rises forever and ever, and they will have no relief day or night."

[34] 1 Peter 4:10: "As good stewards of the manifold grace of God, each of you should use whatever gift he has received to serve one another" (BSB).

[35] Matthew 18:19–20: "If two of you agree here on earth concerning anything you ask, my Father in heaven will do it for you. For where two or three gather together as my followers, I am there among them."

[36] Matthew 25:21: "Well done, my good and faithful servant."

[37] Matthew 8:22b: "Let the spiritually dead bury their own dead."

[38] Psalm 24:4: "Only those whose hands and hearts are pure, who do not worship idols and never tell lies."

Chapter Nineteen

Holy Beginning

The four warriors stood with their backs to the rest of the world. Their focus was on what lay in front of them. They each stared at the evil blanket of darkness.

Ruhamah thought of her people, who were being tormented by Beelzebub. This was a choice they had made. Her people had allowed Beelzebub to enter Zion through the power of agreement. These were people who once loved the Father, but because of the decision they had made, the Father had no choice but to remove His hand of protection. Beelzebub wasted no time devouring his prey.

Ruhamah knew repentance was the only thing that would release the people from the bondage they were in. *The Father will forgive when the people repent,* she thought. The princess smiled, knowing her Father's identity. *This is the nature of the Father. Yes, the Father's nature is unchangeable, the same yesterday, today, and tomorrow.*[1] *He is Jehovah, the unchangeable, intimate God,* she said quietly to herself as she continued to stare at the blanket of darkness.

The princess was standing on a slightly elevated ridge, overlooking the destruction. Shamar landed by her side. The princess looked up at her Forever Friend, who towered over her, then smiled and placed her delicate hand upon his tawny fur. The lion looked upon the child he had witness mature into her full destiny. Shamar smiled and nodded his head in approval of the transition which had occurred. Then the majestic lion looked out towards the destroyed city of Zion and released a loud roar.

Shear-Jashub grinned as he listened to Shamar's roar. Then he gazed out upon the blackness. There was no life, no sound. Emptiness, darkness, and a putrid smell were the only things that presented themselves. The air was perfectly still. The warrior thought of his own walk, remembering the days he too had given into the ways of Beelzebub. *How easy it is to fall away from the Father,* he thought. The warrior would not condemn the people for their actions, their mistakes. He was here to help them, not judge them. Shear-Jashub remembered the lies he had believed and spread, knowing evil saturated the ground it fell on. He realized now that left undisturbed, evil would creep into the soil of one's heart. There it would methodically suck all life out of its victim and claim territory. He remembered the torment he had once lived in. He sighed. This was now the torment the people of Zion were experiencing. The warrior shook his head slightly, feeling the pain and anguish of the people. His turquoise feather moving slowly, emphasizing his motions.

Then Shear-Jashub though about how he now walked with the Father, as one of His soldiers. He knew his heart had been healed. He had forgiven others, he had forgiven himself, and more importantly, he had been forgiven. He was Shear-Jashub, the remnant that had returned! He had come back from the dreadful world he had once freely entered into. The warrior laughed, his elegant feather moving wildly above his head. *Since the Father allowed me back into the Kingdom of righteousness,* he thought, *I know He will make a way for all the people of Zion to return to Him.*

In the east, Samuel stood at attention. He was thinking about the great wall of fire he had willingly travelled through. He knew he had been strengthened by the hands of his Father.

Samuel smiled now as he continued to stare out over the evil blanket of darkness. "I have been purified in the fire by your great love for me, Father.[2] Here I am, Father—send me![3] Use me for Your good, Your glory."

Samuel spoke the words out of a depth in his heart he was just beginning to understand. His passion for the Father had grown. His desire was no longer to prove himself to the Father— his only desire was to love the Father. It was out of this love that he willingly chose to obey and engage with the Father's will.

Ezekiel stood before the bleak darkness. This was the day he had waited for, in anticipation of splendour. He had watched as all three children had grown into a magnificent cloth of righteousness. The remnant had gathered together to create a cloth of purity and strength. Ezekiel looked up towards the heavens and smiled. His skin was sparkling and gold flecks were dancing off his body, creating a gold dust ball around himself. Ezekiel knew the Father was sitting on His throne, pleased with all He had created.

The Son of the Father was also on the throne. He was sitting at the Father's right hand.[4] He too was pleased with the children. Soon the Son would be coming back. The remnant was unknowingly preparing the Son's bride, who was coming to life. Yes, Zion would be the bride for the King's Son. The Son could feel His heart pounding with love and joy, anticipating His precious bride.

The Son knew all the qualities of His bride, His people. He was aware of all her struggles, her defeats, and her victories. He had prayed for her day and night, unceasingly.[5] Only when she became spotless, with no wrinkle,[6] could the Son begin His wedding march. Now the time was coming close. His prayer for her continued and intensified, creating a burning glory in the heavens unlike any before. The smell was the aroma of pure love. The angelic host were singing praises that had never been heard until now. This was a moment so many had waited for, prayed for, believed in. Heaven would soon be able to touch earth with an everlasting embrace.[7]

Gimel flew down beside Shear-Jashub. The seasoned warrior placed his hand on the back of the powerful eagle. At the same time, Ruach descended to Samuel's side. The ram folded in his glorious amber wings and looked tenderly at the young warrior, his large crystal blue eyes penetrating into Samuel's heart. Samuel smiled as he looked down upon his faithful Forever Friend. The warrior then reached for his ram's horn, which had been provided to him by Ruach with perfect timing. *What Beelzebub meant for evil to harm me,* Samuel thought, *the Father turned around and used for my benefit.* "Wow!" he said aloud.

Samuel looked across the lifeless blanket of evil and admired his brave friends standing at their posts. Then with great honour he brought the ram's horn to his mouth, took a deep breath in, and sounded the alarm. As the single loud blast from Ruach's horn entered the atmosphere, all the world stood at attention and listened. Samuel took another deep breath as the world waited. Then the Father's warrior created the same dominant rhythm he had found in battle. Judah was now in its rightful position.

The rebellious hearts of the people of Zion were being shifted. They would soon be freed. Samuel continued his sound—long and full, the music of victory. The black blanket of darkness began to wiggle. Again, there was a screaming and groaning sound. The ram's horn blast continued its forceful beat. The darkness began to rip and tear apart.

The black blanket slowly transformed into a mass of brown, immense worms wiggling over the city of Zion.[8] The worms could be heard as they slithered and moved among each other in a huge, thick pile. The worms were longer than the warriors were tall. The gross, massive worms were trying to escape from the light. The large, wriggling beasts could not stand the light which was penetrating their bodies. Squirming over and under each other, they wiggled, trying to hide, achieving nothing but the creation of a brown squirming mass. The slime that they secreted as they moved birthed a mass of scurrying black bugs.

The black bugs began to eat the worms and grow in size. The mass of worms now became a pile of black bugs moving quickly over Zion. The bugs made a noise that was painful to the ears of the warriors, for it was a sound from the pit of eternal fire. The warriors placed their hands over their ears as they watched the bugs burrow into the ground. The earth shook as the bugs descended lower and lower into the darkness from where they had emerged.

The warriors stood in disbelief as they looked at what remained. There before their eyes was an enormous pile of bones—old, dry bones with no flesh on them. The bones were heaped in a mass of confusion.

The remnant was unsure what to think. Had the people been completely devoured by Beelzebub? Did the monster suck the life out of everyone? Or had the worms and bugs eaten away the flesh of the people? The remnant stared in apprehension. There was obviously no life in the bones. Were they too late to save the people of Zion? No—this couldn't be. The Father's timing was always perfect.

From the west, Ezekiel began to sing and dance. The gold flecks were dancing with him. His cape was illuminating more and more colours. From their positions, the warriors watched Ezekiel dancing, wondering why he was rejoicing.

"The Father is doing a brand-new thing! Do you not see it?"[9] Ezekiel shouted to the remnant. "He has already begun! Look with the eyes He has given you—eyes from the heavenly realm. This is not the end. This is not death. For you must all breathe life into the bones. You must speak to the bones." Ezekiel continued in his dance of joy as the gold dust grew around him.

HOLY BEGINNING

The three warriors looked at one another over the ruin in front of them. They each wondered how they would speak to the pile of bones. What would they say to bring life into a desert of dryness? The dry bones covered the entire valley floor of Zion. They were scattered in heaps randomly all across the dry ground.

The three warriors looked over at the tall dancing friend of the Father. He was laughing heartily. His joyful chuckle echoed all across the valley of dry bones. Ezekiel danced with shouts of joy and pounded his sceptre on the dry land. All the colours danced around and through the majestic man. Ezekiel could not contain the excitement he had waited a lifetime to experience. He knew the great event that was about to be birthed.

"Ha ha ha!" the captivating man yelled. "Those who wait for the Father, who expect and hope in Him, will gain new strength and renew their power; they will lift up their wings and rise up close to the Father like eagles rising towards the sun. They will run and not become weary; they will walk again and not grow tired."[10]

Suddenly they heard a beautiful sound from heaven. Thunder and lightning were released. The remnant stood in their positions. They knew the voice of the Father was one of strength and love, always entwined together. The remnant now had an unearthly fear, one of respect and reverence for the Father—for the Father's love is with those who fear Him.[11]

The Father spoke to the remnant within the sound of the thunder. "Can these bones become living people again?"

Samuel answered, "Oh, sovereign Father, You alone know the answer to that."[12]

As the thunder and lightning continued, they heard, "Speak to these bones and say, 'Dry bones, listen to the word of the Father! I am going to breathe into you and make you live again! I will put flesh and muscle on you and cover you with skin. I will put breath into you and you will come to life. Then you, people of Zion, will know that I am the Father—the Father who loves you and brings you back to life. I, and I alone, can give you life from death and freedom from the destruction you freely entered into."[13]

The three young warriors looked at one another and nodded their heads in agreement. Shear-Jashub's turquoise feather moved like a baton in the hands of a choir director. They spoke to the dry bones in unison.

From the north, Shear-Jashub spoke with authority and power. His feet began to dance, and the fire of love erupted from the ground beneath his feet. An amber glow began to develop around the warrior, and spread out as the flames progressed. The fire of love began to refresh the dry, parched land.

From the south, Ruhamah spoke. Her words became vivid and could be seen visibly entering into the atmosphere—silver and purple, with gold crystal dancing among them. She joyfully continued to release her words. Laughing with Shamar, she watched her colourful words dancing over the dry bones as she continued to speak. Her words were bringing the provision of the Father that the people had been anticipating.

Samuel stood in the east. He felt a mounting wind come from behind and begin to rise over him. The wind increased and became a gale force. The warrior kept his feet fixed upon the earth, bracing himself against the powerful, rushing wind. Ruach effortlessly steadied himself in the wind, his long, silky wool blowing towards the dry bones. Samuel looked down at his Forever Friend. The wind appeared to be blowing though the ram as if they were one.

Samuel spoke to the bones in a commanding voice. "No weapon formed against the people of the living Father shall prosper!"[14] The mighty wind continued to rise up, off of and out of Ruach. The wind began to howl as it blew over Samuel, sweeping across the valley of dry bones.

Instantly, a rattling noise rose up over the howl of the wind. The bones of each body slowly came together and attached themselves as they had been before, bone to bone. Then the remnant watched muscles and flesh form over the bones. Next, skin formed to cover the bodies, but the bones still had no breath in them.[15]

A wind from the north rose up. It, too, was a mighty rushing wind.[16] Shear-Jashub held onto his Forever Friend, who had gripped his talons deeply into the ground. The warrior's regal turquoise feather was bending over in the windstorm.

Ruhamah heard an interesting tinkling sound. It reminded her of small bells being rung. The noise became a delightful symphony ascending over her. Accompanying the melody was an ascending breeze. The princess glanced down at her exquisite gown, which began to flow in the gentle wind. The current of air increased in strength, moving her long hair wildly about. Her magnificent cape was now fluttering in the current of air.

Ruhamah stretched her arms out and smiled up at the sky. She knew her Father's voice was caressing her. Shamar, too, was smiling upwards. His thick mane was flowing in the breeze.

The Father spoke to Ezekiel within the sound of thunder. "Speak to the winds now and say: 'This is what the Sovereign Father says: Come, O breath, from the four winds! Breathe into these dead bodies so that they may live again.'"[17]

Ezekiel danced in a new, radical splendour, moving wildly. The west wind now began to stir. As it gained in strength, Ezekiel's colourful cape blew violently in the wind. The extraordinary man laughed as the sapphire on the top of his sceptre grew three times in size. The sapphire released lightning and bolts of colours. A thunderclap was heard. Instantly, a blast of air surged up over the Father's friend. The thunderclap resounded throughout the land on the currents of the westerly air blast. Ezekiel laughed loudly, the sound becoming interlaced in the wind currents flowing over the valley of dry bones. Then the peculiar man boldly proclaimed the words the Father had just given him.

The four stood and watched the great display of wind, fire, and heaven's embrace massaging the dry bones.

"Samuel!" Ezekiel yelled. "It is time for Judah to hold the sceptre."[18] Ezekiel threw the royal staff across the valley. The mixing currents of air from the four winds captured the sceptre and spun the majestic rod around, creating a tornado of colour. The sceptre rose towards the heavens in the updraft, and then began to spiral slowly downwards. Thunder flashed above the entire valley of bones, as the kaleidoscopic display of colours produced fireworks above the valley of Zion.

Samuel watched in amazement as the world around him suddenly bust into new life, but the trained warrior didn't take his eyes off the priceless sceptre. As the winds carried the treasure towards Samuel, he reached out and grabbed hold of the golden rod. Immediately, his entire body shook as if lightning bolts were going through him.

Ezekiel chuckled, his laughter echoing throughout the land. The great friend of the Father smiled. The young warriors persevered as the four winds pushed past them with endless fury. The four winds mixed with the words that Ruhamah had visibly spoken.

The flames of love from Shear-Jashub's feet were stronger than the hold of death on the people of Zion. The flames had been birthed from the burning love within the Father's heart for His treasured people.[19] The colours from Judah's sceptre danced erratically over the bones. The

Father's judgement had now released Beelzebub's grip on the people. Breakthrough was being forged—the atmosphere was charged with life.

The four winds entered into the bodies and they began to breathe. They all came to life and stood up on their feet—a great army of people, both young and old.[20]

A flash of white light burst forth with a loud clap of thunder. Then the Father spoke: "I will gather the people from among the nations. I will bring them home to their own land from the places where they have been scattered. I will unify them into one nation in the land. One King will rule them all; no longer will they be divided into different nations. They will stop polluting themselves with their detestable idols and their sins, for I will save them from their sinful backsliding. I will cleanse them. Then they will truly be My people, and I will be their Father, their God.[21] I will give them a new heart with new and right desires, and I will put a new spirit in them. I will take out the stony, stubborn heart, and give them a tender responsive heart. I will put My Spirit in them so they will follow my decrees and be careful to obey my regulations. I will cleanse them from their filthy behaviour, for there will now be a great harvest."[22]

Thunder and lightning stretched out over the valley. The loud bursts echoed throughout the universe. All the eyes of the people of Zion, young and old, were gazing intently upwards at the heavens.

"Beelzebub, your enemy, has turned away from you. I put a hook into his jaw and led him to his final destruction.[23] Now you will know and understand: I am the Lord, your Father, *Abba, God*—the One who is now and forever. I am the *Alpha* and the *Omega*, the beginning and the end."[24]

As the thunder and lightning continued, the angelic beings proclaimed the Father's glory. Overwhelmed by the Father's goodness and mercy, the people of Zion fell to their knees, wailing and sobbing. The repentance from the people filled the air with a sweet smell of freshly picked flowers. The aroma was carried up to heaven in the arms of beautiful angels.

The Father's voice once more spoke to his children. "I will sprinkle clean water on you and you will be clean. Your filth will be washed away, and you will no longer sin.[25] To all who are thirsty, I will give the springs of the water of life without charge. I will be your Father, and you will be My children. But as for cowards who turn away from Me and unbelievers: sadly, their choice will lead them down a dark path into the world of Beelzebub. Only those who choose to be my children can remain with me." [26]

Then a beautiful, brilliant white cloud released the healing rains. It fell gently upon all the people, young and old. An awe and wonder came over the people. They stood mesmerized by the voice of their Father and the cloud, relinquishing its healing rain. The people now all stood, raising their arms towards heaven and singing songs of praise to the Father, for they knew they had been redeemed. The healing rains gently washed all the people until a river was birthed. The river flowed out of the city of Zion and into the desert wasteland.

Wherever the river flowed, great trees grew instantly on the river's edge. Grasses grew beyond the trees, and a meadow sprouted. Then the Father said, "There will be swarms of living things wherever the water of this river flows."[27] Deer burst forth from the meadow and walked towards the river. They began to drink from the water of life. The sky was filled with different birds, all singing songs of praise to the Father.

The Father looked down and smiled upon the earth. "By the river on its bank, all kinds of trees will grow for food. Their leaves will not wither, and their fruit will not fail. They shall bear fruit every month because their water flows from the Tabernacle. The fruit will be for food and their leaves for healing. The river is a gift to My people who call Me by My name—Abba, Father!"

The thunderclouds and lightning bolts continued. The angelic hosts were proclaiming all the names of the Father in every language. A glorious wave of peace had flowed towards earth from heaven's throne.

The cloth of righteousness again descended from the heavens. The angelic hosts were dancing with it as it shimmered, alive with sparkles of gold and silver. Crystals and gems bounced along the cloth, which was placed above the people of Zion. The rainbow of colours from Judah's sceptre held the cloth of righteousness in place, with one rainbow at each end of the cloth.

"Never again will you forget My covenant with you. Never again will you rebel. For now My Son will prepare to come back for His righteous bride. Blessed are those who wash their robes so they can enter through the gates of the city and eat the fruit from the tree of life."[28]

Then the praises of the people rose and became a bright star, which rose above the people into the sky of day. The star would be a visible reminder, day and night, to the people of Mount Zion. The star would be a constant reminder of the Father's covenant with His beloved people, reminding the Bride of how she must now prepare for her wedding march.[29] Yes, the children of Zion would be joyful, rejoicing in their King and in His Son, their soon coming Groom.[30]

The three noble warriors and their Forever Friends walked towards Ezekiel, who was still dancing wildly. The tall friend of the Father looked down upon the remnant, which had been woven into a great and mighty army. Ezekiel's arms opened, and his huge embrace wrapped around all three of the warriors. They stood, looking out at the splendour which had been created in front of their eyes. They gazed upon the goodness of the Father. They felt His love, strength, and power in the atmosphere and within their own hearts.

FOREVER FRIEND

Dunamis landed beside them, his glorious wings moving up and down slowly as the glistening white feathers were being illuminated. They all stood in silence, watching the families rejoicing. Ezekiel's tall frame towered over the warriors as he stood in the middle of the group. Beside each fearless warrior was their personal Forever Friend.

Samuel looked down at his loving ram as his hand firmly gripped the sceptre. Ruach's crystal blue eyes looked up at Samuel and peered through to his soul. The ram smiled a big, beautiful, pearly white grin. Samuel placed his hand on the ram's silken wool and stroked his Forever Friend. *Everyone needs a Forever Friend,* Samuel thought to the Father.

The Father's voice answered back, loud, and clear for all who were listening, for all to hear.

"I am the Forever Friend!" The words burst forth loudly, shaking the earth.

"To all who call upon Me, I will be your everlasting Friend—for I will never leave you nor forsake you. I will make an everlasting covenant with all who cry out to Me. I will never stop doing good for you.[31] Nothing can ever separate you from My love.[32] I am forever love. I am *Jehovah-Rohi.* I am the *Forever Friend.*" The Father's voice boomed loudly as the words "Forever Friend" could be heard echoing around the earth's atmosphere.

Samuel looked over at Ruhamah. He thought about the young girl's part in the battle. "Ruhamah, what was the word you spoke to paralyze and then destroy the five devil heads?" Samuel asked.

The elegant princess smiled at Samuel. Her face shone with a fresh brilliance. She spoke with love visibly flowing from her mouth: "Yeshua. Jesus. I spoke the name of the Son."

HOLY BEGINNING

The Father and the Son looked down from heaven with joy flowing from their hearts! Ruach rubbed his head against Samuel's leg; then the gentle yet mighty ram looked lovingly upwards towards heaven.

The Father, *Jehovah-Shalom*, reigns!

The Amazing End

For a New Beginning

Written by Janice Plumton Chassie

Through the Gentle Whisper of the Holy Spirit

Thank You, Father!

Questions to Contemplate

1. Why do you think the author called this chapter "Holy Beginning"? What do you think began?

2. Do you think the name of Jesus can paralyze and destroy evil? Have you ever called out loud the name of Jesus when you were fearful? What happened?

3. Samuel started out as an ordinary boy and become a brave warrior for his heavenly Father. What quality do you think helped Samuel the most in his transition from boy to warrior for God?

4. Throughout this story, the author uses the word "friend" to describe people, celestial beings, and animals. What does the word "friend" mean to you? Who is your closest friend? Why is this person your friend? Who would you like to make friends with? Is God your friend?

5. Why are the people of Zion referred to as the Bride of the Son?

6. Which character in the story can you most relate to? Can you explain why you relate to this character? Which character was your favourite? Why?

7. What have you learned about your heavenly Father by reading this story? Do you think of God as your Father? What have you encountered about the Holy Spirit? Who do you think represented the Holy Spirit in the story? What have you discovered about Jesus?

8. The author writes, *"Heaven would soon be able to touch earth with an everlasting embrace."* Do you think heaven can touch the earth? What might a picture of heaven touching earth look like?

HOLY BEGINNING

[1] Hebrews 13:8: "Jesus Christ is the same yesterday, today, and forever."

[2] Ephesians 3:18: "And may you have the power to understand, as all God's people should know, how wide, how long, and how deep his love is."

[3] Isaiah 6:8: "Then I heard the Lord asking, 'Whom should I send as a messenger to my people? Who will go for us?' I said, *'Here I am. Send me'*" (emphasis added).

[4] Mark 16:19: "When the Lord Jesus had finished talking with them, *he was taken up into heaven and sat down in the place of honor at God's right hand*" (emphasis added).

[5] Romans 8:34: "Christ Jesus who died—more than that, who was raised to life—is at the right hand of God and is also interceding for us" (NIV).

[6] Ephesians 5:27: "He did this to present her to himself as a glorious church without a spot or wrinkle or any other blemish. Instead, she will be holy and without fault."

[7] Matthew 6:9–10: "Our Father in heaven, may your name be kept holy. May your Kingdom come soon. May your will be done on earth, as it is in heaven."

[8] Isaiah 14:11: "Your might and power were buried with you. The sound of the harp in your palace has ceased. Now maggots are your sheet, and worms your blanket."

[9] Isaiah 43:19: "…I am about to do something new. See, I have already begun! Do you not see it?"

[10] Isaiah 40:31: "But those who wait for the Lord [who expect, look for, and hope in him] Will gain new strength *and* renew their power; They will lift up their wings [and rise up close to God] like eagles [rising toward the sun]; They will run and not become weary, They will walk and not grow tired" (AMP).

[11] Psalm 103:17: "But the love of the Lord remains forever with those who fear him."

[12] Ezekiel 37:3: "Than he asked me, 'Son of man, can these bones become living people again?' 'O Sovereign Lord,' I replied, 'you alone know the answer to that.'"

[13] Ezekiel 37:4–6: "Then he said to me, 'Speak a prophetic message to these bones and say, "Dry bones, listen to the word of the Lord! This is what the Sovereign Lord says: Look! I am going to breathe into you and make you live again! I will put flesh and muscles on you and cover you with skin. I will put breath into you, and you will come to life. Then you will know that I am the Lord."'"

[14] Isaiah 54:17: "'No weapon formed against you shall prosper; And every tongue *which* rises against you in judgment You shall condemn. This *is* the heritage of the servants of the Lord, And their righteousness is from Me,' Says the Lord" (NKJV).

[15] Ezekiel 37:7–8: "So I spoke this message, just as he told me. Suddenly as I spoke, there was a rattling noise all across the valley. The bones of each body came together and attached themselves as complete skeletons. Then as I watched, muscles and flesh formed over the bones. Then skin formed to cover their bodies, but they still had no breath in them."

[16] Acts 2:2: "Suddenly, there was a sound from heaven like the roaring of a mighty windstorm, and it filled the house where they were sitting."

FOREVER FRIEND

[17] Ezekiel 37:9: "Then he said to me, 'Speak a prophetic message to the winds, son of man. Speak a prophetic message and say, "This is what the Sovereign Lord says: Come, O breath, from the four winds! Breathe into these dead bodies so that they may live again."'"

[18] Genesis 49:10: The scepter will not depart from Judah, nor the ruler's staff from between his feet, until he to whom it belongs shall come and the obedience of the nations shall be his" (NIV)

[19] Song of Solomon 8:6 "Put me like a seal over your heart, Like a seal on your arm. For love is as strong as death, Jealousy is as severe as Sheol; Its flames are flames of fire, The flame of the Lord" (NASB).

[20] Ezekiel 37:10b: "They all came to life and stood up on their feet—a great army."

[21] Ezekiel 37:21–23: I will gather the people of Israel from among the nations. I will bring them home to their own land from the places where they have been scattered. I will unify them into one nation on the mountains of Israel. One king will rule them all; no longer will they be divided into two nations or two kingdoms. They will never again pollute themselves with their idols and vile images and rebellion, for I will save them from their sinful apostasy. I will cleanse them. Then they will truly be my people, and I will be their God."

[22] Ezekiel 36:26–27: "And I will give you a new heart, and I will put a new spirit in you. I will take out your stony, stubborn heart and give you a tender, responsive heart. And I will put my Spirit in you so that you will follow my decrees and be careful to obey my regulations."

[23] Ezekiel 38:4: "I will turn you around and put hooks in your jaws to lead you out with your whole army…"

[24] Revelation 21:6: "It is finished! I am the Alpha and the Omega—the Beginning and the End."

[25] Ezekiel 36:25: "Then I will sprinkle clean water on you, and you will be clean. Your filth will be washed away, and you will no longer worship idols."

[26] Revelation 21:6b–8: "To all who are thirsty I will give freely from the springs of the water of life! All who are victorious will inherit all these blessings, and I will be their God, and they will be my children. But cowards, unbelievers, the corrupt, murderers, the immoral, those who practice witchcraft, idol worshipers, and all liars—their fate is in the fiery lake of burning sulfur."

[27] Ezekiel 47:9: "There will be swarms of living things wherever the water of this river flows."

[28] Revelation 22:14: "Blessed are those who wash their robes. They will be permitted to enter through the gates of the city and eat the fruit from the tree of life."

[29] Revelation 22:16: "I, Jesus, have sent my angel to give you this testimony for the churches. I am the Root and the Offspring of David, and the bright Morning Star" (NIV).

[30] Psalm 149: 2: "Let Israel rejoice in their Maker; Let the children of Zion be joyful in their King" (NKJV).

[31] Jeremiah 32:40: "And I will make an everlasting covenant with them: I will never stop doing good for them."

[32] Romans 8:38: "And I am convinced that nothing can ever separate us from God's love."

Entrance To the Kingdom Family

The eyes of the Lord search the whole earth in order to strengthen those whose hearts are fully committed to Him. 2 Chronicles 16:9 NLT

If you would like to know the heavenly Father or you want a deeper relationship with the Father, then know your heavenly Father is searching for you. God is passionate about His relationship with you. *Exodus 34:14 explains; You must worship no other gods, for the Lord, whose very name is Jealous, is a God who is jealous about his relationship with you. NLT* God loves you so much, that He sent His only son Jesus to die on the cross for our sins. *God so loved the world, (us) that He gave his one and only Son, (Jesus) that whoever believes in him shall not perish but have eternal life. NIV Johns 3:16*

The Father wants a relationship with everyone. For this relationship to begin, simply invite Jesus into your heart today. Ask Holy Spirit to speak to you, and guide your life. Ask for the forgiveness of your sins and then begin to repent—turn from sin. God will help you with this. Now thank the Father for you are a child of God's! You are now in the Kingdom family with a heavenly Father who loves YOU!

WELCOME

About the Author

Janice Chassie is an Early Childhood Educator, certified horticulturist and commissioned intercessor with a deep love for the Word of God.

She wrote this book in her own picturesque garden, praying to the Lord and writing what was given to her by her very own Forever Friend,

the Holy Spirit.

Janice resides in Lakeshore, Ontario, Canada.
She attends Shekinah Reginal Apostolic Center in Ann Arbor, Michigan, U.S.A. under the ministry of Apostle Barbara Yoder and
Apostle Benjamin Deitrick.

Interested readers can find Janice Chassie at:

Facebook: facebook.com/janicechassiebooks

Instagram: instagram.com/janicechassiebooks

Website: janicechassie.ca

Book page on website: janicechassie.ca/foreverfriend

email address: janice@janicechassie.ca

Made in the USA
Columbia, SC
24 March 2023